MAFIOSA PRINCESS

LIZA MALLOY

To Jeremy, for always making sure the only bad boys in my life are fictional...and for never asking questions about my Google search history. I love you!

CHAPTER 1

Giada

I peered into the trunk again, surveying my collection of bags. Maybe I had overpacked for my winter break trip, but in my defense, we'd spent over three weeks in Italy. That sort of trip demanded lots of outfits and accessories, and I'd come home with even more thanks to a shopping spree in Milan. My heart thumped harder as my eyes landed on the suitcase filled with all of my new fashion nestled beside my brother Angelo's singular suitcase.

I tapped my foot, casting yet another glance across the tiny courtyard. Angelo showed no signs of nearing the end of his heated phone call, and our driver stood behind him, seemingly chiming in on the discussion. I suspected they would not appreciate my eagerness, but my fingers were already stiff beneath my cashmere-lambskin gloves. Besides, there was no reason to wait for them to complete a task I could handle on my own.

I retrieved my duffel bag and backpack with ease, then braced myself as I lugged the larger of my two suitcases out of the trunk and onto the luggage cart. The muscles along my forearm twitched as I grabbed my garment bags and the smaller suitcase.

I reached into my coat pocket and untangled my rosary from my cell phone before checking if my roommate Gabriella had texted to announce her arrival yet. I was dying to catch up with her. She'd spent part of her break with her boyfriend, which seemed infinitely more exciting than my travels with my mom, two brothers who rarely got off their phones, and a father who could only spare a few days away from his business to catch up with the family. Not that I'd ever complain about a trip to Italy, but having someone other than my mother to talk with would've been nice.

Confirming my chaperones were still oblivious, I began to steer the luggage cart towards the building. The front left wheel spun listlessly, forcing the entire contraption to veer to the side. I braced my foot against the wheel, brushed my hair behind my shoulders, then used my hip to ram the cart in the other direction. I was panting by the time I reached the covered entrance to my apartment building.

I paused by the building, appreciating the protection from the wind and the fleeting rush of warmth that blew my way whenever someone else opened the door to leave. No matter how many winters I spent in New England, I'd never adjust to the painful frigidness that settled in by November each year.

I was debating heading inside when a gust of wind hit the cart at just the right angle, causing it to lurch back down the ramp. Visions of a collision ricocheting my precious clothes across the alley flashed before my eyes. I lunged for the cart, but it rolled just out of my reach.

Suddenly, it stopped with a jolt.

"Thank you," I said, inhaling with relief.

I stepped around the cart to see the hero who'd saved my stuff. Heat rushed to my face as I realized it was *him*. The hunky guy Gabriella and I affectionately referred to as Baby Blues.

Admittedly, it wasn't the sexiest nickname for the guy, but since he had the bluest eyes I'd ever seen, the moniker fit. Plus, based on the frequency with which he visited the criminal justice building, I assumed he was studying law enforcement. With broad shoulders, a tall, muscular frame, and a butt that belonged in underwear ads, he sure looked like a cop.

"I really appreciate you catching my runaway cart."

"No problem," he replied with a wink. Up close, his eyes were even more mesmerizing. Their cerulean blue contrasted nicely with the dismal grey sky above us. He steered the cart back to the door and angled it away from the sloped sidewalk. "You moving in?"

"Returning from vacation," I said, appreciating the effort he made not to laugh. "It's possible I overpacked."

"No, not at all," he teased, his smile revealing symmetrical dimples.

"Do you live here?" I asked, nearly positive from my stalking that he didn't.

"No, but I'm studying criminal justice, so I spend a lot of time next door," he said, gesturing at the building.

"Ah, studying to be an officer of the law?"

He laughed, revealing straight white teeth. "An officer of the court actually," he said, adding, "A lawyer."

"Oh. Wow. Fancy," I said. "I'm Giada Conti, and I do live here." My heart thumped harder now that I knew he wasn't going to be a cop. I mean, I had nothing against police, but my father thought they were all self-dealing liars. And not that I'd let my father dictate who I'd date, but…

"Adrian," he said, jolting me out of my thoughts.

I extended my hand towards him, wishing we were gloveless so I could touch his skin. "Do you have a last name?"

"Patras."

"Nice to meet you. I feel like I owe you a coffee to thank you for rescuing my stuff." Out of the corner of my eye, I spotted a dark sedan roll up beside Angelo and Enzo. My brother climbed into the sedan without even so much as a glance in my direction, leaving Enzo alone on the sidewalk. It sure looked shady, but that was nothing new with Angelo. He had long since mastered the art of being creepy and mysterious.

"Hang on," I said as Enzo approached. He paused by his car, closed the trunk, then shook his head at me.

"Stubborn, impatient…" he began lecturing, his tone light.

"Independent and capable?" I proffered. "Angelo didn't want to say goodbye to his favorite sister?"

Enzo held his hands in the air. "He's got fires to put out."

I rolled my eyes. My brother was training to take over the family business, but as far as I could tell, he was hardly that essential to the current operations. Not that anyone ever told me anything about the family business.

"You okay to get all this inside?" He nodded towards my luggage.

"Of course." As much as I wanted to catch up with Enzo, not having seen him much since summer, I was dying to get back to flirting with Adrian.

Enzo appeared skeptical but nodded. "It was good seeing you, Princess."

"You too," I said. I threw my arms around him as he squeezed me so tightly that my feet lifted off the ground. It was the hug I'd wanted to give him earlier, when he met us at the airport, but I figured Angelo would've pitched a fit over me touching the help.

Enzo lowered me to the ground slowly, then stared at me for a moment before winking and turning around. I watched him stroll back to the car then remembered the cute guy standing beside me.

"Sorry," I mumbled. "Where were we?"

He licked his lips and furrowed his brows. "You had offered to buy me coffee, and I was about to suggest I take you to dinner instead, but…"

My heart pounded erratically. "But?"

He gestured to Enzo's car as it drove off. "Isn't that your boyfriend?"

I bit back a smile. "No. That would be my driver."

"Um, I've had my fair share of rides and my drivers never hug me like that. You must be a great tipper."

I couldn't help but giggle at that. "Lorenzo works full time for my family. He has for years. I mean, yeah, he's hot, but he's twenty-six and he treats me like a little sister."

Adrian shook his head slowly. "I'm trying to ask you out and you just called another guy hot. Can we just push this cart back into oncoming traffic and start over?"

"I'd rather start over at dinner this week," I said, acting bold despite the flutters in my belly.

His grin widened as he reached into his back pocket. "What's your number, Giada Conti?"

I rattled off the numbers and let him push the luggage cart into the building for me. I wasn't entirely positive I'd be able to maneuver it off the elevator on my own, but I was so giddy at the moment that I really didn't care.

~

Adrian

Giada had the most beautiful laugh I'd ever heard. I wasn't expecting it, honestly. In my experience, the prettiest girls had the most annoying voices, but Giada's was so melodic that it was captivating. More than anything, I wanted to make her laugh again.

Truth be told, I'd seen her before that afternoon. She was hard to miss, with lustrous dark brown hair that conjured images of shampoo ads, flawless skin, and a body that belonged in Hollywood. She had big round chocolate eyes framed by long, thick black lashes, and plump rosy lips. Everything about her was so perfect that I knew there had to be some major flaw and it was only a matter of time until I discovered it.

Twenty minutes into our first date, though, I still saw no signs that she was anything less than perfect. Fresh out of creative ideas, I'd chosen a cozy restaurant a short ride from campus. Since my palms were sweaty and my mouth was dry, I nearly ordered a drink to relax myself, then stopped. I didn't even know if Giada was twenty-one yet. I knew virtually nothing about her.

Well, except that she, apparently, shared none of my nervousness.

She ordered a water with lemon, asked the waiter about his favorite dish on the menu, then teased me about the quantity of textbooks she'd seen in the back of my car.

"Have you always wanted to be a lawyer?" she asked once we'd ordered.

I shrugged. In all honesty, I still wasn't sure I *wanted* to be a lawyer, but I had already applied to law schools and I didn't have any better ideas for post-graduation. "I wanted to be a superhero until recently. But I couldn't find any solid graduate programs for that career path."

Giada smiled. "I could see you as a superhero."

Impressed that she somehow flipped my confession that I was a closeted nerd into a compliment, I changed subjects. "Is Giada an Italian name?"

She nodded. "Yep. So is my middle name, Francesca. But most people call me Gia. I mean, outside my family."

"Gia," I repeated, liking the sound of it. "What would you prefer I call you?"

She flashed her mischievous grin again. "I have a feeling I'll answer no matter what you call me."

An excited tingle washed over me.

"Where did you go over winter break that required all that luggage?"

"Sicily," she said with a blush. "And a short side trip into Milan. Well, we flew into Rome because my dad and brothers had some business meetings there, but then we flew down to Naples the next day, and I took the ferry with my mom to Palermo. Not the most efficient way to get there but by far the best. The Mediterranean Sea is the most idyllic place in the world. I can just hear the sirens calling to me when I'm there."

"Let me guess, English major?"

She cringed. "No, but I did read *Odyssey* in high school."

"Italian major?"

"My parents wish," she said with a laugh. "My family is Italian. Like *very* Italian. We eat Italian, we look Italian, we act Italian, and everyone except me speaks Italian. I only made it through two semesters of Italian here, and that was a stretch."

"Okay, so what are you studying?"

"Interior design."

"Interesting. How'd you end up in that?"

"Well, I've always loved fashion design, but I can't sew worth crap. And I've always been interested in architecture, but focusing on the exterior of buildings and homes just seems so impersonal."

"I'm impressed you've put so much thought into it. I'm prelaw just because I'm not creative enough to think of something more interesting to do with my life."

"Oh, come on. With the number of legal dramas on TV, you can't tell me lawyers aren't interesting." She paused as the waiter delivered our entrees. "You graduate this spring?"

I nodded. "And you?"

"I'm a junior."

"Tell me something about yourself."

She thought for a moment. "Okay, I hate bugs, reptiles, rodents, basically anything that slithers or scuttles or flies."

"Birds?"

She wrinkled her nose.

"Seriously? What about pets—you like cats and dogs?"

She shrugged. "I'm more of a people person."

"Wow. Okay, what else?"

"Mexican food—I hate it. Too many of the same ingredients as Italian food but with a totally different flavor, so it always tastes rancid to me, like something expired. Oh, and French fries. Totally don't get the appeal."

"Is there anything you *do* like?"

"Food-wise? I could eat olives or tiramisu all day."

"Huh," I said. "This is fascinating. But tell me something personal."

"Like what?"

"I don't know. Maybe if you have a secret tattoo on your pubic bone."

Giada winced. "Ouch, and heck no. My dad would kill me if I got a tattoo."

"It's not like he'd know if it were there," I pointed out.

She hesitated, and a wave of nausea rushed over me. Incest was not the sort of personal information I had anticipated.

She must have read my face because she quickly set the record straight. "No, of course, he wouldn't ever *see* it, it's just, well, my ex-boyfriend and my dad were pretty close so I wouldn't be shocked if he told my dad." She exhaled, but her face was still red. "No tattoos. You?"

I shook my head.

"Siblings?"

"I have a sister, April. She's two years older."

"Matteo is three years older than me, so I guess that makes him the same age as April. My other brother is five years older. Angelo. He was the one talking with my driver the day after break, if you remember."

Judging from the wistful expression on her face, I suspected her relationship with that brother was complex, at best. I tried to recall anything about him, but from a distance, he just looked like some guy in a suit.

"So you're the baby of the family?"

She nodded. "They treat me like it, too. My brothers had a lot more leeway at this age. I'm pretty sure if my father had some way of enforcing curfew at college, he would." She paused. "And the whole driver thing—my brothers almost never have an actual driver. I think Lorenzo is as much a babysitter for me as anything. Either that or my dad doesn't trust my driving ability."

"Can you drive?"

An indignant scowl crossed her face. "I'm an excellent driver. Zero accidents, zero tickets."

"What does your father do?"

"He owns a shipyard. Well, a couple."

"A couple?"

Gia wrinkled her nose in a way that reminded me of an adorable bunny. "Honestly, I don't know a lot about my dad's business. He works a lot, and it sounds stressful and boring. Whenever I ask questions, he and my uncles tell me not to concern myself with men's work or some other sexist crap like that."

"Wow. So I guess they're not priming you to take over the family business."

She laughed the most innocent, melodic laugh I'd heard in ages. "No. That would be my brothers, and I don't envy them for a second. It's a twenty-four-hour-a-day business, so they are constantly on call." She motioned for the waiter and ordered an espresso.

"Not planning to sleep anytime soon?"

"Definitely not," Giada replied with a smile.

I asked the waiter to make it two. If she needed all that energy for something, I sure wanted to be ready.

"So, what do you plan to do after graduation?" I asked once we were alone again.

She shrugged. "No clue. I love art, interior design, and fashion, so I figure I'll move to the city and try to do something with that."

"That's cool."

"I'm not sure my parents love that idea either, though."

"No? What do they want you to do?"

"Ideally I think they'd like me to stay a child forever."

"That ship has sailed, hasn't it?"

"They call me La Principessa. Not just my parents, but everyone. My brothers, aunts, uncles, everyone. It means 'Princess.' And that is what they all expect me to be when I graduate. I just haven't figured out exactly what all it entails, being a career princess. I mean, without a country to rule or anything."

My lips tugged at a smile. Gia was gorgeous and extremely feminine. She also epitomized innocence, so it was understandable the patriarchy in her life wanted to protect that. But it was equally clear she was feisty and independent. She would follow her own path whether Daddy liked it or not.

"What about you? What made you settle for lawyer when the superhero dream didn't pan out?"

"My dad is a lawyer."

"Ahh, so it's in your blood. How about your mom?"

"She's a kindergarten teacher."

Giada cocked her head to the side. "Why didn't you consider that as a profession?"

I laughed. "I'm not patient enough."

"Your mom must be a saint," Giada said.

My mind flashed back to my senior year of high school when I rescued a stray cat from the side of the highway. I'd brought her home, and she promptly delivered seven kittens on top of a basket of clean laundry. My mom simply rewashed the laundry and set about figuring out how to raise kittens. "She absolutely is a saint," I agreed. I told Giada that story, and we both laughed.

"Does this mean you have eight cats back home?"

I cringed at the notion. "No. We found homes for the babies once they were a couple months old. My mom had bonded with the mama cat by that point though, so she named her Lola and she's still a happy member of the Patras household."

"Cute name," she said with a smile. She accepted an espresso from the waiter and raised her miniature cup. "Salute."

"Salute," I repeated. I watched her drink it like a shot and did the same. I'd never drunk espresso, or any coffee I didn't sip, so I was startled by its intensity as I swallowed.

I offered my credit card to the waiter after confirming Giada didn't want anything else, then turned back to her. "So now that you've gotten me all jittery, what do you plan to do with me?"

Her dark brown eyes twinkled mischievously. "How do you feel about dancing?"

"Dancing with you? Very good."

~

Giada

It was nearly two a.m. when Adrian dropped me off at my apartment, but I couldn't have been less focused on sleeping. Every fiber in my body tingled with excitement. I ached to invite him in, but I sagely convinced myself a night with Adrian was worth the wait.

I'd been intrigued by him since I first bumped into him, although I couldn't pinpoint why. He was devilishly handsome, of course, with sandy brown hair, bright blue eyes, and that kind of perfectly coiffed facial hair usually only seen on actors. Adrian was a good six inches taller than me, so probably about six feet even, and he was well-muscled but not bulky. His dark jeans accented a butt I yearned to grope, and his thin, long-sleeved Henley clung to his chest muscles and drew my eyes to his forearms when he rolled up the sleeves.

He was polite and charming but not the slightest bit boring. He was funny, too. During our date, I laughed the way I usually only did with my bestie, Gabriella. He held his own just fine on the dance floor too, even though he clearly hadn't been forced through cotillion as a teen. Adrian struck me as confident without being cocky.

I realized as he walked me to the door that I'd somehow learned much less about him than I'd shared about myself, but that only made me eager to find out more.

"Well, Miss Giada Francesca Conti, I thank you for a memorable evening."

"Memorable?" I repeated with a smile, impressed he'd recalled my full name.

He smiled, flashing adorable dimples. "Nothing about you is forgettable, Gia."

I tried to think of a cutesy reply, but he'd already placed his hand on my cheek. It was a simple, affectionate gesture, but it completely cut out the awkward never-ending moment of wondering when that first kiss would happen.

I couldn't focus on anything but his gorgeous eyes, pulling me closer and closer as though under a spell. I leaned in, desperate for more. He smiled, closing the gap between us and planting his lips on mine. The kiss started out tender, then intensified quickly. His tongue darted between my lips, sending a jolt of pleasure straight to my core. He left one hand on my cheek but brought the other to my back, cradling me against him.

My hands reached his hips, and I held his shirt tightly in my fists, not trusting my self-restraint alone to keep me from groping him. I was dizzy and breathless and certain my lips would go numb, but I didn't want the kiss to end. Not then, not ever. I'd have been content to kiss Adrian until the sun came up.

Of course, he was too much of a gentleman for that. When he ended the kiss, my lips ached from the absence. I was tempted to launch myself at him again, but he just reached for my hand and kissed my fingers.

"Sleep well, Giada."

He turned and started back to his car, leaving me practically panting for more.

CHAPTER 2

Giada

I was still daydreaming about the kiss when I headed out for mass with my best friend in the world, Gabriella Giordano. We'd gotten in the habit of attending Saturday evenings because then we could avoid the Catholic guilt without enduring the sleep deprivation that Sunday morning services would've imposed.

Gabriella and I were always in sync on such matters. We liked the same music, the same food, and even the same nail polish colors. We'd met first semester in Italian 101. She was a natural at romance languages, and I was a complete mess. Still, having her at my side helped me survive the two semesters of Italian my parents demanded, and with little damage to my GPA. We'd remained friends since.

We were roommates in an off-campus apartment, but next year, she would be moving in with her younger brother. We'd both stay in the same building, though, with my one-bedroom unit just below a two-bedroom unit for Gabriella and her brother.

I was equally terrified and excited to live alone for the first time. Having been in boarding school since Junior High, I'd always had roommates. I'd never truly lived alone. Sure, I'd have some privacy in my family's 18,000 square foot estate on a private eight-acre lot over the summer, but with a constant revolving door of extended family members visiting, I'd never actually be alone.

Gabriella never smothered me, but the amount of freedom and privacy I'd have with no roommate was astounding. If Adrian came back to my apartment now, we could be alone in my bedroom, but next year, we could have privacy anywhere; in the kitchen, on the couch, in the shower…

"Hey!" Gabriella smacked my arm and snapped me out of my thoughts. "What are you so distracted by? I can tell by the goofy grin on your face that you're not thinking about the homily."

I felt heat rush to my cheeks but reassured myself that only Gabriella knew me well enough to read my mind.

"I can't stop thinking about him."

"Who, Adrian?"

"Yes, Adrian. Who else?"

She shrugged. "I don't know. Father Eric isn't too hard on the eyes." She winked as we walked past him towards our seats.

"Oh my gosh, Gabby, you're going straight to hell."

She laughed. "Oh, lighten up. I'll get it all off my chest in confession." We took our seats, and she turned back to me. "So, spill. When is the next date?"

"I don't know. He texted today but didn't ask me out again."

"Hmm. So he's showing you that he's not playing hard to get, but he's also not desperate. Smart man."

"I really want to see him again. Soon."

Gabriella laughed louder this time. An elderly woman in front of us turned, her eyebrows furrowed in disapproval. I smiled politely but rolled my eyes once she faced forward again. I mean, the service hadn't even started yet.

"You just want to get enough dates over with so you can sleep with him without feeling like a total slut," she teased.

I didn't necessarily disagree, but that still didn't answer my question. "Is it pathetic for me to ask him out?"

"You already have plans tonight," she reminded me.

As if I could forget. I'd promised to be her 'plus one' at some frat party. Not my scene at all, but for Gabby, I'd do anything. "Tomorrow. Maybe a matinee or something?"

"Tomorrow is good, but not a movie. That's lame, and you are *so* not lame."

"Ice skating?"

"Yes! That's perfect."

I pulled out my phone and texted him right as the priest took his spot at the front of the sanctuary.

~

Adrian

*I*ce skating with Gia was a blast. My feet throbbed after a half hour, but I'd never laughed so much in my life. Gia fell multiple times, but somehow managed to look graceful even while sprawling onto the ice. I had no problem kissing her to distract her from her lack of coordination.

We stopped for hot cocoa after, and as we sat on a bench outside, it hit me. I already felt comfortable with Gia. There was none of that normal awkwardness that usually took a handful of dates to disappear completely. We were like old friends already. Well, old friends that needed to sleep together soon.

Gia stole a marshmallow from my paper cup and popped it into her mouth before running her tongue along her lip to clean the residue.

"Hey!" I played along by protesting, even though I'd happily give her all my marshmallows just to see her lick her lips like that again.

"You had more than me," she replied. "But I'll share."

She leaned forward and planted a gooey marshmallow kiss on my lips.

I swiped my tongue along the slight part between her lips, plying her mouth open further. Her frisky giggle shifted into a soft moan as the kiss deepened. She groaned when I pulled back.

"Hot chocolate, ice skating…this is starting to feel like we're in a Christmas movie."

"If this were a Christmas movie, you'd be a newcomer to my small town, having grown sick of big city life. But you'd struggle with the transition, and I'd have to prove the merits of the simple life before you learned to accept me as more than just a country bumpkin."

"Are you mocking my love of Christmas movies?" I asked.

"I wouldn't dare." She crossed her arms and tilted her head to the side.

"I'm serious. Scout's honor. You could ask my sister. We spent the entire break binge-watching the Hallmark channel."

She laughed at me. She probably thought I was exaggerating, but I wasn't. Christmas movies were a tradition in my house, and after everything my family had been through, I wasn't about to buck tradition.

"You were a boy scout? Why does that not surprise me?"

I shrugged, wondering if she'd still find me so sexy after seeing my collection of Eagle Scout badges.

"So, what's your favorite? Christmas movie, I mean."

That was a no-brainer. "It's a Wonderful Life."

Giada groaned and clutched her chest like she'd been stabbed.

"What? Everyone loves that movie."

"Exactly. It's such a cliché. Besides, it's so sad. Christmas shouldn't be sad."

"Okay, weirdo, what's your favorite?"

She pursed her lips together and her eyes shifted upwards as she considered my question. "National Lampoon's Christmas Vacation," she finally said.

I couldn't help but raise an eyebrow. "Be serious," I finally said.

"I am. It's a classic. It's funny and festive, and I always wanted a family like that."

"That family is crazy!"

"Every family is crazy. But theirs is crazy in such a fun, easy way. It just all seems so normal and simple."

I gazed at her, wishing I could read her thoughts. Or at least meet her family. If a slapstick comedy life represented the type of normalcy she craved, the Conti family must be fascinating.

By the time I left Gia at her apartment Sunday night, I had spent twelve straight hours with her. Despite that, I couldn't stop thinking about her or wanting more of her. Her laugh, which she shared freely and often, was contagious. When we walked along the street and she laughed, strangers smiled without even knowing what was so funny.

Her dimples matched the laugh and completed her smile. I struggled to tear my eyes away from her mouth, but Gia's smile was one of those that wasn't limited to her gorgeous full lips. When she smiled, her eyebrows raised and her big round brown eyes twinkled. Her silky hair nearly reached her waist and so far, I'd never caught a strand out of place, but what intrigued me most about her hair was the strong vanilla scent. Every time I got close to her, I craved her the way a dieter might crave ice cream.

Her body left nothing to be desired either, though I'd be lying if I said I wasn't eager to see more. Her clothes were all classy but not overly conservative. Despite the doe-eyed expression she'd mastered, Giada was far from the innocent daddy's girl she dressed as. She wore a thick silver cross around her neck at all times, but judging from the way she danced and the way she kissed, she wasn't completely forsaking earthly desires for her spiritual beliefs.

At less than a week into the relationship, I was already so hooked that I wanted to prepare myself for any possible disasters. Frankly though, it was hard to see any. Giada was younger than me, but not impossibly so. She didn't strike me as the most independent person, but that wasn't her fault, and nothing about her made me think she was incapable.

If anything were to pose a problem, I supposed it could be the money. She didn't make a big deal about it, but I'd picked up on several comments she'd made that strongly suggested she was rich. The driver, the vacation in Sicily, and her wardrobe supported that theory as well. I hadn't grown up poor, but my parents spent the majority of their income on medical bills and college tuition for my sister and me. There wasn't much leftover for foreign travels.

But if I were a betting man, I'd say Giada couldn't care less that I wasn't loaded.

~

Giada

Adrian and I spent three hours talking on the phone Monday. I completely skipped my gym date with Gabriella, but I also missed dinner, so maybe it all evened out. Adrian asked me to go out again Tuesday, but he wouldn't give me any hints about what he'd planned for the evening.

When I climbed into his car that evening, there was a mason jar wrapped with a teal ribbon tied into a bow on my seat. I picked it up without looking too closely, leaned over to kiss him, then fastened my belt.

He watched me expectantly as I finally eyed the gift. It was a jar of olives—fancy ones from a local organic grocer. I licked my lips in anticipation.

"I love it. Thank you," I said, kissing him again. "Is this dinner?"

Adrian laughed and pulled out onto the road. "No. That's for you to eat later. Don't open that in my car." His tone was serious, but the sparkle in his pale blue eyes told me he'd probably overlook the transgression if I did snack a bit.

"So, where are you taking me?"

"Marzetti's," he said, grinning with a confidence that told me he knew it was my favorite.

"Lucky guess?"

"Helpful roommate," he replied.

I should've known Gabriella blabbed. That's what I got for taking too long to get ready. Hopefully, she hadn't shared anything embarrassing with him.

"She didn't tell me anything incriminating," Adrian said, reading my mind.

When we reached the restaurant, I took charge of ordering, being an expert on their menu. I selected multiple items for us to split—the calamari appetizer, chicken rigatoni, gnocchi with sausage, a Caesar salad, and the tiramisu.

"That's too much food for two people," Adrian said as the waiter took our menus.

"Not up for the challenge?" I teased.

Conversation flowed smoothly while we ate, and as we tucked into the tiramisu, Adrian shook his head and laughed.

"What? It's good," I said, licking the cream off the tip of my spoon.

"It's delicious. All of it," he agreed.

"But you're still laughing at me."

"I can't help it. The sounds you make when you're eating…"

I felt my cheeks blush. We were enjoying all of my favorites, but I hadn't realized I was so vocal.

"And where do you put it all? You look like the type of girl who eats nothing but lettuce all day."

"I detest that type of girl."

"Me too. She's no fun!" Adrian shook his head. "And you are a lot of fun."

"Plus, I have excellent taste in food, right?"

He nodded and took one last bite. "So, how do you feel about stars?"

"Like movie stars?"

Adrian laughed. "More like astronomy."

I shrugged. Astronomy had never been my sort of thing, but gazing at the sky with Adrian at my side sounded pretty sweet.

We drove to the planetarium, where we watched a movie in a bubble-style theater about the way meteors have shaped the planet. Then we took an elevator up to the rooftop observatory where we could see the stars.

It was all insanely romantic.

I was still swooning when I got home.

Gabriella winced when she saw me. "This is bad. You've been seeing this guy for two weeks, and you already have that sappy grin on your face. He must be really good in bed."

I groaned, wishing I knew. I told her about our date so she could help me overanalyze his every word. I loved that Gabriella didn't resent me for suddenly spending so much time away from her and that she was so supportive of my ridiculously strong feelings for my new beau.

≈

Adrian

*A*fter the planetarium, Giada invited me into her apartment, but I declined. I was determined to be a gentleman, even if it killed me.

We met up for lunch in between our classes the next day. It was one of those unseasonably warm late winter days, which lent the illusion that spring was much closer than it really was. We'd eaten as much of our food as we were going to and had moved to the make-out portion of the picnic when Gia's phone buzzed loudly.

Gia groaned and ignored it. Finally, the buzzing stopped. It was less than a minute before it resumed. She groaned again but this time glanced down at it. I did too and caught that the name on caller ID said "Lorenzo."

"Why is your driver calling you?"

"Not sure." She clicked to answer. "Yes?"

Gia was quiet a moment then swore and hung up.

"Everything okay?"

She nodded *yes*, but everything about her facial expression screamed *no*. She quickly stood up and began gathering her trash.

"I can clean up, Giada. What's wrong?"

She was visibly flustered. "Nothing. Enzo was calling to tell me he just dropped my brother off by the fine arts building."

I gazed across the field towards the fine arts building, where Gia's next class was.

"Did you know he was coming to visit?"

"Nope."

It struck me as odd for someone to drop in for a surprise visit, especially since campus was hours from their hometown. "Does that mean something is wrong?"

"No, but I have to go. If he sees you…" She shook her head, "I just don't want him to ask too many questions."

"Questions like…?"

She pressed a firm kiss against my lips. "Angelo can be intimidating. I'm not subjecting you to that today. Thank you for lunch, though."

I started to remind her that she provided today's lunch, but she'd already taken off across the field. I packed up before walking a little closer, then watched her from a safe distance as she greeted a man in a dark business suit. From my vantage point, the guy definitely had the same dark hair as Giada, but he was significantly taller and heavier than her. There was another man with him, whom Giada also hugged. I watched as they spoke for a few minutes and then waited for her to head into class, but instead, she walked with the men to a sleek black Audi idling nearby.

Gia climbed into the back seat of the car with the guy I assumed to be her brother while the other man waited outside as though he were guarding the vehicle. He clasped his hands in front of him, like he was trying to appear casual, yet everything about his posture suggested he was on high alert. Having nothing to do until my two o'clock class, I pulled out a book, curious how long they'd sit there before leaving. To my surprise, they never drove off. Instead, after maybe ten minutes, Gia climbed out of the car.

She glanced down at her phone then scurried on into the arts building. I kept watching as the third man got into the car, and they drove off. I sighed. Something was definitely odd about the whole encounter, but what, exactly? I considered that perhaps her brother had a bodyguard. That would explain the behavior of the one man I watched, and I supposed if they were filthy rich and her brother was about to take over the family empire, that could make sense. But it still didn't fully explain why they'd have a discussion inside a car, especially on such a gorgeous day.

Most likely, I was just pissed that our picnic had been interrupted. Or maybe it was Gia's unwillingness to introduce me to her brother that had me all prickly.

CHAPTER 3

Giada

That weekend, Adrian and I were finally alone. I assumed we were both on the same page about the purpose of our encounter, and it wasn't to talk. But after a few minutes of kissing, Adrian nudged me away to do just that.

"Was everything okay with your brother the other day?"

I winced, struggling to shift gears from my lascivious thoughts about my boyfriend to my super dull brother. "Yep," I finally said.

"Does he do that often? Just drop by?"

"He's done it before, usually just when he wants to tell me something in person. It's a haul from Connecticut, so he doesn't come often."

"He didn't stay very long," Adrian said.

I turned to him. "Were you spying on me?"

He at least had the decency to blush as he shrugged.

"If you're mad I didn't introduce you, I'm sorry. I promise I'm not embarrassed by you. Angelo is a tightly wound guy, and he thinks of me as his sweet innocent baby sister. If Matteo were in town, I'd invite you out with us in a heartbeat, but Angelo just… isn't so…welcoming."

I paused, realizing it was inevitable that Adrian learn why Angelo had dropped by. "Besides, I knew he'd be in a bad mood. He only comes when he has news to share."

"What kind of news?"

"Well, this time he was telling me that our uncle was arrested."

"What? Oh my God, Gia! Arrested for what?"

Now I was the one shrugging. I had asked Angelo the exact same question, and he had declined to tell me, reinforcing my fear that he still saw me as a child. "I don't know, but Angelo didn't seem too concerned. He said it was bullshit, and it would be straightened out soon."

"So, he's innocent?"

"Of course!"

Adrian raised an eyebrow. "I didn't mean…it's just, well, I don't know your uncle. Wait, which uncle is it anyway? Didn't you say you have a big family?"

"Yeah, it was Leo. Anyway, Angelo just wanted to make sure I didn't talk to anyone about it."

"Anyone, like me?"

"No, I think he meant reporters or cops."

Adrian's forehead was still all scrunched up. I groaned internally. I'd hoped our time alone together would take a very different turn. I was eager to resume the kissing portion of our evening and hopefully progress into bigger and better things.

"Leo and my dad are in business together. It's a profitable business, and they have some enemies. So whatever it is someone accused him of, I shouldn't be surprised. He's a big guy, and he can handle himself. Justice will prevail, right, Mr. Law Student?"

Adrian rolled his eyes. "I'm not a law student yet."

"You were already accepted though. That's basically the same thing."

At that, I was done talking. I stood up and sauntered off to the bedroom. I stretched out along the bed with my arms above my head and hoped that Adrian would catch on.

Luckily, he did. He followed me into the room and made a soft, eager noise in the back of his throat. Then he pounced and kissed me. I traced my tongue along his lip before darting it into his mouth. He sucked on my lip in return and then worked his way down my jaw to my neck, kissing and licking me until I was tingly and panting.

Adrian suddenly pushed away and reached for his phone. I couldn't suppress my groan. What text could possibly justify interrupting? He laughed at my frustration.

"I'm sorry. I just, well, I don't want to be presumptuous or anything, but I did get tested recently. I'm clean," he mumbled, then thrust his phone towards my face.

It took me a moment to figure out that he was showing me the results of his latest STD screen. Now his obvious discomfort made sense. I was torn between wanting to draw out the awkwardness and mock him further and just getting back to what was clearly going to be amazing sex. The former urge won, but only because it would extend the foreplay and make the sex that much better.

"Oh wow. Umm, so I'm a virgin," I said.

It was challenging not to laugh as Adrian's eyes opened wider than I'd thought possible. His mouth curved into a grimace of sorts that he quickly attempted to mask.

"The Church forbids premarital sex," I continued, glancing down at my feet to ensure I kept a straight face.

"What church?"

"The one and only Church," I began with an overly dramatic eye roll. "Oh my God, you're Catholic, right? I can't marry a protestant!"

"Well, yeah, I'm Catholic, but…"

I gazed up right as Adrian's panic peaked.

He frowned and then shook his head. "You're just messing with me, aren't you?"

I shrugged apologetically. Adrian was so cute when flustered.

"There may have been one or two guys before you to experience my sacred grounds. But I've been screened since then, and I'm all good." I paused, annoyed that I hadn't thought to bring a medical chart or some other proof.

Adrian slipped the phone out of my hand and dropped it on the floor. "I believe you. Now, if you're done tormenting me, I think you were about to take off your shirt."

"Mmm, was I? I thought I was about to take off yours," I said, slipping my fingers under the hem of his shirt to lift it over his head. I barely got a glimpse of him before he pulled me in for a kiss. I ran my fingers along the ridges of his abdomen and up his chest, my pulse increasing with every inch of flesh I eagerly explored. When that wasn't enough, when I needed to feel more of his skin flush against my own, I tugged off my own top.

Adrian released me from the kiss, and I dropped my top on the ground, suddenly affected by the intensity of the look in his eyes as they wandered down my body. His gaze finally settled on my face.

"Giada, you are gorgeous. Every inch of you is perfect."

I felt my cheeks flush. I let him admire me for another moment before reaching behind my back and unfastening my bra. The moment it slipped off my arms and onto the bed, Adrian launched himself at me. His hands cupped my breasts, sending intense tingles through me as he guided me onto my back. His lips replaced his hands, and I moaned loudly, so loudly that I would've been embarrassed if I had any capacity for an emotion other than pure pleasure at the moment.

I fumbled with his jeans until we were both frustrated with my efforts. He pulled back, slipped out of his jeans, then helped me out of mine. He started to kiss me again then stopped to reach for his wallet.

I figured out what he was going for and cleared my throat. "It's up to you, but I'm on birth control," I said, my voice coming out raspy.

He frowned. "Like the pills?"

"No, the shot, but same idea."

"So we don't need…"

"I won't get pregnant, and we're both clean," I said, although by this point, I was so ready to have him inside me that I really didn't care how, as long as he'd hurry up.

He dropped his wallet and rejoined me on the bed.

~

Adrian

The next few days passed in a blur of Giada. Since having sex, I'd thought about her even more than before, and we still had the same lengthy phone calls and easy chemistry. That night, she had invited me out to sing karaoke with her and some friends. Since nothing could make me turn down the opportunity to spend time with Giada, I agreed but offered to cook her dinner beforehand.

I'd been nervous about the menu, worried she wouldn't like my cooking, but she had no complaints.

"How's everything with your uncle?" I asked as I wiped my lips on my napkin. "Was he officially charged?"

Giada didn't look too concerned as she answered. "He's out on bail. Not sure about the actual charges, but my dad says not to worry and that it won't make it to trial. No witnesses or corroborating evidence, or something like that."

"That's good," I said.

"Yep. So how am I just now learning you can cook?" Giada asked, licking her fingers.

"You've literally only known me a few weeks."

"This should've come up right away. You should have said, 'hello, I'm Adrian. I can cook the best steak you'll ever eat and I'm awesome in bed.'"

"Awesome, huh?"

She blushed but nodded. I sighed peacefully. I was satisfied in every way possible, and watching this gorgeous girl enjoy my cooking was the icing on the cake.

"How do you eat like this and still look like that?" I asked, realizing only as the words left my mouth that it would put a damper on the evening if she had bulimia or something. Luckily, she wasn't offended. Of course she wasn't. Giada took everything in stride.

"No clue, but it really pisses off my roommate." She pushed her now-empty plate towards the middle of the table. "That was delicious, Adrian. Seriously. If this whole law school thing doesn't pan out, you should become a chef. Where did you learn to cook?"

I'd never given anyone an honest answer to that question before, but with Giada, I didn't hesitate. "My mom had cancer when I was a freshman in high school. My sister drove her to all her appointments and took care of her when she was sick, and I wanted to pitch in too. So I started following some basic recipes and gradually worked my way up."

"I'm sorry about your mom. Where was your dad?"

"He didn't handle it all very well. I mean, he threw himself into his work saying he had to do all this stuff to keep our insurance and pay for her treatments, but I think he was just avoiding it all and it was easier to be at work."

"I can't imagine it's easy to watch someone you love suffering, but that had to be hard on you."

"On the good days, when my mom was just feeling tired, she'd sit on a stool in the kitchen and talk me through some of the more complicated recipes. It was a great bonding thing, and I did really enjoy cooking, but I was always terrified that she'd die and it would become my permanent duty, and I'd grow to hate it."

I glanced up and noticed Giada's sullen expression. "Wow, I just managed to dampen the mood in here, huh. Sorry!"

She placed her hand over mine. "I'm sorry you went through all that, and I'm so glad your mom is okay. How long has she been in remission now?"

"Six years."

"That's amazing." She gazed up as though gauging my mood through my eyes. "Do you want to talk about something else? I mean, we still have a while until the karaoke bar is hopping, and I need a little longer to digest my food before I can make a final decision about whether your greatest skills are in the bedroom or the kitchen."

Just like that, the mood was happy and light again. "Yeah, maybe you should tell me about your most traumatic childhood memory." It was a joke, but by the way her expression changed, I could tell she was dredging one up.

"Totally not the same as your mom being sick and you becoming the top chef supreme, but a little known fact about me is that my grandfather was murdered. Like, in front of me."

I felt my jaw drop. A million questions rushed through my brain, but I couldn't even formulate a single sentence. Luckily, she proceeded to explain.

"I used to love going to the shipyard with my dad. It was my absolute favorite place in the world, and I was always begging him to let me come, and every once in a while, he did. It was my granddad's business before my father took over, so he was there. It was an overcast day, and I remember praying it wouldn't rain because it was so boring in the office, and I just wanted to run around the docks and see all the boats coming and going."

She paused and took a deep breath. "Anyway, my grandpa came out to get me and bring me back inside, and we were just holding hands walking along the boardwalk when these two guys came up to us. They were in suits and looked like they were headed to work, but they didn't say anything, and then there was this terrible sound."

I pulled her into a hug, certain she was distraught even though her face seemed calm. When I finally released her, she picked up where she'd left off.

"I didn't even realize what had happened until I saw the man slip a gun back into his jacket, and then when I turned to my grandpa to ask what the noise was, there was all this blood. He collapsed to the ground but didn't let go of my hand."

"Jesus. That's terrible, Giada. How old were you?"

"Eight."

"Did they catch the guys who shot him?"

Her eyebrows furrowed for a moment. "Yeah, I think so."

"Was it a robbery?"

"My mom just said they were bad men who didn't like my grandpa." She sighed. "He was a really likable guy, though, so it had to be some business deal gone wrong. He was the life of every party, always joking and making everyone around him laugh. Everyone liked my granddad."

I cleared the dishes off the table, unsure of what else to say. She'd grown up in a suburban town along the Connecticut coastline and not some a crime-ridden area, so it had to be a deal for the police there. It was horrible regardless.

"Were you and your grandpa close?"

"Not exactly. I really liked him, and he was always nice to me, but I didn't know much about him. He was a very private guy, kind of like my dad, I guess." She paused as I returned to the table. "It was horrible losing him, of course, but in the long run, I actually think the hardest part was knowing my dad blamed me."

"It was a crime, and besides, you were 8. It wasn't your fault."

"Well, yeah, but if I hadn't been there, maybe my grandpa wouldn't have been distracted. Maybe he would've seen them coming and known something wasn't right."

I shook my head. "Your father couldn't possibly blame you."

"Since that day, he's never once let me go with him to work. He doesn't talk about his work with me. He doesn't even let me drop by the shipyard for anything. He completely shut me out. If I directly ask about it, he'll say it's 'men's work.' And the minute I was old enough for boarding school, he sent me away. It was like he couldn't stand to have me around as a constant reminder any longer."

I sighed. I couldn't even imagine. I needed to change the subject. "So, how was boarding school?"

She laughed at my awkward transition. "Boarding school was not bad. I was super homesick at first, but I transferred to a new school my sophomore year, and after that, I probably felt more at home when I was at school. I had a good group of friends, a hunky boyfriend..." She paused and flashed me the kind of smile that told me she was hoping for a reaction.

"Are you trying to make me jealous?"

"You don't strike me as the jealous type."

I agreed with her assessment, generally, although given that I already felt a tad possessive of her so early in our relationship, I could definitely see myself getting jealous later on.

She didn't make me answer. "There's not much to be jealous of. He was the perfect boyfriend and my best friend, but then he graduated and left me."

"He was older?"

"One year."

"Was he supposed to flunk out to stay with you another year?"

"Of course not. But we went from being so in love and talking about a future together to him flying off to Italy without me and never looking back."

"He moved to Italy?"

She nodded. "He's Italian. I mean, he grew up there."

I suppressed an eye roll. It figured that the hunky boyfriend was Italian.

"He called a couple times over the summer and then came to visit at the start of the school year, so I thought we were going to do the long-distance thing, but then he stopped calling. And the best part, he apparently told all the other guys at school that we were still together and so no one else would go out with me because they didn't want to piss off Luca."

"Luca, that's your ex?"

"Yeah."

"Is he still in Italy?"

"I'm not sure at the moment. He talks to my brothers some, and he came to Thanksgiving last year, so he's definitely in town at least some."

"Your ex-boyfriend came to your house for Thanksgiving?"

Gia made a face as though just now realizing that wasn't the norm. "Our dads are business associates or something. It's not exactly an intimate family gathering at my house anyway. We have a huge Italian family, and basically any other Italians in town are counted as family even if they're not technically related."

"Ah. Any other former lovers I should be aware of?"

She smiled shyly. "Well, after essentially being blacklisted my entire senior year, I was so traumatized that no guy made it past the second date with me freshman year. Last year I dated someone for most of first semester, and I thought things were going well. He even came and met my family over Thanksgiving break." Giada paused and made a face. "But then he ghosted me and never spoke to me again."

"Oh wow. Think he was scared off by your family?"

"Everyone seemed perfectly cordial, and he was in good spirits when he left, but…" She shrugged.

"Should I be watching my back?"

She rolled her eyes. "Matteo is a puppy dog. Italian charmer, party boy, couldn't hurt a fly unless the fly wound up under his tire after he drank too much. Angelo is more serious, but in a business sort of way, since he's the one Dad is training to take over the shipyards when he retires. Neither is overly involved in my life."

"Well, none of my ex-girlfriends have left the country or been threatened by my family, and none of them share holiday meals with me, so I guess I'm boring."

"Any still at this school?"

I hesitated, certain nothing good could come from Gia learning my ex's names but also knowing no excuse not to answer. "Carolyn Cutler, Josie McCarthy, and Abigail Wolfe."

Gia pulled out her phone, not even attempting to disguise her stalking.

"Seriously? You're looking them up now?"

"I'm a terrible speller. I might need your help finding them."

"Josie is a junior, but the other two are graduating this spring. Or at least I assume they are. I have a class with Carolyn, but don't talk with any of them anymore."

Gia was fully engrossed in her phone and didn't answer immediately. "Wow, you have nice taste in women. Do you happen to know who Abby's hairstylist is?"

"Uh no," I said, totally flummoxed by the turn the conversation had taken.

The karaoke bar with Gia's friends was a blast, just as she'd promised. Her friends were all nice to me, but it was easy to tag Gabriella as her closest friend because she was the only one who dug deeper. She was friendly and polite but inquisitive. I sensed Gabby's questions were her own, that Gia hadn't instructed her to drill me.

Gabriella probably worried her friend was too trusting and too willing to overlook my imperfections. Surprisingly, that relieved me and endeared Gabriella to me. Gia needed a friend like Gabriella, watching her back and protecting her when her tendency to be too accepting, too loving crossed the line into naivety.

In my twenty-two years, I'd successfully managed to avoid karaoke until that night, but with Gia, it was pure fun. It wasn't awkward or embarrassing or offensively painful to my ears. Gia didn't have the voice to excel as an a cappella singer, but her enthusiasm captivated the entire room whenever she took the stage. Over the course of the night, she sang with her whole group of friends, as a solo, and then even dragged me up for a duet.

I'd never known someone as joyful as Gia. She was so light and innocent that it was hard for me to fit that persona with some of the horrific things she'd told me earlier. After witnessing a horrific crime, most people would be cautious, perhaps even paranoid, but Gia seemed to embrace the whole 'people are good' Anne Frank sort of mindset. Spending adolescence feeling blamed for a tragic death in the family would fill most people with self-pity and bitterness, but Gia exuded gratitude and hope. She was a complete enigma.

The biggest puzzle to me was Gia's relationship with her family. Listening to her stories, it seemed that her parents were overbearing, judgmental, and unforgiving. Her father especially struck me as cold, which contrasted sharply with the warmth emanating from Gia. Her brothers and ex-boyfriend sounded over-protective, possessive, and controlling. Yet she spoke of her family with love, and I could tell she valued and respected their opinions.

In college, where nearly everyone seemed to be eager to break free of their families and forge their own way, Gia remained content to find her own joy within the confines of their unreasonable expectations for her. Whatever the explanation was, I was eager to learn more. Everything about Gia intrigued me.

CHAPTER 4

Adrian

"Don't you have class soon?" Gia asked, tracing her fingernail along my forearm, playing connect the dots with the handful of faint freckles scattered along my skin.

I lifted my head to glance at the clock, feeling my ensuing groan like a rumble in my chest. My criminal justice clinic began in exactly 54 minutes. If I left immediately, I could squeeze in a quick shower and still have time to find a decent parking spot.

Gia shifted her weight so she was stretched out on top of me, raising her eyes to meet mine. "Or you could just ditch class and tell your professor that you were trapped under a sexy lady."

"True, except I'm hardly trapped," I said, certain I could flip her lithe body with minimal effort.

"Well, I don't see you escaping."

"I'd have to be crazy to want out from under you."

She smiled, but then her expression deepened, and her eyes filled with worry. "This is just too easy."

"What is?"

She cocked her head to the side, causing her hair to cascade over my face. I swept her hair behind her ear so it didn't obscure my view of her.

"This. Falling in love with you," she said.

I felt my lips part, but I wasn't sure if I wanted to kiss her, reply, or just smile. I hadn't expected her to say that, especially not so casually.

"There should be drama, or fighting, or — I don't know — some uphill challenge. It's never just easy."

Now I outright laughed. I understood completely what she meant, and I'd had the same thought. With other girls, I wondered if they were playing games, wondered if they were being straight with me, wondered how I could tweak my behaviors just enough to actually please them. With Gia, there was none of that. I didn't question her feelings for me or work to impress her or stay in her good graces.

"You're right," I finally said. "If this were a romance novel, we'd make extremely boring characters."

She wrinkled her nose. "I hate being boring."

"But you love me," I said, emboldened.

Gia smiled. "I do."

I felt my own smile widen. "I love you too."

She kissed me tenderly, but with her naked figure pressed against mine, the kiss didn't stay tender for long. As we rolled to our sides, preparing for me to take the top again, I glanced back up at the clock. I was down to 50 minutes.

"You have time," she said, reading my mind.

"I need a shower."

"I prefer you dirty."

I laughed, but if the girl I loved didn't mind me skipping the shower, why fight it? "I won't find a parking space," I said, kissing her again.

No matter how much I pretended to resist, we both knew I wasn't leaving her bed until we were both fully satisfied.

"I'll drop you off and park it for you. I'll get your keys to you at lunch."

I pulled away to stare at her. "You can drive?"

Gia giggled. "Yes."

"But you have a driver."

"It's a luxury, not a necessity."

I truly hadn't realized that. "Huh. So you have an actual driver's license and everything?"

She nodded and squirmed beneath me. "Yep. And if you do that thing with your tongue, I probably won't even crash your car."

I growled eagerly at the challenge and worked my way down her body.

~

Giada

It was premature to invite Adrian on a vacation with me less than two months into our relationship, but already I couldn't stand the thought of a week away from him. Besides, Gabriella and I had planned a girls' trip to Florida, but her boyfriend was happy to tag along too.

Adrian was much more reasonable than me. So, I had to be sneaky with the invitation, less his rational thinking kick in and spur him to say no. Accordingly, I waited until we were in bed one night. I had just spent five minutes showing him how talented my mouth could be, and after a brief recovery period, we would explore some other mutually satisfactory ideas. It was definitely the perfect time.

"Hey, I need a date for something. If I promise you it'll be fun, would you agree to go and not throw a fit about me paying?"

"Hmm, so I get an all-expenses-paid date with the hottest girl on the east coast?"

"Yes."

"I'm in. When do you need me?"

"Always. But this specific date is over spring break."

"What part?"

"All of it. I'm taking you to Florida."

He wrinkled his nose. "I told my parents I'd come visit."

"But just now you told me you'd say yes to my date." I told him all the other details that would definitely convince him.

"Babe, I'm not saying it doesn't sound perfect. It's just, well, I already booked a ticket home and everything. My mom will be so bummed if she doesn't get to see me."

I considered that and then offered a compromise. "I got it. You'll fly home as planned to see your parents, spend a few days with them, then fly from Chicago to Florida. It's perfect."

After a few more minutes of cajoling, Adrian agreed.

~

Adrian

Visiting my parents was great, but I was eager to share a hotel room with Giada. When I called her upon landing, she said she was at the pool, so I decided to surprise her. I dumped my bags in the room and changed into my swim trunks.

As I stepped out of the room, a hand clapped down on my shoulder. The grip was tight and pulled me backwards, but just as I turned to face the person, he released me.

I glared, fairly sure I recognized the guy as Giada's driver. "Lorenzo?"

The man looked equally confused by my presence as I was by his. "What were you doing in there?"

"I'm Adrian. Giada's…"

"I know who you are. I asked what you were doing."

I gritted my teeth together. "Dropping off my suitcase." I brushed past him, more eager than ever to meet Giada now.

"She didn't tell me you were going to be here," he said, taking off down the hallway after me.

"Well, she didn't mention you'd be here either."

"She doesn't know."

I swiveled back to face him. "She does too know I'm here. She's the one who invited me."

Lorenzo's expression softened. "I meant she doesn't know that I'm here. Her father asked me to come since he didn't want her traveling alone with a girlfriend."

"Well, I'm here now, so you can head back to Connecticut or wherever you stay when you're not stalking Gia."

Now Lorenzo appeared amused. "I doubt Mr. Conti would be very reassured as to his daughter's safety in your presence."

I figured that was a dig at my combat skills or whatever, but I was over the discussion. My girl was poolside in a bikini, and that was where I needed to be. I shook my head.

"Are you just sitting outside her room all day?"

"No." He pointed to the room across the hall from ours. "I'm in there if she needs me."

"She won't," I said, stomping off.

The moment I laid eyes on Giada at the pool, all my tension melted away. She was on her stomach on a chair, a wide hat covering most of her head and a magazine flat on the chair beneath her face. Her magenta bikini covered the smallest portion of her butt possible, but her knees were bent with her feet in the air, her legs crossed at the ankles. I glared at the handful of men nearby who were leering at my hot, oblivious girlfriend, then snuck up behind her and gently swatted her butt.

She shrieked and jumped, the hat falling to the ground. Once she saw me, her expression changed to pure joy. She stood and threw her arms around my neck, pulling me down for a much-welcomed kiss. Her skin was hot from the sunlight, and her moist lips made me wish we were back in the room instead of poolside.

I groaned and nudged her away before the kiss turned x-rated.

"I missed you," I said. Only then did I realize Gabriella was seated beside Giada. I smiled and waved to Gabriella, who returned the gesture without removing her earbuds.

I turned back to Gia as she did a little twirl to show off her bikini. "You like my new swimsuit?"

I laughed, wondering how she could even think someone could not love it. "Every man within a two-mile radius likes your new swimsuit," I teased.

She made a face then settled back onto her chair, raising the back of the chair so she could sit upright. I plopped onto the chair beside her, kicking my sandals off onto the concrete. Gia lowered her sunglasses to look at me, but her beautiful brown eyes were frowning.

"Please tell me that shirt is coming off," she said.

I complied. "Better?"

"Much," she said, leaning back with a pleased sigh. "Although now that you're here and half naked, maybe we should take a quick break up in the room. I'd hate to get too much sun..."

I loved where her mind was headed, but when she mentioned the room, I remembered what I'd meant to tell her before the sight of her in a bikini wiped my brain clean.

"Did you know Lorenzo was here?"

Giada's face remained blank.

"Your driver?"

She leaned forward. "Wait, Enzo is here, in Florida?"

"He's in the room across the hall from yours."

Gia shook her head. "I shouldn't be surprised, I guess. My dad doesn't trust me to go anywhere alone."

"Well, apparently he thought you were here with just Gabriella, not me."

Now she snickered. "I perhaps neglected to tell my parents I was sharing a room with my boyfriend instead of their beloved Gabriella."

"They like Gabriella?" I hadn't meant to sound so surprised, but honestly the girl struck me as a bad influence. She was certainly loyal to Gia, but I could see her being the instigator of most trouble the pair got into together.

"Of course. She's Catholic and Italian. She even speaks Italian."

Under the cover of my sunglasses, I rolled my eyes. If those were the requirements for her parent's approval, I was screwed. I mean, I guess I had the Catholic thing covered, but only by birthright and not as a result of actually attending mass outside of Christmas. But I couldn't fake any Italian heritage any more than I could fake knowledge of the language.

When I snapped out of my thoughts, I noticed Giada was dialing someone on her phone.

"Dad, it's Giada. I am an adult, and I don't need a babysitter. Plus I don't think Lorenzo appreciates the warm weather. Please send him home. It's embarrassing."

She paused, then hung up.

"Voice mail," she explained. She reached for the pink frozen drink beside her chair and took a long swig from the purple straw before daintily tugging the garnish off the rim and popping the fruit into her mouth. "So, up to the room, or should I order another?"

I grinned and stood, reaching for her hand to escort her upstairs.

As we lounged in bed after reacquainting ourselves with each other, I had to admit I was happy. I'd never seen the appeal in the whole Florida spring break thing, but relaxing in a plush king-size bed in a four-star hotel with a beautiful woman draped across my chest—well, that I could get used to.

"This is nice," I said aloud.

Gia snorted then popped her head off my chest to look at me. "Nice?"

I rolled my eyes. "You know what I mean. I think I could stay right here the rest of the week, just like this, with no complaints."

"But what about the beach? Or the pool? Or the swim-up bar? Or the renowned restaurants?"

"We could get room service, and the rest I could do without."

"No deal. You'll get your fill of me way too quickly if you do nothing but me all weekend."

I laughed at her terminology, although the idea of doing her all week was extremely appealing. "I will never get my fill of you, Giada."

"Promise?"

I nodded, then kissed her on the lips. "I love you," I whispered before drawing her back in for another kiss. She shifted her body on top of mine and returned the kiss with renewed vigor.

~

Giada

By the time I finally dragged Adrian out of bed, we'd missed the majority of the day at the beach, but I had no complaints about the way we'd passed the time together. We were meeting up with Gabriella and her boyfriend Mitchell for dinner at eight, so we still had time for a romantic walk on the beach and a drink at the pool bar before showering for dinner.

I changed back into my magenta bikini and tugged a gauzy white cover-up on top before stepping into my sandals. Adrian was patiently sitting on the chair by the door, watching me with a soft smile. Something about his admiring gaze made me suddenly feel shy.

"Why do you look at me like that?" I asked.

"Because you're beautiful."

"It's distracting," I said, tugging my hair into a loose ponytail.

Adrian laughed and held open the door for me to leave. He threw a pointed stare in the direction of the room across the hall, and I remembered Enzo was there. My father, not surprisingly, hadn't returned my call, but maybe I could make some progress speaking directly with Enzo.

I slowed by his door. "I'll meet you in the lobby. I'm going to talk to Enzo for a minute."

Adrian's eyes wandered down my outfit skeptically. Clearly, he disapproved of me wearing the same swimsuit he'd admired so openly a moment before in front of anyone but him. "I can wait here," he offered.

I kissed his cheek. "I'll meet you in the lobby," I repeated. I waited until he started down the hall before knocking on the door.

Enzo opened his door a moment later.

I asked to come in, and he swung the door wider. I glanced down the hall where Adrian was waiting at the elevator bank and smiled at him just before stepping into Enzo's room.

I gazed around. The room was fairly similar to my own but surprisingly less cluttered. Apparently, Enzo didn't have the same quantity of wardrobe options as I did. I didn't want to snoop too much, and it felt weird to sit on his bed, but there was a suit jacket draped over the nearest chair. I turned back to Enzo awkwardly.

"What's up?" he asked. His gaze lingered briefly on my attire, and then he turned, crouching down by his minibar and retrieving a soda.

"This doesn't strike me as your dream vacation," I said.

"I'm more of a ski-trip sort of guy. I don't love sand," he said. He moved the jacket off the chair and motioned for me to sit before lowering himself onto the foot of the bed.

"I called my dad and said you should go home."

"You shouldn't have done that."

"I'm not afraid of my father."

"That makes one of us," he replied with a wink.

"I'm not completely helpless. Nor is Gabriella. We can manage to take care of ourselves just fine without getting lost or date raped or whatever my dad is worried will happen."

Enzo frowned. "I don't think those are his primary concerns."

I wanted to ask what else was left, but that was beside the point. "Okay, well, regardless of what old-fashioned, sexist logic you two had for thinking us poor defenseless girls needed a babysitter in the first place, it's a moot point. We have two perfectly capable guys with us already, so I just don't want you wasting your time by sticking around when you aren't needed."

"I'm on the job, Giada. I don't mind your father paying me to hang around here any more than I would to run errands for him back home."

"Well, I don't want him wasting his money when your services aren't needed."

Enzo laughed. "Your father has plenty of money."

I flung my hands in the air. "Enzo, come on. I'm trying to have a relaxing vacation with my boyfriend, and having a babysitter is totally distracting."

He sipped his drink calmly. "Do you want me to call your father and tell him that your boyfriend is staying in your room with you?"

My stomach clenched. I had mentioned to my mom that I was dating someone, but I had neglected to emphasize that it had become so serious in such a short time. As far as my parents knew, I was still a virgin and would remain so until I married some boy they hand-picked for me. If my dad knew I was sharing a room with a boy—particularly a non-Italian, well, then I'd probably wish I had Enzo around to keep me safe from my dad.

Enzo laughed, presumably at my expression. "I didn't think so, Principessa. So don't worry about it. I'm not spying on you, and unless you give me a reason to report back to your papà, I won't. Just stay out of trouble and let me know if you need me."

I sighed. As always, he seemed so rational. Enzo wasn't a bad guy by any means. Over the past couple of years since he'd come into our lives, I'd gotten to know him fairly well. Unlike my earlier drivers, he would usually chat with me when we drove. He treated me more like a friend than a baby sister, even though he was a few years older. I'd never understood what exactly his motivations were for working for my dad or what career ambitions he held that made him content to provide menial babysitting tasks whenever my dad asked, but Enzo wasn't so close-lipped about other things.

"Alright," I said finally, standing slowly. "We're headed out for dinner later. The head chef supposedly learned in Sicily. You want us to bring something back for you?"

He smiled. "Grazie, but no."

I reached for the doorknob as he spoke again.

"Giada, don't let your father see that swimsuit."

I turned back and pouted. "Gabby and Adrian both seem to like it."

His eyebrows rose. "Trust me when I say your father won't share their appreciation."

"I thought I looked okay."

"You look hot. If your papà saw the way grown men were looking at you in that swimsuit, he'd shoot them and ship you off to a nunnery."

I rolled my eyes but couldn't ignore the unexpected compliment. "Thanks for saying I look hot," I teased.

Enzo shook his head but smiled. "Go find your boyfriend, Giada."

CHAPTER 5

Adrian

Florida was a blur of oceanfront make-out sessions, breakfasts in bed, late-night dinners and dancing, and playing around with Giada in the pool. I'd never realized a woman could be as fun or interesting or funny as Gia, not to mention as gorgeous. I'd had girlfriends before, but never ones whose company I preferred over that of my other friends. My past girlfriends each had some fatal flaw, like being too clingy or jealous, too self-obsessed, or too predictable and boring. Gia was none of those things. As far as I could tell, she was perfect.

After spending the last few nights with Giada's warm body curled against me, sleeping alone my first night back on campus was brutal. We both needed the time apart to catch up on sleep, unpack, and even do some of the homework we'd neglected since we'd started dating. But still, the brief separation was a wake-up call. Giada's presence in my life was already a necessity, much like food or water. I needed her around to breathe, let alone smile. She told me all the time she loved me, and she never hesitated to brag about me to anyone willing to listen, so I trusted she felt the same. But it was still too early to bring up the future with her.

I'd applied for a local internship before we'd even had our second date, and right as we left for spring break, they offered me the position. It was an unpaid internship with the prosecutor's office designed for pre-law students. That sort of opportunity was rare for students who hadn't even begun law school yet, so I couldn't say no.

The fact that the internship was unpaid wasn't ideal, but it was also only four weeks long, leaving me the rest of the summer to earn a paycheck. I could sublet my apartment during the summer session if I headed back to Chicago in early June. Gia was planning to head home for at least part of the summer, but her home was an easy driving distance from campus. That meant I'd get to see her regularly through May, and then surely we could figure out a way to meet up a couple of times the rest of the summer.

It was an ideal plan, so I shouldn't have been surprised when the prosecutor called to let me know they'd decided to cancel the program. He offered some lame excuse about how they had enough first-year law student applicants to fill the unpaid internship positions. The missed opportunity sucked, and without a compelling reason to stay on campus, the only responsible thing to do was to head home and start working in May.

Gia would not like to hear that. I decided to break the news to her sooner rather than later. I steered into the last open spot along the alley beside her apartment complex and ran my fingers through my hair as I slammed the door. I'd only made it a few feet when I heard a deep voice call my name.

I turned to see Lorenzo leaning against a black town car.

I waved as though we were friends, then walked over to him.

"Does she know you're coming?" he asked as soon as I was within earshot.

"Yes," I said, my tone clipped. "Does she know you're here?"

"She does now." He glanced down at his phone and read an incoming text before turning back to me. "If I were you, I'd walk around the block a few minutes and then go up."

"Huh?"

Lorenzo laughed. "Giada's brother is in the apartment now, but he needs to be on his way soon. If you do a lap, you'll probably miss him altogether."

I considered that. "Which brother?"

His smile widened. "Matteo."

Matteo, I recalled, was the nice one, according to Giada. "I'd hate to be rude," I said. "Thanks for the warning though."

Lorenzo tipped his head to me as I walked to the apartment.

I took a deep breath before knocking. A minute passed, and no one answered, so I knocked again. Finally, I heard the click of the lock and Giada opened the door, poking her head out a few inches.

"Hey," she said. "I'm just finishing up something, so if you want to come back in a few…"

"I saw Lorenzo downstairs," I interrupted. "I thought I'd introduce myself to your brother."

Giada stared at me like I'd just offered to walk across a bed of nails. She hesitantly opened the door.

Her brother stood by her kitchen counter, his eyes focused on his phone. He was about my weight and height, or maybe an inch shorter. His dark brown hair had a coppery tinge to it and was trimmed short. He wore black suit pants, a white button-down shirt, a black tie, and a black suit jacket, all of which gave the appearance that he'd just come from a funeral. As he dropped his phone into his pocket and glanced up, I could immediately spot the family resemblance. The curve of his lips and the shape of his nose matched his sister's perfectly.

"Matteo, this is my friend Adrian," Giada said, her voice uneasy.

"Nice to meet you," I said, offering him my hand. His handshake was firm, but his smile was genuine.

He turned to his sister then back to me, his eyes clearly questioning.

"Well, Matteo just dropped by for me to sign some papers, and he can't stay," she said, thrusting the papers back into his hand.

In her hurry to shoo him out the door, she dropped a few pages. I bent to pick them up, noting they appeared to be part of a legal contract.

"What kind of papers?" I asked.

"I didn't even read them," she said, snatching the remaining pages out of my hand and shoving them towards her brother. "Thanks Matteo. See you soon!"

Her brother's grin widened, and he sunk into a chair at the table. He folded the documents then slid them into the inside pocket of his suit jacket. "I can spare a few minutes."

Giada glared at him, but he simply chuckled.

"Tell me about yourself, Adrian," he said.

"I'm from Chicago, I'm graduating next month, and I'm starting law school here in the fall. What about you?"

He ignored my question. "Law school? What's the end game with that? Any chance you want to be a criminal defense attorney?"

I shrugged. "I'm not sure yet. Hoping to figure that out during law school."

Matteo smiled. His phone chimed, and as he gazed at the screen, the smile disappeared altogether.

"Adrian is a really good cook," Giada volunteered.

This seemed to amuse her brother. "Are you aware she has zero skills in the kitchen?" he asked me. "I'm not even sure she can operate a microwave."

Giada flipped her middle finger to her brother right as his phone chimed again.

"I guess I really do need to leave," Matteo said, standing slowly. "It was nice to meet you, Giada's *friend*," he said, his eyes twinkling at the funny emphasis he put on the final word.

Giada hugged her brother. "Don't tell Angelo or dad, please? Mom already knows."

"She does?" Surprise filled his eyes.

"Well, I mentioned I was seeing someone."

"Seeing someone as a friend," Matteo said.

"Leave already," she said, her tone light.

"Maybe we'll get a drink sometime," he said to me. "Assuming you stay 'friends' a little longer."

I smiled. Giada watched him walk down the hall before shutting and locking the door.

"He seems nice," I said. "I don't think he believes we are just friends though."

She rolled her eyes. "Just don't be surprised if someone runs a background check on you now."

I wasn't completely sure if she was kidding or not, and I had so many more questions about her brother, but I didn't want to get distracted from the reason for my visit.

I let her pull me close for a tame hello kiss, breaking away before it developed into something more.

"So I wanted to tell you something," I began.

"If you're about to break up with me after meeting my brother, I will kill you," she said, her expression suggesting she didn't really think I was about to dump her.

"I wouldn't dream of breaking up with you, and your brother seemed great." I paused, curious to know more about the papers he had her sign but decided to spit it out instead. "My internship fell through."

"Oh. I'm sorry." She patted my hand soothingly. "Wait, is this the internship at the local prosecutor's office?"

I nodded.

"The unpaid internship?"

"There's nothing else available within commuting distance of my apartment."

"Okay, but you could just not work at all and still not get paid, right?"

"Gia, I was doing the internship for the experience. I'd like to try the different areas of law before committing to something, and it would improve my chances of getting an award that I could apply towards tuition."

"Could you find something similar back home? Surely Chicago has a lot of prosecutors. Isn't it like the most murdery place in the U.S.?"

"No," I said, answering her last question first. "And probably not, because it's really last minute to look for a similar program. Most internships are for students who've already completed a year of law school. Besides, I didn't want a long internship. I still need to work and earn money at some point this summer."

Giada cringed. She'd mentioned before that the idea of working full time was so repugnant to her that she had concerns about ever being able to do it after graduation, but I'd assumed she was kidding. Surely she at least realized others had to work to support themselves.

"Chicago is too far from me anyway," she said finally. "What if you stay on campus the first month as planned, and spend whatever time you're not with me researching different types of law and internships for next year. Then you'll be ahead of the game."

"You could come visit me sometime," I said.

"Absolutely. I've never been to Chicago," she said. Her tone remained upbeat, but her face fell.

"You okay? You look like someone just murdered your pet unicorn," I said.

"I would love a pet unicorn," she said. "And no, not okay. This is your way of telling me you're moving back to Chicago right after graduation, isn't it? That's a terrible idea. I'll miss you too much."

"Me too, but..."

She abruptly perked up. "You don't have to be back in Chicago till June 10, right? So you can stay in Connecticut until then.

"Where in Connecticut?"

"My house."

"Your family's house?"

She nodded eagerly.

"I hardly think your parents want your boyfriend shacking up in your house for a month."

"We have guests all the time. It's a big house."

I opened and closed my mouth several times while trying to phrase my next sentence carefully so as not to upset her. "Gia, I would love to come stay with you for a weekend. I could meet your family and see where you used to hang out growing up, but I can't move in. And there's no internship there."

"What if there were?"

"There isn't."

She frowned. "Challenge accepted." She rose to her toes and kissed me before I could protest. "Now, let's order a pizza and make out until it arrives. Then, you have to go. I'm going to flunk my architecture course if I don't start cramming now."

I couldn't find fault with that itinerary.

Giada

As soon as I shooed Adrian out of my apartment, I started brainstorming ways to convince him to spend the summer in Connecticut with me. All I really needed was to find him a job. I trusted that he really had looked into all of the options since he was responsible like that, but he lacked my creativity and out-of-the-box style of tackling problems.

Before I got too far into my planning, my father called. I'd expected that after Matteo met Adrian, but not so quickly. Had Matteo even had time to get home yet? My dad spent about two minutes pretending he called to check up on me before launching into an interrogation about Adrian. I half expected him to ask for his social security number and credit history, but before he delved in that deeply, it hit me. It was the most brilliant idea ever.

Normally, I'd downplay the relationship and pretend we really were just friends. But in this instance, the opposite tactic might prove beneficial. And as creative and resourceful as I was, my dad was even more so. If anyone could find Adrian a job, it would be him. Nothing would motivate him more than the fear of me running off with a boyfriend.

"Dad," I interrupted. "This is perfect timing for you to call. I'd love to figure out a time that you can all meet Adrian because we've been talking a lot about summer, and I think I'm going to head to Chicago with him."

"Chicago?"

"Yes, that's where he's from." I paused, then explained about Adrian's internship. "Since his internship fell through, there's no way he could find a similar job at a prosecutor's office anywhere near here, and he absolutely needs to work this summer. But since *I* won't be working anyway, we figured I could just go and stay with him."

"You want to stay in Chicago this summer?" he repeated, skepticism filling his voice.

"Well, no. I'd rather stay at home, but unless a job suddenly pops up for Adrian at a prosecutor's office near home, I just don't see that happening." I paused before going in for the kill. "Actually, if you know of anyone who might be hiring in town, let me know. He's practically got a 4.0, and he's such a hard worker."

Then, I quickly changed the subject back to my own upcoming final exams, hoping I'd planted the seed in his mind.

Adrian

The next morning, I re-read the email multiple times before glancing away from the screen. Blowing out a sigh, I reached for my car keys. There was only one person who could explain this, and she needed to do it in person.

Gia was home, thankfully, so I simply handed her my phone and let her read the email. I watched her expression as her eyes scanned back and forth. Then she gazed up at me, grinning widely before glancing back down.

"Adrian, they were delighted to hear of your interest in their internship. How flattering is that?"

"Gia," I stopped at that. I literally had no words.

"What? This is perfect, right? The dates work out, and it's the exact type of internship you want."

I frowned again. "Yes, the dates line up precisely to the ones I wanted, which is coincidental. Also interesting is the fact that I never applied for this internship, and when I checked their website, there isn't even a mention of them having such an internship."

She backed away into the kitchen and opened the fridge. She rummaged around then retrieved a jar of maraschino cherries. "Geez. Talk about looking a gift horse in the mouth. This is a good thing, Adrian. Can't you just be happy about it?" She wrestled with the jar for a moment before handing it to me. I twisted the lid off easily and held it out to her. She stuck her fingers in and pulled out a cherry, then popped the whole thing in her mouth, stem and all. I watched as she wiggled her mouth around and then a moment later, she reached up and retrieved the stem, now tied in a knot.

She handed it to me and smiled proudly, then grabbed two

more cherries and threw their stems in the sink before popping one into her mouth.

"It's ten am," I said, questioning the randomness of eating candy this early.

"I needed some fruit."

"That isn't fruit."

"Cherries are fruit," she insisted. She bit the last one in half and stuck a piece in my mouth. "See? Delicious, right?"

I shook my head, frustrated that she'd managed to distract me from my mission with something as simple as the sexy way she devoured candied cherries. 'Gia, how did they get my email address? Did you send in an application for me?"

She hesitated. "No. I hinted to my dad that he could do me a favor by getting your resume to someone in the office if he had any contacts there."

"Why would your father do that for me?"

"I may have told him I would spend the summer in Chicago if he didn't."

"Gia, that's not how I wanted to get a job! I like to earn things."

She reached for my hands and placed them on her own hips, settling in between my arms. "I know, and that's so admirable. You *did* earn a job, and it fell through. And you're more than qualified for this one, so it's not like you owe them anything. Besides, everyone uses their connections to get jobs. That's networking. When you start the job and totally blow them away with your prosecutorial whatever, well, that'll be when you'll prove to them that you're worth it."

I groaned as she hugged me. It was hard to think straight with Gia pressed up against me, distracting me with the sweet scent of her shampoo. I was definitely conflicted, but I'd need time to sort out the specifics. I was a smart, hard-working guy. I'd never had to pull strings or call in favors to get a job.

If I'd contacted the prosecutor's office in Gia's hometown on my own accord, I'd have no problem with the scenario. So I supposed it was the fact of being given something I could've—should've— earned that bothered me.

"Why didn't you tell me you were going to do this?"

She pulled back and gazed up at me with adorable puppy dog eyes. I clenched my stomach at the certainty that I'd never be able to say no to that face.

"I wasn't sure what they'd say. My dad has a lot of local connections, but I still figured it was a longshot."

I took a few breaths to think about it all.

"Please say yes. Summer will feel so long if you're off in the middle of nowhere for months."

I started to remind her that Chicago was a major metropolitan city, but that wasn't the point. I had a beautiful girl snuggled up against me, practically begging me to spend more time with her. I'd have to be an idiot to let my pride get in the way of that.

"Fine. I'll call them about the internship, and if it seems like I could actually be useful to them, I'll accept it."

Gia squeezed me so tightly that we both nearly toppled over. "Thank you."

I hugged her back for a few minutes, dropping my face down to meet hers for a kiss. Then, I realized what was still bugging me.

"I'm not staying at your house though. I'll either sublet an apartment or get a hotel or something."

She dropped me instantly and pouted.

"Non-negotiable. You can sleep over whenever you want, but..."

"How will you pay for this temporary abode?" she interrupted.

I smiled. "With my salary. You forgot to tell your dad I was looking for an unpaid internship."

CHAPTER 6

Adrian

The rest of the semester flew by in an exhilarating whirl of activity. My parents flew out for graduation and met Giada. They loved her, of course. I knew they would, but since I told them I was staying out east for law school, I also worried they'd blame her for keeping me out of Chicago longer than they'd like. I'd be lying if I said Giada hadn't played any role in my choice of law school, but she truly hadn't been the deciding factor.

Even though I was only vacating my apartment for the summer, packing still took a ridiculously long time. By the time I finished, I was exhausted and more disorganized than I'd ever been before. Luckily, I had already secured lodging near my internship. The Martins were a couple of empty-nesters who rented out the apartment above their garage. The price was right, and the location was squarely between Giada's house and the municipal building which housed the prosecutor's office.

As I drove to Giada's hometown, I tried contacting the

Martins, but no one answered. So instead of heading to their place, I decided to surprise Giada. She'd given me her address, but I got lost even with GPS. Between the navigation running constantly and my multiple calls to the Martins, my cell phone died right as I pulled up in front of what appeared to be a country club.

The address on the massive metal gate blocking the property's drive matched what I thought was the street for Giada's house, so I'd clearly remembered wrong. And without my phone working, I couldn't call her.

I popped the trunk in search of my suitcase, certain my phone charger was in the front pocket. I shoved a duffel to the side and was just unzipping the larger suitcase when I heard a noise behind me. Before I could turn, a hand grabbed my shirt and flung me backwards.

"Hey!" I shouted.

The man who held me was in his mid-fifties and looked less than thrilled to see me. He wore dark suit pants with a button-down shirt and a scowl on his face. A slightly taller, similarly dressed man stood beside him.

"What the hell?" I said.

"Who are you?" the taller guy asked.

"My name is Adrian. Let go of me."

The guy did not let go.

"This is private property, Adrian. What are you doing here?"

"I'm trying to find my girlfriend's house. I thought she lived around here, but now my phone died, so I can't check her address or text her."

The tension on the back of my shirt released. I wanted to welcome the slight relief, except I was still trapped in between two men who outweighed me by fifty pounds apiece.

"Do you know Giada Conti?" I asked. "She has to live around here somewhere."

The men exchanged a look. Then the taller man walked away and pulled out a cell phone. There was a lengthy pause. I tried to think of something tough and brave to say, but it was all just too weird.

"Do you know Giada?" I repeated to the other guy. "If you don't, I'll drive to a gas station and charge my phone then call her. I don't have all day."

"This is the Conti residence," the man answered. His tone was curt. "We weren't expecting an Adrian today though."

I blew out a sigh. At least I'd found the right place, but Jesus, Gia wasn't kidding about the overprotective bullshit. "Gia doesn't know I'm coming. I thought I'd surprise her."

"Giada," the man said. It took me a moment to realize that he was correcting me. Before I could argue, the taller man hung up the phone and motioned for us.

As much as I didn't want to walk with the men, I wasn't certain I had any viable alternatives. I followed the first one up the long paver-driveway, with the other right behind me. The driveway ended with a circle around a small fountain. The house stretched on before us, with the far corners curving in towards the street. The façade was a grey stone, with a burnt-orange shade of wood on the front door. The majestic property was exquisitely well manicured yet void of any warmth.

I half expected to find gargoyles perched on the roof, or at least a few sculptures of roaring lions guarding the front entrance.

We climbed the two steps to the front porch, and the taller guy turned to me and ran his hands over my body like a pat down.

"Hey!" I protested. He ignored me and kept molesting me until, apparently, he was assured I had no weapons. They swung open the thick door, leading me inside a vast foyer.

The ceiling was easily twenty or more feet, framed by a

wrought-iron catwalk splitting into two identical stairways that curved down towards the foyer. A massive vase of flowers perched on top of an ornate-looking round table placed over a circular rug in the middle of the foyer. A decorative chandelier the size of my childhood bedroom hung over our heads. The sleek cherry wood floors contrasted nicely with the thick white columns separating the rooms ahead of us. To my right was a formal dining room featuring a table for twelve, with room to spare. To my left was a large den, and just past that, I saw another wrought iron-spindled staircase with wooden steps leading down. Straight ahead, beyond the catwalk, there was a wall of windows I supposed formed the far wall of the great room.

The size and grandeur of the home was overwhelming. As the breath whooshed out of my lungs, I briefly forgot why I was even there.

When I heard footsteps on the stairs, the guys stepped closer, and each grabbed one of my arms. I started to shake my arms free, ready to bolt, but then I saw Gia. She wore a casual sundress, and her hair was pinned up on the sides. She looked like a princess waltzing down the steps of her palace.

Giada

"*A*drian! What are you doing here?"

"He says he knows you," my uncle said.

"Yes! Jesus, let go of him Vinny. Leo, you too!" I glared at my uncles until they released their grip on my boyfriend.

Adrian hesitantly approached me.

"I'm so sorry," I began, but Leo interrupted.

"He was snooping around the entrance, so we brought him in for a chat."

"I wasn't snooping. I came to surprise Gia, and I hadn't expected the gated entrance," Adrian snapped back. He turned to me. "I was going to call you, but my cell phone died, and I was trying to find a charger."

The men were still staring at both of us, adding to my mortification and to Adrian's obvious distress. I grabbed his elbow and guided him down the hall. "Come on," I said.

"Giada Francesca," Vincenzo began with his paternal voice, but I cut him off.

"No! Back off."

I tugged Adrian past the kitchen and into the sunroom at the back corner of the house. His eyes were wider than saucers, and I chided myself for not better preparing him about the size of my home. I'd give him the full tour later when he didn't look like he was about to pass out, but for now, I owed him an apology for my stupid uncles.

The sunroom was my favorite room of the house, aside from my own bedroom, of course. It felt like a hidden alcove off the back of the kitchen, framed on three sides by extensive windows. The fourth wall shared a fireplace with the breakfast room. I shut the door as we entered, although since the door was glass-paned, we still didn't have complete privacy.

"You said your house was big," Adrian said as I nudged him onto the couch. His mouth hung open, and he hadn't blinked since he arrived.

I shrugged. "Okay, yes, I didn't elaborate as much as I could have. The main house is about eighteen thousand square feet. Eight bedrooms, twelve bathrooms. And then there is a small guest house and pool house on the property, too."

Adrian nodded as though it was all totally normal. "And your uncles…?"

"Total asses, apparently. I'm so sorry. We don't get a lot of unexpected visitors, and with the nature of my dad's work and the size of the property, well, sometimes people get a little paranoid."

He shook his head. "I don't even know what to say."

I chewed my lip. "Well, can I get you some water? Or something stronger?"

"Water is fine."

He watched me anxiously as I stood, then returned a minute later. He drank the water thirstily then rose and walked towards the windows.

"You grew up here?"

"Yep. We moved when I was four or five. My grandpa lived with us until…"

"It's gorgeous."

I blushed. For some reason, I always felt slightly ashamed about my family's wealth when I was around someone who didn't grow up in a similar environment. I knew it wasn't a crime to be rich, but I could tell when someone else thought it was excessive.

"The property has been in my family for years. I think my great-grandparents originally bought it. It took over a year to build this main house, and then the pool house came a few years later. The guest house over the extra garage is the latest addition. We have a lot of family who stay with us regularly, so it's occupied more often than not."

"Is that where you wanted me to stay?"

"No." I shuddered at the vision of trying to sneak out at night to go see Adrian all the way in the guest house. "I wanted you to stay in the guest room down the hall from my room. My uncles are in the guest house most of the time anyway."

"The uncles who accosted me outside?"

I winced at his terminology. "Yes."

"How many brothers do your parents have?"

That was a weird question.

"You seem to have a lot of uncles," he clarified, apparently reading my perplexed expression.

"Oh. Yeah, they aren't all like actual brothers. It's an Italian thing. We just call them my uncles because they're close like family." I shrugged. "I have a lot of cousins that aren't blood relatives too."

Adrian frowned. "Are any of them actual relatives?"

"My mom is an only child, but um Vincenzo, Vinny —you met him— he's my dad's younger brother. And Antonio, or Tony, is married to my dad's sister Sofia, and they're basically like brothers. I also have a cousin Vinny and a cousin Tony, so that's confusing."

"They named their kids after themselves?"

"Uh, Vincenzo, yes. But then my cousin Antonio is Leonardo's son with his first wife Noemi."

He blew out a sigh. "You might need to draw a family tree for me."

I smiled. "You got it."

He'd downed most of his water, so I pried the glass out of his hands and set it on the coffee table. I squeezed his hands then leaned forward and kissed him. He was so tense that he didn't even respond to my lips on his for the first minute. Gradually he warmed to me and finally, slipped his hand onto my back.

Just as things were getting good, there was a loud thunk and a voice clearing. Adrian instantly tensed up again and nudged me backwards.

I turned to see my brother Angelo glaring at us from the doorway. He looked like he was about to speak when my other brother pushed past him. Matteo grinned warmly at us.

I stood to greet him, letting Matteo scoop me up into a big hug and spin me around once.

"When did you get back?" I asked him.

"Just now. This jackass ditched me at the airport, so I had to borrow Lorenzo."

"I'm sure Enzo was happy to do it," I said, glancing back to Angelo, who was still focused on Adrian like a bird of prey about to pounce.

I reached for Adrian's hand and tugged him off the couch. "This is my oldest brother, Angelo. This is my boyfriend Adrian."

Adrian politely extended his free hand to each of my brothers.

"What's your last name?" Angelo asked.

"Patras."

Angelo's frown deepened. "Is that Greek?"

Adrian glanced at me uncertainly. "Um, maybe? I mean, I'm from Chicago, so…"

"Back off, Angelo. We like him," I said.

Angelo's expression softened. "I guess we can talk more at dinner?"

Adrian turned to me again.

"He literally just got here, so I don't even know yet if I can convince him to stay for dinner. He's working at the prosecutor's office for the month, so originally I—"

"You a cop?" Angelo interrupted me again.

Adrian shook his head. "No, I'm starting law school in the fall. Thought I'd explore my options before I settle on one specific type of practice."

"He had an amazing job offer, but it fell through last minute, and dad's friend in the prosecutor's office here needed some help for a few weeks. So, it worked out great."

"Well, nice to see you again. We'll chat later," Matteo said to Adrian. Then he started out and winked at me to show he approved.

Angelo reluctantly retreated as well, so I shut the door behind them.

"You have to at least stay for dinner," I said.

Adrian grimaced. "This is overwhelming, Gia. Maybe I could just take you out for dinner somewhere?"

Before I could answer, there was another tap at the door. This time, it was Enzo. I motioned for him to come in.

"If you give me your keys, I'll pull your car in," he said to Adrian.

Adrian stood and reached into his pocket. "Oh, yeah. I forgot it was out there. No, I can do it."

"I'll do it," Enzo insisted. He pried the keys from Adrian's hand and started out while Adrian still looked shell-shocked.

"It's okay," I assured him. "He's not going for a joyride."

~

Adrian

I still couldn't reach the Martins, so hours later, I found myself walking into the crowded kitchen with Gia. She filled a long-stemmed glass nearly to the rim with red wine and handed it to me before leading me out to the equally crowded patio. I inched along, terrified to spill the dark liquid on a thousand-dollar rug.

"I am so sorry. I had no idea everyone would be here when I convinced you to stay for dinner," she said under her breath. She turned to me, facing away from the crowd, and stole the wine glass back. She chugged more than half of its contents before handing it back and closing her eyes peacefully. Just as she started to relax, a black-haired guy about our age smacked her on the back.

"Hey, la principessa is back! Are you hiding over here?"

She turned slowly to the guy. "Don't call me that, and yes, we are hiding. Why is the entire family here?"

Another man joined the first. He leaned forward and planted a kiss on each of her cheeks and then offered his hand to me.

"Federico Regio," he said.

I shook his hand. "Adrian Patras." I turned to the first guy as well, and he accepted my hand too.

"Georgio Lomba."

Gia turned back to me. "They're both, um, cousins," she explained. "Adrian's my boyfriend. Be nice."

The two men exchanged a look that I couldn't quite decipher, and then Georgio laughed. "I guess that answers my question about Marino being back in town." He patted me on the back. "You better hope the prince doesn't hear about you."

He laughed again but stopped abruptly when Gia narrowed her eyes into a menacing glare.

"It's good to meet you," Federico said, then he nudged his brother or cousin or whoever they were to each other.

"Marino?" I asked her.

She shook her head dismissively. "Doesn't matter." Gia swiveled back to me and reached for my wine glass again.

I tugged it away. "Oh no, I need this more than you. These are your people, not mine."

"Just ignore them. They're harmless."

I frowned. I hadn't thought they might be dangerous, but I was curious about why everyone seemed so surprised and amused when Gia introduced me as her boyfriend. Sure, I wasn't wealthy, and clearly, I wasn't Italian, but I was the type of guy most parents were thrilled to see with their daughters. I graduated magna cum laude and was headed to law school. I considered myself to be a nice, good-looking guy. Why was that inadequate for this family?

"Who is the prince?" I asked.

She shook her head "No one. Georgio is just being stupid."

I felt certain she was omitting something. Georgio hadn't been the only person to mention some prince, and since they all called her the princess, I assumed it had to be one of her brothers. But why just one?

I gazed around the crowd. "Is your dad here yet? I feel like I should meet him."

"You'll know when he gets here," came her reply.

I wasn't sure what she meant by that, but we were accosted by a couple of her aunts before we could talk anymore. With each person I met, there were two more waiting to be introduced. Nearly everyone had an Italian name, and even if all their other language was accent-free, they all pronounced each other's names with such authentic flair that I could hardly understand, let alone recall the names.

Everyone was friendly and polite, for the most part, but I couldn't shake the feeling that I was the topic of most of the discussions taking place around the room. I was also surprised by how outnumbered the women were. Of course there was Gia and her mom, and then she had three aunts, but the only other woman even remotely close in age to Gia was the girlfriend of one of her male cousins.

"Don't you have any female cousins?" I whispered as she led me to the banquet-style table where her aunts were delivering food.

"A few, but they're all older and live with their families."

I lifted my wine glass to hide a confused frown. After an eternity, we sat down at the table, but before I even draped my napkin across my lap, a cheer rippled along the table. I turned to see three men waltz in. Several of the men at the table stood as though welcoming royalty. Two of the men greeted people around the table, then took their seats.

The third man, who made his way to the head of the table, was clearly Gia's father. He had her same deep brown eyes, but his hair was much darker, and his hairline receded. She'd said her parents were both in their fifties, but Marco seemed quite virile still. He effortlessly commanded the attention of everyone around him, almost as though the entire gathering were in his honor.

If Gia was the princess, he could easily be the king.

Once he sat, everyone else returned to their seats and resumed eating. Gia began speaking to the aunt beside her, so I kept watching her father. He frowned and glanced down at his phone, then whispered something to the man beside him. That guy then nodded across the patio. I turned to see a man I hadn't even noticed before nod back then dash around to the front of the house.

Before I could turn back to Gia, her father caught my eye. His expression was hard to read at first, but then a wide, warm smile erupted on his face. Instantly uneasy, I glanced over at Gia, relieved to see she was smiling back at her father.

She squeezed my thigh under the table. "Babe, breathe. You're staring at my father like he's about to serve you for dinner."

"Who's that guy?" I asked, nodding to the mystery man who had been across the patio and was now whispering something to her father.

Giada gazed over to him, and we both watched him return to his post by the back corner of the garage. "Don't know," she said casually.

"Is he like a security guard or something?"

She breathed a giggle, as though it were a ridiculous notion. "He's probably just a new employee of my dad's. I haven't been around the house for a while."

"Employees don't get to eat?"

"Not with the family," she said.

I started to remind her that technically, half these men weren't her family, but then I noticed her father was on the move and headed towards us. I didn't have time to panic or even stand before he reached us, but he bypassed me altogether to greet his daughter.

"It's so good having you back at family dinners. Having all my children back home again," he said, a genuine smile on his face.

He pressed his lips into the top of her head. "I'm sorry I was away for work when you returned. We'll catch up soon?"

She nodded then tilted her head towards me. "This is Adrian," she said.

Her father smiled, but his eyes remained wary. "Nice to meet you. We'll talk later, Adrian," he said. He placed a hand on my shoulder and squeezed tightly before returning to the head of the table.

The rest of the meal was uneventful. No one at the table seemed too curious about me. They did, however hit Gia with one interrogation after another. She had clearly been missed while she was at school, and I didn't blame them one bit for that sentiment. Since Gia always described her family as chatty and overly-friendly, I'd expected more of them to have some questions for me. Or at least to include me in the discussion. As they didn't, though, I focused my attention back on Marco.

I had been dreading meeting Gia's father, but not because I didn't think he'd approve of me. No, I just already resented him for blaming an innocent child for a tragic crime committed by strangers. From everything Gia told me, I'd pieced together a decent picture of her father.

My first impression vindicated all of my assumptions, as Marco Conti was cold, distant, and unapologetic in his distrust of those around him. When he walked into the vicinity, the mood instantly shifted, and the ambient temperature dropped noticeably.

But what I saw when he interacted with Gia perplexed me. His expression softened, his posture relaxed, and his voice warmed. He watched her with pure adoration. By the end of the evening, it was obvious I'd been wrong. Marco Conti wasn't a man filled with resentment for his daughter. He was a man who would move heaven and earth to please his daughter. Marco was completely enamored by Gia, as was everyone else. Though he struck me as fearless in most aspects, it was equally clear that he was frightened by the intensity of his love for Gia.

In a single evening of observation, I'd learned something that had somehow evaded Gia for over a decade. Marco Conti didn't blame her for her grandpa's death. More likely, he blamed himself for letting her witness it. He didn't resent her, he worshiped her. He may have come off as tough as nails, but Marco Conti was filled with terror at the prospect of losing his greatest treasure. There wasn't a doubt in my mind—he felt he had to protect her from something.

From what, I didn't know.

CHAPTER 7

Adrian

$\mathcal{I}$mmediately after dinner, the ladies stood to clear the table.

"Giada," her mom said, the meaning behind her words clear.

"Sorry," she mumbled to me. "I'll hurry back."

I began to stack a few plates, but one of Gia's uncles—Tony maybe—shook his head at me. Gia took the stack of plates from me and followed her mom into the house. Marco disappeared after them, but Tony came closer.

"Come on. Let's have a drink in the study. Marco wants to get to know you."

I followed him off the patio, hoping to see Gia so she'd know where I went, but we took a different path that wound around the garden and ended up at a separate entrance off the side of the house. Marco was inside the office already, speaking in hushed tones with another of the uncles.

The room was larger than I'd have expected and more ornately decorated. The tray ceiling had planks of wood flooring along the inside, and cherry wood trim and detailing coated the walls. A large executive desk was the centerpiece of the room, but a sofa was against the other side, and a handful of chairs offered plenty of additional seating.

After a moment, Marco noticed my presence and nodded to the other uncles. They left, shutting the door with a clank. Suddenly, my body tensed, acutely aware of the stakes. If I wanted any kind of future with Gia, I needed this man to like me.

"Nice to meet you, Mr. Conti. Gia has told me a lot about you."

He shook my hand and smiled with his lips, but his eyes seemed to frown. "You call her Gia?"

My stomach clenched. Two sentences in, and I'd already screwed up. "A lot of people call her that at school."

His displeasure was apparent. "I wasn't aware." He reached for a decanter on his desk and two glasses. He filled each glass about an inch with the amber-colored liquid then handed one to me.

"Salute," he said.

I expected the bourbon to burn when it hit the back of my throat, but it was so smooth, it slid right down. I suspected I'd never tasted anything even close to this pricey.

He motioned for me to sit, so I did. He sat behind his desk, lounged backwards.

"I figured we should get to know each other. Giada seems enamored."

I felt my face flush. "She's a great girl." I cringed at my word choice, not having intended to make her sound like a child.

"So, uh, Patras. That's Greek?"

I shook my head. "I'm not sure. I'm from Chicago."

"You're not Italian, though," he said with a mischievous grin. "Giada tells me you're Catholic at least."

I nodded.

He went over some other basics, and I started to feel like I was at a job interview. We covered my parents' jobs, my undergraduate course load and hobbies, my interest in the law, and the basics about where and how I'd met Giada. When he finally paused the inquisition, I realized it was late.

"I'm so sorry, sir, but I have to go. I am subletting a room from a family in town, and they are expecting me. I don't want them to wait up."

Mr. Conti raised his hand. "Sit down, Adrian. I had Giovanni call the Martins earlier and let them know you'd be staying here."

I swallowed hard, unsettled by the dread creeping up my neck. "That's not necessary sir. I appreciate the offer, but I don't want to impose. I'll be working a lot, and—"

"It's already done. We offered to pay your rent to the Martins, but they already found a new subletter, so it's all taken care of. I believe Lorenzo moved your bags into a room upstairs."

He watched me as though hoping to gauge my reaction. I chewed the inside of my cheek but kept my expression as blank as possible. Like he said, it was done. There was no point arguing with him.

"Well, that was very thoughtful of you."

He shrugged. "Giada said to treat you like family. Family stays at the house."

As if on cue, there was a tap on the door, and a man named Giuseppi appeared. He said nothing aloud, but I suspected his body language conveyed some important message.

Marco nodded and stood. "Well, if you'll excuse me Adrian, it looks like some business has come up. I'll let Giada show you to your room. Please let her or my wife know if there's anything else we can get for you while you're here."

"Thank you, sir."

～

Giada

$\mathcal{M}$y mother caught Adrian pacing outside the study and dragged him upstairs to the guestroom, so he was already unpacking when I realized what had happened.

I rushed into his room.

"Looks like you'll get to see a lot more of me now," I said cheerfully, shutting the door behind me and flopping onto the bed.

Adrian stood by the dresser. He glanced over at me then refocused on his unpacking. "Was this your plan all along?"

He sounded pissed.

"You mean my dad? I'm sorry he cornered you like that. Tony said you guys were just talking."

"We were. I mean this, me staying here. You never intended to let me stay with the Martins, did you?"

I dug the nail of my ring finger into the pad of my thumb. He was not going to ruin my good mood. "I told my mom where you planned to stay, and that was it. My parents didn't even mention that they spoke with the Martins."

He paused and turned back to me, his expression apologetic. "Oh," was all he said.

Adrian let me pull him onto the bed beside me, but he still looked grumpy.

"Come on. This is a good thing. I didn't ask my dad to move you here, but I'm glad he did. Now I can see you first thing each morning and last thing before bed."

He glanced at the door warily. "There's no lock on the door."

"My bedroom door locks. We can head to my room whenever we need to do anything that requires a lock on the door," I said, wiggling my eyebrows.

He shook his head. "I can't sleep with my door unlocked. I'm just not comfortable here. No one likes me. They don't really want me here."

"They went out of their way to get you here."

Adrian furrowed his brows. "I don't think that's why they moved me here. They're trying to scare me off."

"Ah, of course. That's why they had a huge family dinner for you to meet everyone. That's why they set you up in this cushy suite. Makes total sense." I rolled my eyes. "They're being hospitable."

His eyebrows shot up now. "Seriously? Gia, they basically kidnapped me. Hospitable would be inviting me to stay and offering to pick up my stuff, not trapping me in an office."

"If you're so determined not to be here, go. No one is forcing you to stay."

"Where do you want me to go? They made sure there's no place else for me to stay."

"I don't *want* you to go anywhere. I'm happy that you're here, although maybe I'll change my tune if you keep being an ass about it."

He sighed, then didn't answer for a minute. "Your father overstepped. That's all I'm saying."

I bit back my reply. He was entitled to his opinion, even if it was wrong.

"It's hard being a houseguest. I don't know anyone, and I can tell no one likes me."

"They're trying to get to know you. Everyone was friendly."

"I don't even understand half of what the guys are saying."

I rolled my eyes. "I don't speak Italian, and I get along just fine."

He narrowed his gaze at me. "Gia, no one wants us together. You know that, right? No matter what I do, I'll never be good enough for you."

"You're being ridiculous."

"Am I? Because I feel like I could be a billionaire genius who cured cancer, and if I still wasn't Italian, they'd all still hate me."

I sighed and patted his hand. "My family can be a little overwhelming, but they're really nice. Just give them a chance before you make up your mind."

He stood abruptly and resumed unpacking. "Your uncles all look like they could kill me in my sleep and not miss breakfast," he said, jamming the rest of his socks into a drawer and slamming it shut.

"What?"

He turned around. "You heard me. They may be nice to you, but they all made it very clear to me that if I mess up at all, I'm out."

"Out of what?"

"You seriously don't think all those guys that aren't really your uncles look like a bunch of scary thugs?"

"Jesus, Adrian. Seriously? First my father kidnapped you, and now my uncles are thugs? Fine." My eyeroll was lost on his back.

"Why do they need guns at dinner?"

"Who had a gun?"

"Ricky, or Ricardo? And Tony. The younger one. And…Mario?"

"Was Luigi threatening you too, perhaps with a giant toadstool? God, I don't even have a relative named Mario."

"Why were they all in suits?"

"Because it was a family dinner. Sometimes people dress nicely to show respect."

"Suit jackets cover up guns nicely too."

I stood. "Alrighty then. I'm going to bed now. If you want to say goodbye in the morning before you head to work, my room is down the hall on the left. I'll leave it unlocked. Maybe you should push the dresser in front of the door or something, you know, to protect you from my evil thug relatives. I just don't want anyone to sneak in and stab you in your sleep."

"Gia," he began.

"Nope, I'm done. Goodnight."

I walked out and shut the door behind me. In my own room, I left the door unlocked as promised, hoping Adrian would come to his senses and drop by to apologize. I spent the next half hour browsing random pictures on social media with no visitors and no texts from him. Finally, I switched off the lamp and went to sleep.

It was our first real fight, and he actually chose to go to bed angry rather than apologize.

~

Adrian

I didn't wake Gia before I went to work in the morning. I wasn't sure what to say. I was nervous enough about my first day of work without having our disagreement fresh on my mind. I grabbed two large coffees on my way and drank them both myself. I hadn't slept well that night. As stupid as Gia thought it was, I did have some slight concerns that one of her overprotective relatives would visit me in the night. Not so much to kill me as to tell me to stay away from her or something equally inappropriate and overbearing. Plus, I felt terrible about how I'd left things with Gia. I hadn't been wrong—her father had grossly overstepped by forcing me into staying with them. But maybe I could've restrained myself a little about my comments on her cousins and uncles.

The drive to the office was quick, and I secured a parking space with time to spare. My supervisor for the program, Jeremy Newman, met me in the lobby. He was a friendly-looking redhead with glasses and an oversized soft briefcase. He showed me the ropes and gave me a quick tour of the office.

Basically, I'd be handling some filing and data entry from some of the charges. Nothing about the work was particularly challenging or stressful, but it also wasn't too interesting. Still, I was grateful for the opportunity. I hadn't expected to be performing actual lawyer tasks, so I just needed to sample enough of the prosecutorial duties to get a true taste for the job.

At half past noon, Jeremy knocked on the side of my cubical. "I'm headed to lunch with a few of the other summer interns. Want to join us?"

I quickly agreed. The other interns, I learned, had all just finished their first or second year of law school. We spent the walk to the nearby deli chatting about law school and the goings on in the prosecutor's office, but by the time we'd all ordered and were seated awaiting our sandwiches, the discussion turned to me.

"So, how did you snag this job without any law school under your belt?" asked Brian, one of the interns who just finished his first year of law school.

I told them the truth about my other internship falling through and my girlfriend's dad calling in a favor. To my surprise, none of the other interns seemed bothered by the fact that I'd bypassed the normal hiring procedures.

Kyle, another first year, chimed in next. "I grew up around here. What's your girlfriend's name?"

"Giada Conti," I replied, just as our sandwiches were delivered to the table.

I was so focused on how appetizing my sandwich looked that I nearly missed the glance the others exchanged.

"What? Do you know her?"

His eyebrows made a funny movement, and then he shook his head. "Uh, no. I don't know that I do. There was an Angelo Conti a year or two ahead of me in school though."

"Yeah, that's her brother. Gia went to boarding school, so she hasn't been around much."

Another look passed between the others.

I bit into my pickle. "What is it?" They all shrugged and suddenly focused intently on their food. I hadn't imagined their reactions, though, and I needed to know what they were think-ing. "Don't tell me their house is haunted," I joked.

"Why?" Brian asked.

"Well, I'm staying there."

"You're living at the Conti mansion?" Jeremy asked.

I nodded.

"Like just with your girlfriend, or is her whole family there?"

"Her whole family. Some extra guys she calls her uncles, but apparently aren't blood relatives, are there too."

Jeremy's eyes widened as he turned to his food with renewed interest.

"But you're not, like, part of their family?" Kyle asked.

"Eww, no. I'm dating Giada. I'm not into incest."

"Are you even Italian?" he continued.

"No, and I had no idea how big of a deal that would be, but apparently not being Italian is practically a deal-breaker for her family. Her father looks at me like I'm a criminal."

Jeremy choked on his soda and began coughing loudly.

Kyle looked at him with concern, and Jeremy made a definite face at them.

"So, are any of you baseball fans?" Kyle asked, patting Jeremy on the back.

I survived the rest of the day at work, even enjoying parts towards the end, but the ominous sense of dread washed over me again as I neared the Conti residence that evening.

Gia met me at the door, excited to let me know that just the six of us—her immediate relatives and me, were going out to eat. One of their favorite restaurants apparently. I was already exhausted and desperate to unwind, but I didn't dare tell Gia that a dinner out with the people who make me the least relaxed in the world wasn't my ideal evening.

Neither of us apologized for the fight. Apparently, we were at a draw.

CHAPTER 8

Giada

After spending Adrian's first day at work moping over him being a jerk, I was ready for some fun the next day. My mother and I headed to the mall. As much as I relished designer clothes, I'd never outgrow my love of the quaint local boutique shops casually wedged between the big name labels at the mall. Between bouts of small talk, I snagged a few new tops, a pair of white shorts, and some adorable workout clothes. My mom's only purchase was a pair of slim-cut capri khakis, but that was enough to make me feel like we were engaged in the shopping mission together.

We stopped at a café on the way home for some yummy salads, then elected to make another detour to the nail salon. Over manis and pedis, I opened up to my mother more about Adrian. She had been supportive of him from the start, much more so than my dad anyway, but that was inevitable.

"He seems to be very fond of you," she said, adjusting the vibrations on her chair as her feet soaked.

"Well, duh," I replied. I chuckled at how much I sounded like a younger version of myself. Apparently, three years of college hadn't matured me.

"And becoming a lawyer, that's a noble career choice," she continued.

"Yep."

"You said his family lives out in Chicago?"

I nodded. "They do. He applied for law schools out there, and he was accepted everyplace he applied, but he decided to stay put. So he'll be on campus for another three years."

Her eyebrow quirked, but she didn't comment on that. "Have you met his parents?"

"Yeah. We went to dinner with them when they were in town for his graduation. Their names are Kathleen and Parker. He has a sister, Annie, who's Matteo's age, but I haven't met her. His whole family is super nice and normal."

I rambled on for a few more minutes about the Patras family, and then we both fell quiet as the aestheticians began to work on our feet. When my mom spoke again, I noticed her expression had changed.

"Do you think you'd ever consider moving there?"

"To Chicago?" I felt my mouth form a grimace I hadn't intended. I figured Chicago had some selling points, but nothing about the Midwest appealed to me, and all I ever heard about Chicago was how damn windy it got.

"It's a nice place."

I wondered how she knew that, but instead of asking, I mentioned I planned to visit Adrian there later in summer.

"I think that'll be nice," she said. "You may end up falling in love with Chicago. You never know."

"I doubt it," I said, but really, all I could think of was how it sounded like my mom wanted me to move halfway across the country. I always suspected boarding school and college weren't far enough for my father, but apparently my mother needed more distance from me as well.

"Trim them shorter," I said, turning my focus entirely to the aesthetician.

Adrian

*B*y Friday afternoon, I was exhausted but relieved. I'd finished my first full week of the internship, and as far as I knew, I hadn't fucked up anything too badly yet. Giada and I had never officially resolved anything, but we'd fallen into a new routine, a new normal, and that was okay. She texted me at work each day and greeted me eagerly at the door each evening. Since the dinner out with her parents, we'd spent the evenings alone, just the two of us, but tonight she warned me there would be another big family dinner at her house.

This time, I was ready. I knew what to expect, and I tricked myself into thinking I could handle it. I even brainstormed a few innocent topics to discuss with her brothers or uncles or other random family members so we didn't fall into awkward conversational lulls.

Gia pounced on me the moment I got home from work, dragging me up to her room. She suggested a quickie, but I refused since her entire family was in the house. We both settled for an hour of snuggling and talking.

When she glanced at the clock, Gia sighed. "We should go downstairs now. I bet everyone is here."

I relaxed into a smile, flattered that she was so clearly regretting that our solo time was ending. "I love you," I said.

Gia grinned. "Right back at ya, sexy."

We were just heading down the stairs when there was a commotion at the door. When we reached the dining room, the table was set for a formal affair, but no one was in the room. Gia flung her hands up in apparent frustration, but just then, Leo popped his head into the room.

"We have a guest! Come see, sweetheart."

Gia tugged me behind her but dropped my hand before we reached the foyer. It was hard to see who they were greeting with a mess of men in suits hugging and slapping each other on the back, but then the crowd parted, and a younger man stepped forward. I assumed he was yet another cousin, though perhaps one they hadn't seen so recently, based on the level of buzz surrounding his arrival.

He looked about our age and stereotypically Italian, with short black hair, an olive complexion, and dark eyes. He was maybe slightly taller than me but with a similar build, although the suit made it hard to tell. He waltzed through the crowd like a prince greeting his loyal subjects, then gave one of the uncles a familiar handshake before spotting us.

"Luca?" Gia's face was a mixture of surprise and excitement.

The man brushed past everyone else waiting to greet him and lifted Gia off the ground as he hugged her.

"Carissima," he said with a smile, his Italian accent sounding authentic to my untrained ear. The hug continued for an awkwardly long time before he finally set her back on her feet then proceeded to kiss one cheek, then the next. He lingered on the second side, whispering something into her ear.

I watched her face blush, feeling the pit in my stomach grow. I couldn't hear his words, and I suspected that was probably intentional.

He finally pulled back but left his hands on her arms, holding her in place as he checked her out. The rest of the family simply beamed happily at this quizzical reunion, so I told myself he was simply another relative, although the way he was eying her was creepy if they actually were blood relatives.

"You've gotten even more beautiful with age," he said to her.

Gia smiled and crooked her head to the side. "Oh, stop. You

don't call, you hardly write, you can't just waltz back in here and start flirting."

"I brought you a present though," he said, accepting a gift bag that the guy behind him thrust into his hands.

"My birthday isn't until tomorrow."

His grin widened. "You know I like being the first. Open it."

Gia's eyes lit up even before she tugged the object out of the gift bag. When she saw it, she shrieked and held it up. Everyone else ooh'd and ahh'd at what appeared to be an oversized mauve purse.

She turned to her mother, beaming. "It's a Valentino."

Even I knew that had to be an expensive accessory.

"When I saw it in the boutique in Rome, it reminded me of that Valentino gown you wore to your senior prom."

Gia laughed. "I can't believe you remember that. The dress is still hanging in my closet upstairs."

"I bet it still looks fabulous on you," he said, leaning in for another hug. "Happy birthday, tesoro."

As they pulled apart and Gia gazed adoringly back at her new bag, I could've sworn the guy smirked at me.

Her father stepped forward, patting the guy on the back. "You must join us for dinner, son."

Gia smiled, then turned to the side. She caught a glimpse of me, and from her expression it was apparent she'd completely forgotten I was there. She rushed back to my side. I was about to ask who this guy was when she began introductions.

"Adrian, I'd like you to meet Luca," she said. "He's a family friend."

Luca turned and gave me a disapproving once over before shaking my hand.

"Luca is not just a family friend. He's Giada's longtime boyfriend," her father said, ushering Luca into the dining room.

"High school boyfriend," Gia quickly added, but everyone

except us had already moved on. "High school," she repeated, turning to me.

I nodded skeptically. I didn't want to be a dick, but the last five minutes had been painfully emasculating. "You sure look close still."

Gia frowned. "I told you he moved to Italy after graduation. I've only seen him a handful of times since then." She tugged my arm. "Come on, let's go eat."

My appetite had vanished. I didn't want to sit through an hour-long reunion with some beloved ex-boyfriend of hers, but the best way to win was to get to know my enemy.

Luca sat near the head of the table, right next to Marco and directly across from Angelo. They sat his friend, Alessio, next to me. Nearly everyone at the table was hanging on Luca's every word.

Mrs. Conti wasn't quite as thrilled as the rest of the group, but her irritation seemed more directed at her husband. Every time he dared glance in her direction, she stared pointedly and raised her eyebrows as though sending a telepathic message.

There was something going on between Luca and Angelo too, but I couldn't tell what. They were both outwardly respectful to each other, but when no one else was looking, I caught a few menacing glares. I wondered if the tension had to do with Gia, like maybe her big brother was feeling protective of her, or maybe it had something to do with Marco. To some extent, the two reminded me of brothers competing for their father's attention. At the moment, it seemed that Luca was winning.

Somehow, I survived the meal, but then when everyone moved to the great room for drinks, Marco made a big show of telling everyone that Luca would be staying at the house for a while. Apparently, he'd be residing in the room next to mine. That was too much for me.

I stepped outside and dialed my freshman roommate. Hearing a familiar voice, talking with an actual friend, would've calmed me, but I wasn't shocked when my call when to voice mail. Friday night wasn't the easiest time to reach a buddy.

I hung up the phone and then glanced around. The night was completely dark, thanks to the same clouds which trapped the sweltering heat down at ground level. I craved the air conditioning, but the silence and solitude offered on the patio was nearly as refreshing.

Suddenly, I heard a rustle and realized I wasn't alone. I quickly rose to my feet, ready to bolt for the door, when Luca stepped out of the shadow.

"Sorry." He cocked his head to the side as though inspecting me, his expression a sharp contrast to his words. "I didn't mean to interrupt your call. I just wanted some fresh air. It's stuffy in there."

I nodded, planning to excuse myself back into the house, when he blocked my path. He reached into his pocket, and I had just enough time to wonder what he could be reaching for when his had emerged with a cigar.

"Do you smoke?" he asked, offering it to me.

I shook my head.

"Me either," he said. "But it's always handy to carry around. A lot of these guys do." Luca sat on the floral cushion of the nearby wicker couch.

I should've walked off then, but I hesitated and lost my chance.

"Giada says you're studying to be a lawyer," he said, motioning for me to sit across from him. Against my better judgment, I did. In my defense, I got the impression that everyone did what Luca asked.

"Yes. And you're studying business, right?"

Luca nodded. "More of an apprenticeship. I took some classes in Italy, but I'm mostly training directly with my father's company."

"What business is he in?"

A quizzical expression crossed his face. "A little of this, little of that. Sales, entertainment. And exports?"

I decided not to press the point further.

"How much do you know about Marco's business?"

I shrugged. "Giada's told me a bit about his work. I know he owns several of the shipyards. Clearly, he's doing well," I gestured at the luxury around us.

Luca frowned. "You should be careful. There are things you don't want to snoop around."

"What's that supposed to mean? Are you trying to threaten me?"

"I am not *trying* anything. I'm giving you a friendly warning." Luca laughed. "If I were threatening you, you'd know."

I gritted my teeth together, then changed the subject. "Look, I know you and Gia have some history together, but that was a while ago."

"I look forward to getting reacquainted with her."

"She's not the same person anymore."

"I dunno, she's still her papà's little girl, and I don't see how anything else matters."

"Gia's a big girl, and she makes her own decisions. She's doing just fine at college without her dad there."

Luca appeared to consider that. After a moment, he nodded, his face relaxing. "That's good. Does she like it there?"

"Yeah. We're happy there."

Luca snorted at my emphasis on the "we." "Look amico, I get it. Giada's dating you now. I haven't exactly been sitting around pining for her either."

I hadn't expected such sudden agreement. Luca's phone buzzed, and he glanced at it, furrowed his brow, then turned back to me.

"So you're not trying to win her back?" I asked, suddenly emboldened.

He hesitated. "I don't have to win her back. It's not a contest."

I wasn't sure if he was conceding or not. This guy spoke in riddles. Luckily, he continued before I had to decipher anything.

"Like I said before, she's a daddy's girl. You'd be well advised to remember that. In the end, it doesn't matter what Giada wants. She'll do what her papà tells her to do."

Now I was the one chuckling. Gia was the most stubborn person I knew. The notion of someone else telling her what to do was outright comical. "You honestly think just because her dad likes you that she'll dump me for you? You really don't know her very well."

Luca sighed and stood. "You seem like a nice guy, and I don't want you to get hurt. But trust me when I say that one way or another, her father will get his way. You're a fool if you try to stop him."

He turned abruptly to a man that I hadn't even noticed was looming in the shadows. "Alessio, let's roll. Shipment's in."

I stayed in my seat until they'd gone back inside. The temperature had dropped considerably, and the lack of wildlife chirping was disheartening. I swallowed, the sound echoing in the dark night.

CHAPTER 9

Giada

Adrian looked so peaceful in his sleep, but I hadn't gone through the trouble of sneaking into his room just to watch him sleep. Weighing my options, I decided to slide my hand down under the covers and into his pajama pants. I stroked him softly at first, stifling a giggle at the fact that he was responding to my touch without even waking. Just as I shifted the sheets lower to take over with my mouth, he woke abruptly. He jumped backwards, elbowing me in the cheek.

"Ouch!"

Adrian leaned forward, squinting. "Gia? Shit. Babe, I'm sorry. I didn't realize it was you."

"Who else would it be?"

An awkward silence followed my question.

"I'm a little on edge," he said. "I had a weird talk with Luca earlier, and I just don't feel welcome here."

I crawled under the covers beside him. "What exactly happened with Luca?"

"I don't know. We were talking outside for a while, and then he left with that guy, Alessio, to deal with something at the docks. You don't think that's strange, them leaving that late?"

"Not at all. It's a 24/7 business. A lot of shipments arrive at night, and Alessio is like his best friend. They go everywhere together, according to my brothers."

"Luca said you're a daddy's girl and that you'd do whatever your dad told you to do," Adrian continued.

"When have you ever known me to do as I'm told?"

"He said I shouldn't try to come in between you and your dad, and that my only hope of any future with you is to play nice with your dad."

I raised an eyebrow. I'd never known Adrian to be the defensive or jealous type, so I wasn't sure how to react. "That all sounds reasonable. And I know it's not easy for you staying here when everyone already knows Luca so well, but he's just trying to give you advice. It wouldn't hurt you to make an effort to get along with everyone."

Adrian stared at me for a minute and then closed his eyes. "I sound insane now, don't I?" he asked after a pause.

I shrugged.

"I think I'm just groggy. It made sense in my head. It just...it felt like he was warning me." He shook his head. "I'm sorry. How's your cheek?" He reached out and stroked where his elbow had bonked me.

"I'll live, but you could kiss it and make it better," I suggested.

He smiled and kissed my cheek before moving on to my lips. We kissed softly for a few minutes. Then he nudged my leg over his lap so I was straddling him. He pulled back abruptly.

"Hey, it's your birthday," he said.

I nodded.

"Happy birthday!"

I smiled and slipped my nightgown up over my head, Adrian watching with a wolfish grin on his face.

"You are so gorgeous," he said. "I don't think I'll ever get bored of seeing you naked."

I gripped his cheeks in my hands and leaned close for another kiss, moaning as I felt his hands reach up to my breasts. We followed our usual pattern of foreplay, having already found a comfortable intimate routine. As I began to rise up and down over Adrian, guided by his firm hands, all traces of his paranoia were swept out of my mind.

The next morning, I awoke gradually to someone calling my name. I peeled my eyes open slowly, smiling when I realized I had fallen asleep on Adrian's chest. He had—hands down—the sexiest chest imaginable. It was tanned and well-muscled—but not so bulky that I couldn't get comfy on it—and had only the smallest patch of light brown hair. I glanced at his sweet face, confirming that he was still asleep, and then I heard someone call my name again.

Suddenly, I was wide awake and very cognizant of the fact that I was not in my bedroom.

"Crap," I whispered, frantically searching for my nightgown.

Adrian shifted and rubbed his eyes. "What's going on?"

"We fell asleep," I said.

A knock on the door caused us both to jump. Adrian fished my nightgown out from under the covers and thrust it to me before quickly hopping up and pulling on his pants. The knock repeated, this time louder. I tossed a shirt to Adrian and motioned for him to answer the door. I flattened myself against the wall behind the door, praying my brother didn't sniff me out and murder Adrian in front of me.

Adrian opened the door slowly, but the voice that greeted him wasn't one of my brothers' but rather Luca's.

"Hey, sorry to wake you, but Tina was looking for Giada. She's not in her room. I thought before they call in the guards, I'd just confirm you hadn't seen her this morning."

I groaned internally but didn't see any way to avoid the truth.

I stepped away from the wall and let Adrian nudge the door open wider. I was still hidden from anyone else passing down the hall, but Luca sure saw. His eyes roamed down my body then back up again before focusing on Adrian with a less than friendly glare.

"She just came by to bring me the newspaper," Adrian said lamely.

Luca winced, like the excuse was so dumb that it offended him. Then he turned back to me. "Your mom is worried. Put on some clothes and get downstairs."

I exhaled the breath I'd been holding and gazed out into the hall.

"Come on," Luca said, motioning for me to follow him. "The coast is clear."

Luca grabbed my hand and practically dragged me down the hall. When we reached my room, he stepped in after me, shutting the door behind him.

I flung my hands in the air in frustration. "I'm not changing with you in here.

Luca rolled his eyes. "I've seen it all before."

I chewed the inside of my cheek, not needing that reminder. Honestly, it would've served Luca right, to tease him by stripping in front of him, just to remind him what he was missing. I had no intention of doing that to Adrian, though. I stomped over to my dresser to find suitable clothes and then shut myself in my closet.

"Happy birthday," he said.

I thanked him.

"Were you trying to get caught?" Luca asked, quickly switching topics.

"We fell asleep."

"What if your father had found you and not me? Or one of your uncles? Are you trying to get your new beau killed?"

"Jesus, Luca. We fell asleep," I repeated. "It wasn't intentional, and frankly, it's not your business."

"Yeah, well, your papà asked me to keep an eye on you."

I laughed, stepping into my shorts and fastening them. "Thanks, but no thanks."

"He didn't exactly give me a choice."

I tugged the T-shirt over my head and stepped out of the closet in time to roll my eyes. "You always were a total patsy."

Luca closed the distance between us in two quick strides. He gripped my wrist and locked his dark eyes on me. "What are you doing with this guy, Giada? He seems like a nice guy. You shouldn't fuck with people like that."

I tugged my wrist free. "I like Adrian. A lot." I shook my head and turned to the mirror, ready to work on my makeup. "You don't get to disappear for three years and then come back and tell me how to live my life. I'm an adult. I choose."

Luca frowned at me, but a knock on the door interrupted us before he could say anything else. He opened the door to reveal my mother.

"Birthday girl was in her bathroom and didn't hear you," he quickly told her. "I tried to tell her she doesn't need all that makeup to look pretty, but she never listens to me anymore."

My mother rubbed her thumb across his cheek affectionately, and he glanced over his shoulder to me before leaving.

I knew he expected gratitude, but that was not my primary emotion at the moment. I focused on my mother instead. She wished me a happy birthday and gave me an overly suffocating hug.

"What's up, Mom?"

"I thought we could go shopping today."

I counted to four before answering. "That's what was so urgent? I haven't even had breakfast yet."

"Bianca wanted to be home in time to make you lunch."

"Is she already here?" I couldn't imagine having slept through that level of activity. Bianca, like most of my aunts, couldn't make a quiet entrance if she tried. What she counted as a whisper was more of a shout for normal people, and she stomped around so much you'd think she weighed three hundred pounds.

"No, of course not. Antonio said we can pick her up on the way."

"Mom, it's my day. I haven't even had breakfast yet, and I told Adrian I'd show him around town."

She stared at me, her face expressionless, for a moment before relenting. "Fine. Be back in time for your birthday lunch. Ladies only though." She kissed me on the cheek then left.

I brushed my teeth and then returned to Adrian's room. I knocked softly, and he answered tentatively.

"Just me," I said.

He opened the door for me. I noticed he had taken the opportunity to get dressed, too. I went in and plopped on the couch while he shut the door.

"We have the morning free, so I can show you around town, but you're on your own for lunch. My aunts are coming over. Ladies only birthday thing. You don't want to be around."

He smiled. "Do you have as many aunts as you do uncles?"

I started to point out what a dumb question that was, but then I thought about it from his perspective. "No. But half of my uncles aren't technically my uncles. They're just guys who work for my dad."

Adrian raised an eyebrow. "How come some guys that work for him are called uncles, and some aren't?"

I shrugged. "I'm not sure. Probably something to do with age. I'm starving and need coffee. You ready to go? We can get breakfast out."

Adrian held a small box up to me. "Do you have time to open your present first?"

I nodded giddily. Few things lately thrilled me as much as presents, especially when they came in a jewelry box. I untied the ribbon and opened the box. A sterling silver necklace with a solitary pearl rested on top of some tissue.

"It's your birthstone," he explained.

"I know. I love it." I pulled him close and kissed him, then turned so he could put it on me.

"It's no Valentino sack," he added.

"Bag," I corrected, giggling. "And there's no comparison. Luca just buys stuff because he can. This is gorgeous, and I love having something you picked out for me so close to my heart."

~

Adrian

The diner was packed when we arrived, but Gia assured me it was the best in town. The hostess estimated it would be a half hour for a table for two and asked for a name.

"Conti," Gia replied.

The man beside the hostess perked up. "Are you Marco's daughter?"

Gia nodded.

He turned to the hostess. "She's a special guest," he said, swiveling back to us. "We'll get you a table right away."

The man ignored the hostess's grimace and introduced himself to Gia as the owner. He grabbed menus and walked us to a table.

"Please give your father my respects," he said, placing a napkin on Gia's lap. "We really appreciated his, uh, advice for the business last month, and I hope he received the bourbon we sent."

She nodded politely, and I cringed watching the wait staff practically trip over each other to fill her coffee mug.

"I guess your dad is well known around here," I said.

"He's been doing business here for forever. Before him, my grandpa ran it."

"What kind of business advice would he have for a restaurant owner?"

Gia shrugged, focused on her menu.

We ordered and had just started into the small talk, when another man approached the table.

"Giada? Is that you?"

She glanced up and smiled, her face not revealing whether or not she knew the man. He looked like a middle-aged business-man, with his only distinguishing feature being a scar across his left cheek.

"Eddie Gallo," he said.

"Oh hey, Mr. Gallo. How've you been?"

"Good, thanks. Yourself? You've been away at school, I hear?"

She nodded. "Yeah. Um, I'd like you to meet my boyfriend, Adrian Patras."

"Nice to meet you sir," I said, standing to shake his hand.

"You too," Mr. Gallo said. Then he turned back to Gia. "I won't interrupt your breakfast, but I just wanted to say hello. And please tell your father I'd love to hear from him when he isn't too busy with his beautiful daughter."

I gazed past Gia to watch Mr. Gallo as he left. Just as I was about to turn back, I saw Lorenzo fly out of the SUV and approach him. The two of them appeared to have some verbal altercation, and then the older man climbed into a gray Genesis sedan and drove off. Lorenzo paced back and forth beside his Navigator for a minute before leaning back against it.

"Was he a friend of your father?"

"Yeah, I think so. I haven't seen him in ages, probably not since I left for boarding school."

"That's funny that he recognized you."

Gia shrugged, her go-to response for all the oddities. Our food still hadn't arrived, so I pressed further.

"Your dad seems to have a lot of friends."

She gazed up at me, eyebrows raised, mouth drawn in. "What's your point Adrian?"

"Are you sure your father's business is entirely legit?"

I expected her to yell at me like she had the last time I'd brought up the weirdness of the situation. Instead she just reached across the table and squeezed my hand.

"Adrian, I get it. I have a huge, overbearing family, and we're all crazy Italians, and it's a small part of town so everyone knows my dad. But sometimes people are rich because their business does well. Isn't that like what you're learning in school?"

I started to answer her then, but Lorenzo came into the café, spoke with the owner, then quickly left again.

"Why do you have a driver? I could've driven us today."

"Enzo knows the area. I thought it would be more relaxing this way." She pouted dramatically. "Please don't ruin my birthday with your conspiracy theory crap. Let's just enjoy the morning, and then when I'm having lunch with my aunts, maybe you can get to know my brothers or uncles better. It wouldn't kill you to be friendly with everyone."

"I am friendly," I insisted as the waiter set our food down in front of us.

"Babe, you basically keep accusing everyone I know of being in the mafia."

The waiter's eyes widened. "Um, is there anything else I can bring you right now?"

We both shook our heads.

"I'm trying to be friendly, but befriending this many people is intimidating. It doesn't help that Luca is here one-upping me on everything. Did they like him from the start?"

She laughed and nodded. "Loved him. Actually, we met through our fathers. It was almost like an arranged courtship," she said with another giggle.

"I thought you met at boarding school."

"Yeah, but we'd known each other as children.

I sighed, struggling to take in this revelation. "I don't understand. You knew each other before but didn't start dating until boarding school?"

"Yes. Growing up, Luca spent most of his time in Sicily, but when his family was in town, our families would hang out and we were friends. Then a few years went by, and I didn't see him much, but when I went to a new boarding school my sophomore year, there he was."

"And you just started going out then?"

"Not right away, no, but he was the only person I knew there so we became friends. When I realized he was flirting, I certainly wasn't going to shoot him down."

"Why not?"

Giada laughed, then brushed her hair out of her eyes. She reached onto my plate and selected the crispiest piece of bacon, bit off a piece, then moaned appreciatively. I offered her the rest of the piece, but she shook her head and resumed her story. "He was a year ahead of me, so that was a big deal. Plus, he was popular and hot. All the girls wanted to go out with him, and he wanted me."

"So that's all it takes?"

"To get a fifteen-year-old girl to go out with you? Yes, it really is." She laughed dismissively. I realized how ridiculous I was being, but I still didn't understand it. Giada was so upbeat and full of life. She exuded warmth. She couldn't possibly have ever been truly interested in someone like Luca. He was perpetually grumpy, cold, and bossy.

"But you guys went out for a long time. Surely the novelty wore off at some point?" I asked.

She shrugged, then fidgeted and glanced to the side.

"I'm sorry. I know I'm making you uncomfortable. I just…I've never been the jealous type, but having your ex living in your house is…a lot. I think I'll relax if I understand it more."

Gia offered me a sympathetic smile. "Understand what?"

"Back in high school, what did you like about Luca? I mean, why did you stay with him so long?"

"We made a lot of sense. In my teenage brain, I was certain we were supposed to be together." Her smile widened. "But also, we had fun together. Luca was adventurous, and funny, and the life of every party, and everything we did was a blast. He taught me to let loose."

I couldn't imagine a version of Giada that didn't know how to let loose, but more than that, I couldn't imagine Luca being fun. "You're telling me the Luca guy staying at your house used to be fun?"

Her eyebrows raised. "Stop it," she said, playfully swatting me. "I'm not saying he hasn't changed any since high school, but you asked me what he was like then. You don't get to mock my answer."

I nodded. She was right. Honestly, I barely recognized myself when I was acting this jealous. It had never been an issue for me before. Josie, a girl I'd dated my sophomore year of college, tutored her ex-boyfriend while we were dating. I'd had no problem with that. Carolyn once got asked out while we were on a date. It turned out the guy thought I was her brother or something, so it was all weird, but still, it hadn't bothered me.

But for some reason, every time I looked at Luca, I could swear he was mentally undressing Gia. When I saw them interacting, no matter how innocently, my mind would jump to images of them together. Maybe it was that I knew he was her first, or maybe it was just because he had this obvious connection to her family that seemed to link them together forever no matter what she wanted, but I couldn't help but feel I was in competition for my own girlfriend.

It didn't help that when I did an internet search for Valentino bags, the pricing was in the thousands, not hundreds. How was that an appropriate gift for an ex-girlfriend, or even just a friend? And how could I ever compete with that?

"He has a girlfriend. Chiara something," Giada said as if reading my mind.

"You've met her?"

"No, but I've seen pictures. And my brothers have mentioned her.

"He's been with her for a long time. Like almost two years. They're probably getting married."

For some reason, that did make me feel better.

Gia reached across the table and squeezed my hand. "I love you. I'm sorry my family is so loud and overbearing, and I promise they do like you. They just know Luca better. You're new and different, and it'll just take some time before you're one of them."

She paused, and I considered her words carefully. I knew she meant it innocently enough, but at this point, I wasn't sure I'd ever be "one of them." I wasn't even sure I *could*.

"And I know it's so weird having my ex-boyfriend staying in the same house as both of us, but trust me, he is in my past. When I look at Luca, all I see is an old friend. I think of him more as one of my dad's lackeys than anything else. You are the only one I want."

I nodded, feeling like a total douche. "I know that, Gia. I'm sorry. I don't know why I'm being so insecure. I think maybe Luca just looks like a better fit for you," I said, not realizing how true the words were until I heard them aloud.

Her eyebrows furrowed. "Well, he's not, and I hate that you feel that way. I'll talk to my dad and see how much longer Luca will be in town and have them figure out someplace else for him to stay. There's no reason for him to be at the house."

I shook my head. Kicking out their beloved Luca would definitely not be the way to win over Giada's family. "No, really. It's fine. I trust you, and I just need to be a grownup about it all."

"You sure?"

I didn't answer, instead motioning for the waiter to bring us the bill. The waiter frowned uncomfortably then shook his head.

"It's been taken care of. Have a lovely day. We hope to see you again soon."

Gia and I both eyed each other suspiciously, and then she shrugged as though people often paid for her meals without telling her.

The rest of the morning was idyllic. We left Enzo where he was and walked along the marina hand in hand. The sun rested high above the trees but cast brilliant rays across the water, turning it a vivid blue. Gia rested her head against my shoulder as we strolled slowly onward, sighing peacefully.

"I see why you like it here," I said. "It's gorgeous." I stopped and turned to her.

She smiled widely, gazing up at me instead of the water. "Yes, it is." She lifted onto her toes to kiss me. Between the heat emanating off her beautiful body and the warmth from the sun, things heated up quickly. We kissed, oblivious to any passersby, until Gia's phone trilled loudly, jolting us both.

"What?" she growled into her cell, barely breaking away from me. She paused, then groaned and stuck her phone back into her pocket. "Enzo says we need to get back to the car now, or I'll be late for lunch," she said, pouting dramatically.

"It's okay. We'll finish that later, alright?"

She nodded.

∼

Giada

*L*unch with my aunts was overwhelming and ear-piercing, as always. I loved my aunts dearly, but they could be a lot to handle. Whenever all the ladies gathered, we would congregate in the kitchen, with everyone moving about comfortably as though it was their house. A photo of my family preparing for an informal lunch would offer the perfect definition of the phrase "too many cooks in the kitchen."

Still, there was a certain comfort to being surrounded by

family, especially when I hadn't seen so many of my relatives since second semester began. Even as aunt after aunt pulled me in for a hug, I felt my blood pressure lowering. There were tons of questions about my classes and my apartment at first, but then, of course, the discussion shifted to Adrian. They'd all heard of him by this point, even those who hadn't met him, and it was interesting trying to guess who'd learned which facts from whom based on the various slants.

After my late breakfast with Adrian, I wasn't too hungry for lunch when we started cooking, but by the time everyone was seated at the table, it was after one o'clock, so I could eat enough to safely avoid any accusations that I was dieting or—gasp—didn't like the food they'd prepared. Aside from Diego's wife and my cousin Giulia, I was the only younger lady, but somehow I ended up squished between my mother and my aunt Sofia instead of at the other end of the table with my contemporaries.

We had just reached the dessert course, which I had zero room for, when Luca burst into the dining room. He surely knew we were in the midst of a luncheon and was equally familiar with the ladies-only rule, but still managed to squirm his way into the room. All my aunts and cousins greeted him jovially and feigned annoyance that he'd interrupted our gathering, but it was obvious everyone was happy to see him. It was equally apparent that he was thriving with the attention. I focused intently on my food, which I had no desire to eat, but he crept up behind me and whispered in my ear.

"Can I talk with you for a moment Giada?"

I sighed and glanced over at my mom, who nodded encouragingly as if leaving the table mid-meal were now an acceptable habit. I followed him back into the kitchen. He grinned and checked out my outfit, making no attempt at subtlety. I crossed my arms over my chest.

"What do you need, Luca?"

"We are headed out for some golf. Your dad wants to take Adrian. I thought I'd clear it with you first."

"Did you guys ask him?"

"Of course. We aren't kidnapping him."

I shrugged. "If he wants to go, it's fine by me. He can make his own decisions."

"Alright."

"Be nice," I cautioned.

He laughed and sauntered out.

I took a few calming breaths, then headed back in. Adrian was a big boy, perfectly capable of expressing his own opinions. Surely he'd speak up if he didn't want to join in the golf outing.

CHAPTER 10

Adrian

Giada's family celebrated her birthday the entire weekend. I loved seeing her so happy, but the more everyone included me on the surface, the more I felt like an outsider. One day back into the office, and I already felt like I belonged more there than I ever did with Giada's family.

I had just finished the last stack of filings when something on Jeremy's desk caught my eye. It was a picture clipped to the front of a manila folder, and I was near certain I recognized the subject. I peered out into the hallway to make sure no one was nearby, then leaned closer. I had seen that man before. He was staying in Giada's guest house, and I was fairly sure he was one of the actual uncles. The picture had been taken from a distance with a zoom lens, and though he was looking in the direction of the camera, his expression suggested he was unaware that someone was photographing him.

My stomach tightened. Surely there was a rational explanation for someone in the prosecutor's office to be photographing Gia's uncle, but...what? I glanced into the hall again, then flipped the folder open using the tip of a pencil as if my fingerprints could somehow be incriminating

According to the file, it was Stefano G. Bruno. The list of potential charges included bribing a public official, embezzlement, and money laundering. His current address was the Conti residence.

I jumped at a clicking sound in the hall, letting the folder flip shut. A moment later, Susan popped her head into the office.

"Hi Adrian, are you all done in here? Jeremy said I could head out for the evening, but I can wait if you're still finishing up."

I shoved my trembling hands into my pocket. "No, I'm good to go." I started out of the office, unable to make eye contact. I walked quickly, then stopped once I reached my car. I was being stupid. Gia had already told me about her uncle who was arrested. None of this was news, so why was I reacting so strongly?

I dialed her number before I had a chance to overthink the situation. Unfortunately, it went straight to voice mail. I left a brief message, trying to sound normal, and said I'd see her soon. Just as I pulled into her driveway, she texted a response that she had gotten delayed at the nail salon and would be home soon.

I started inside, planning to head directly to my room. A long run and then a shower was exactly what I needed. I had just stepped out the back door after changing into my running gear when I literally bumped into Marco.

"Sorry, Mr. Conti," I mumbled.

Mr. Conti smiled warmly. "You're good to keep in shape like that. Believe it or not, I used to be a runner back in high school. If I tried to run a mile now, I'd probably drop dead of a heart attack."

He laughed heartily, so I joined along, although frankly, he still seemed in decent shape for his age. He patted me on the back, and an awkward silence ensued.

"Giada is at the nail salon I guess," I said, desperate to fill the silence.

Mr. Conti smiled. "She does a good job of keeping herself in fine form too, in her own way," he said.

I couldn't quite decipher his meaning, so I changed the subject. "Hey, I meant to ask, but a while back, Giada had mentioned there was some misunderstanding, and one of her uncles had been arrested. Did everything get resolved with that?"

Mr. Conti's eyes narrowed, and I immediately regretted speaking. I hadn't meant to embarrass him, but this seemed an easy way to quell my nerves without bothering Gia.

"When was this?" he asked.

"Oh, um, before spring break, I guess. I think Angelo came to campus to tell Giada just in case there were some questions. She said it wasn't a big deal, that it was just a misunderstanding, so..." I stopped talking, but Marco's face was still blank, so I decided to offer a sliver more detail. "Stefano, I think it was," I said.

At the exact moment that I spoke, Mr. Conti also spoke. "That was Leonardo. The charges were dropped a few weeks later," he said. Then he frowned. "What did you say?"

I felt my cheeks redden. "Oh, uh, nothing. For some reason, I thought it was Stefano."

"Stefano...?"

"Uh, Mr. Bruno, I believe." I paused, swallowing the uncomfortably large lump in my throat. "I must have been confused."

"Stefano is my cousin and one of my oldest friends. He hasn't been arrested."

"My mistake," I said, wishing the ground would open up and suck me in. "I just..." I stopped myself, realizing the significance of what I was about to say before I even blabbed the rest. I glanced around, confirming we were alone. "I saw his name and picture in a file on my boss's desk today at work."

Mr. Conti's expression remained unreadable. There was a long silence. Then he motioned for me to accompany him. We walked to his office, and he immediately offered me a drink. I declined since I was about to go running, but I probably should've accepted the drink.

"Tell me everything you read," he said.

And even though I had a sickening feeling that I was crossing some ethical boundary that would haunt me for years to come in my career, I did.

Mr. Conti showed no emotion while we spoke. When he seemed assured that I had relayed everything I'd seen, he stood.

"I'm so sorry, Adrian. I hadn't meant to keep you from your run. I appreciate your honesty. Hard to come by honest men these days, isn't it?" He chuckled to himself then walked towards the door. I hopped up and followed, eager to escape the oppressive office.

"How is your internship going so far? Do you like working there? Think you can see a future for yourself in the prosecutor's office?"

"Uh, yeah, it's okay so far. I'm not sure that it's the right area of the law for me, but we'll see. I've got a few years to figure it all out."

Mr. Conti nodded as though I'd just said something fascinating. As we walked down the hall, we passed Leonardo. Mr. Conti pulled him close and whispered. I strained to hear, but all I made out was a list of Italian names.

I tried to appear oblivious as we walked down the hall. Mr. Conti left me at the kitchen, where his wife was beginning to cook something, and I ducked into the bathroom, desperate for a moment alone before my run. As I stood in the ornately decorated room, I overheard Leonardo, apparently on the phone.

"He wants all the captains," he said. "Nine o'clock. Usual spot."

I squeezed my eyes shut, wishing I hadn't heard—or seen—anything that day.

I avoided Gia all evening, not wanting to pick another fight with her over the same "conspiracy theories" of mine. I'd slept terribly, and by the time I left for work the next morning, I was sweating profusely. I was fairly certain that telling someone about a file I saw in the prosecutor's office breached all the confidentiality rules I'd signed only a week before.

My concentration was nonexistent at work. I couldn't stop wondering what had gone on at the meeting last night. A quick internet search for references to "captains" confirmed all my suspicions about Mr. Conti and his business, but that knowledge was useless since I couldn't do anything about it. If I brought it all to Giada, she'd make me feel like an idiot for even assuming captains referred to the mafia and not to the drivers of boats docking at her father's shipyard.

I knew I was right, but maybe we both were. Maybe Mr. Conti's business wasn't entirely legit, and yeah, he was an intimidating guy, but I couldn't picture him hurting another person. Surely he wouldn't do anything bad with the information I'd brought him.

But what if Stefano wasn't so kind and forgiving? What if he didn't like Jeremy collecting a file on him?

I gazed around the office, almost as though expecting something out of the ordinary, but everything seemed normal. Clerks and interns buzzed around with papers, secretaries answered phones, and Jeremy sat at his desk towards the back of the office. I froze, confirming I was seeing everything correctly, and then I chastised myself for even thinking anything would have changed. Maybe Giada was right. My imagination was a tad too vivid.

When I finally pulled into the Conti's driveway, I was ready for dinner, ideally alone with Giada, then bed. She greeted me in the foyer, and after the basic preliminaries, she quickly agreed to making our own sandwiches to eat on the patio, just the two of us. She started to the kitchen, and I went upstairs to drop off my work bag before heading down to help.

As I rounded the corner towards the catwalk, I saw Mr. Conti standing with Stefano. They spoke quietly, looking serious. As soon as they saw me, they both smiled.

Stefano breached the distance between us quickly. "Adrian, how are you doing?" he asked jovially.

"Fine, sir. You?"

He glanced at Mr. Conti and grinned as though something about my response amused him. "I'm doing well, too. Marco tells me you helped straighten out a little confusion at the prosecutor's office."

"Oh, no, I didn't do anything. I just …"

He held up his hand to shush me. "I understand. I appreciate the heads up. When you're in business, there's always people who don't like the way you do things or can't handle when others are more successful. What I've learned is that you've got to find out who you can trust, who you can count on. You know what I mean?"

I gazed over the catwalk, wishing I saw anyone who could spare me. "Uh, yeah. I guess I do."

Mr. Conti stepped closer and grinned. "Alright, Stefano, you're keeping the boy from my daughter."

They both laughed, and Stefano handed me a grey rectangular box. "Just a small token of my appreciation," he said.

"Oh, no, that's not necessary. I couldn't…" I started to say, but Stefano had already turned, around and Mr. Conti was shaking his head.

"In Italian culture, you never decline a gift. It's rude. Besides, you deserve it."

I cleared my throat awkwardly. "Well, thank you Mr. Bruno."

He waved a hand in the air dismissively and said, without turning, "Call me Stefano."

Mr. Conti clapped his hand on my shoulder. "You didn't happen to mention any of what we discussed last night to Giada, did you?"

"No, sir."

"Call me Marco, please. You make me feel old with this 'sir' business." He laughed. "And good. Giada is such a bright and inquisitive young lady. It's so important not to stress her out over these things. There's no reason for her to know there was ever any concern about Stefano. Leave it to us men, you know?"

"I, uh…"

"I'm glad we agree," he said, patting my shoulder again before dropping his hand. He turned towards me again as if he'd just remembered something else important. "I don't know if you heard at work, but they threw out the file on Stefano. Total misunderstanding, of course."

"Of course," I repeated, my thoughts swirling.

"Anyway, enjoy that watch. I want to see you wearing that at dinner tomorrow!" With that, he sauntered off down the hall.

I stared down at the box in my hand, noticing the Bulgari label etched into the smooth cardboard. I sighed and retreated to my bedroom, shutting the door before opening the box. Inside was a shiny titanium band with sleek numerals and hands. The label told me it was the Octo Finissimo, and though I'd never been a big fan of jewelry, the watch was a sight to be seen. It oozed masculinity, yet all the mechanical pieces seemed so delicate and precise. I slipped it onto my wrist, appreciating its coolness and comfort. The weight of a watch on my wrist might take some getting used to, but the fit was perfect, and the time had already been set.

I sat on the bed, gazing at the watch again, then reached for my phone. A quick google search revealed the price. My breath caught in my throat.

There was a knock on the door, and I startled, dropping my phone.

"Adrian?" Gia popped her head in the door. When she saw me on the bed, she frowned. "I thought you were coming down to help. You okay?"

"Fine," I said, still processing what I'd just discovered.

She stepped inside, shutting the door behind her. "You look like you've just seen a ghost." She perched on the bed beside me and brushed her hand across my forehead. Then she gasped and reached for my wrist.

"Wow. Where did this come from? It's gorgeous."

"Your father," I said. "Or, technically, your uncle Stefano."

"Aww, that's nice. Hey, and score—this definitely means they like you!" She kissed my cheek, clearly wanting me to turn towards her for a real kiss. "And you kept saying my family didn't like you."

"Gia, it's a thirteen thousand dollar watch."

She sighed but her stare was expressionless.

"Did you hear me?" I asked.

"Yes. I don't know what you want me to say. It's an amazing watch. It suits you perfectly."

"That's not a normal amount to spend on a gift."

"My family has money. A watch like this is the equivalent of a few books and a nice sweater to someone else. Don't overthink it."

I frowned.

"Did they say what it was for?"

I opened my mouth to speak, then realized I'd basically promised not to say anything to Giada. *Shit.* Giada and I had always been completely open with one another, and now, I was keeping secrets from her that weren't even mine.

Gia sat back abruptly. "He didn't ask you to stop seeing me or anything, did he?"

I shook my head. "No, of course not. Nothing like that." Family was everything to Gia. I wasn't going to create a chasm in hers where there wasn't any good reason for it. "You're right. Maybe they do like me. I just feel strange accepting such a big gift."

My answer clearly pleased her, as she smiled again and swung a leg over my lap so she was facing me, her arms roped around my neck.

"I knew they'd like you because you're a very irresistible guy. And you may just have to get used to fancy presents if everyone else has finally figured out how awesome you are."

We kissed for a few minutes, then made our way downstairs to the kitchen.

~

Giada

It was such a relief finally seeing Adrian starting to accept my family and them welcoming him into the folds. I had tried to understand why he was so standoffish before, but now that it was passing, I realized he had just been overwhelmed. I could understand that. I'd been nervous about meeting his family, and I'd only had to impress his mom and dad. Adrian had to prove his worth to dozens of my relatives at the same time.

Adrian also had to contend with Luca, although that really wasn't an issue. I mean, it was strange that he was in town and staying at the house. When I'd asked Angelo why Luca was there or for how long, he'd simply rolled his eyes and laughed like I was missing some inside joke. Luca didn't have a good explanation either.

I understood why Adrian felt threatened by Luca. After all, he was my first…everything. Luca Marino had been my first real boyfriend, my first true love, and my first lover. If I was honest, he was my first best friend, too.

Before Luca, I'd had friends, sure. Tons of them. More than I wanted—or needed—most of the time. But Luca was the first person I'd truly felt comfortable confiding in about everything. I had trusted him with all of my quirks, all of my secrets, and all of my body.

But then he left. I would never be naïve enough to give my whole heart to someone like Luca ever again. I had learned my lesson, and even if I hadn't, Luca had moved on, too.

The shrill chiming from my phone jolted me out of my thoughts and brought an instant smile to my face. I only used that ring tone for Gabriella, and since she'd left for Italy for the summer, I hadn't spoken with her.

When she was accepted into the study abroad program, I'd hoped to at least visit her for a few weeks, but my dad was appalled at the idea of me flying out there alone. Even if I did make it there, I wouldn't be able to stay with her in campus housing anyway. If I could've convinced one of my brothers to accompany me, we maybe could've justified renting an apartment, but they both claimed to be busy working all summer.

"Giada! Oh my god, how are you?" she shrieked.

I squealed in response but also felt my eyes get a little teary. It was the longest we'd gone without talking since we met. "Tell me everything about Italy," I commanded.

She did, gushing about her classes, the overly friendly men, the other students, the food and drink, and of course, the amazing sites. Then she mentioned the sweltering heat.

I laughed. "Yes, well, now you see why I couldn't get anyone in my family to accompany me." Rome was gorgeous year-round, and even though the summer heat and humidity wasn't much worse than Connecticut, it felt much more intense. Perhaps it was because of the crowds, perhaps it was the lack of ice in beverages, or maybe it was the underutilization of air conditioning, but something made it feel unbearably warm.

"If you can escape down to Sicily for a weekend, or maybe even Naples, the breeze more than compensates for the heat," I reminded her.

Gabriella breathed a laugh. "Oh Giada, I would love to, but do you have any idea how much it costs to fly there? It's not exactly a short trip."

"There's an overnight train," I mentioned, cringing at the thought.

"True," she agreed. "So, how is everything going with Adrian?"

I told her, and after fifteen minutes of dishing about boys, I felt the distance between us shrink.

CHAPTER 11

Adrian

When I went downstairs to grab some breakfast before heading into the office the next morning, Mr. Conti was seated at the island. He appeared to be in the midst of a phone call, but he hung up as soon as he saw me.

"Morning," I said. "Sorry to interrupt. I was just going to get something for the road."

"No interruption at all," he said. His eyes lit up as he smiled, reminding me of Giada. "I'd been wanting to talk with you anyway. Join me?"

Unable to think of an excuse, I poured my coffee, made myself a bowl of cereal, then sat beside him.

"Work going okay?"

I nodded.

"What exactly do you do there?"

"I'm basically a glorified secretary, but with less experience," I joked. "Most of my time is spent filing. I'm not sure how useful I am, but it's been great for me to get to observe what prosecuting attorneys actually do all day. When I head back to Chicago, I'll see the civil side of things since I'll be working as a filing clerk at my dad's law firm."

Marco moved his head up and down as though this interested him, but he quickly changed the subject. "Do you happen to know if people in the community can report crimes directly to the prosecutor's office?"

"Well, I think the normal route is to go through the police first."

"Right, but what if someone doesn't want to involve the police?" He shifted in his seat. "Let me be candid with you. I don't fully trust our local police department. I'm sure some of the officers are great guys who take the job seriously, but like most wealthy communities, we have a few dirty cops, the kind that can be bought. And frankly, the kind that have gone after a few of my associates with false charges just to settle some vendetta."

I frowned, wishing I'd insisted I had to leave for work immediately.

"So my problem is that, working at the shipyard, it was brought to my attention that the JD Douglass Firm has been smuggling drugs."

"Oh wow. Locally?"

Marco nodded. "You'd be surprised how often criminals try to shift their under-the-table dealings to towns outside of New York in hopes of avoiding the competition. Anyway, if I go to the police with this information, I'm worried they'll confiscate the drugs and resell them and not do anything to JD Douglass or his corrupt business. And then my business is in danger. My family might be in danger. So what can I do? If I stay quiet, our community suffers from the influx of harmful drugs. But if I go to the police and the wrong cop gets involved, it could be worse."

I swallowed the growing lump in my throat. My thoughts flitted to Giada and the violence she'd already witnessed at the shipyard. Whatever was going on, she needed to be protected. "I'm not sure I'm qualified to advise you on all this, Mr. Conti.

Don't you have attorneys for your business that could give you some advice?"

"Sure, but I want someone I can trust. I don't want this getting out."

I wondered what kind of attorneys he had if he didn't think they'd maintain attorney-client confidentiality.

"Well, I suppose if someone brought the tip to the prosecutor's office and mentioned the concerns of corruption, then someone from the office would be present for the entire arrest and sting operation. Would that help?"

"Yes. That would be perfect." He pulled a small notepad out of his pocket and jotted down a few notes. "Alright, there's all the details they might need."

I accepted the paper, unsure of how I'd inadvertently volunteered myself for this task.

Marco reached for my arm. "Adrian, it's important you keep my name out of this. If they ask where you got the information, tell them you overheard it."

"Overheard it from who?"

"Say it was someone you don't know." He appeared to be thinking. "I know, say his name was Eddie Gallo. He's got a lot of credibility in the community."

I shoved the paper into my folder and went to rinse my cereal bowl. I'd heard that name before, but it took me a minute to remember where. He was the man at the café who spoke to Giada and then appeared to have some disagreement with Lorenzo outside.

"Just leave that for the housekeeper," Marco said, gesturing to my dishes.

I nodded uncomfortably and left.

When I first arrived at work, I went directly to my boss's office, not wanting to wait and risk losing my nerve. I closed the door behind me and then launched into the story. I omitted the part that I'd heard it all from Marco, saying that I overheard the conversation at a diner instead.

"You should take this information to the police," Jeremy quickly advised.

"That's just it. The guy, the one I overheard, he said he knew for a fact that there was some corruption in the department and that this Douglass Firm had some dirty cop in their pocket. So I thought if someone from our office could be there to supervise it all, then there's no risk of the cops losing evidence or anything else happening."

Jeremy considered this long and hard. "Yeah, we can do that. I mean, it's not a common occurrence here, but it's definitely not unheard of for a prosecutor to ride along with the cops in situations like this. I can go myself."

"Thank you," I said, exhaling with relief.

"Hang on. Who did you say you overheard it from again?"

"Some guy. I don't remember his name."

"This address, isn't it your girlfriend's father's shipyard?"

"Uh, yeah." I felt beads of sweat form along my forehead. I needed to think fast. "That's, well, when I heard them talking about that location, that's why I started listening so closely."

"Uh-huh. But you're sure it wasn't any of her relatives you overheard?"

I sucked in a deep breath. "You know, actually, I'm pretty sure the one guy's name was Gallo. I've seen him around before. Eddie, I think that's his first name."

Jeremy nodded and thanked me again. I left the office and took several deep breaths.

That night, while Gia was distracted by some discussion with her mother, Marco invited me into his office. Three of the 'uncles' were in there already.

I hesitated to talk with all of them there, but Marco assured me they wouldn't breathe a word of it. So, I told him what had transpired and that Jeremy assured me he'd take care of it all.

As I spoke, the mood in the room shifted, lightening palpably.

"That is such a relief, Adrian," Marco said, standing and pouring me a drink. He patted me on the back. "Having lived in this community, raised my kids here, it just kills me to see bad things happening. We need more good guys like you to help stop it."

He reached behind his desk and pulled out a large, black leather duffel. It was the type of bag I'd expect to see filled with cufflinks and thousand-dollar suits.

"I was out the other day and saw this and thought you'd like it. It's Italian, of course," he said with a chuckle, amusing everyone else in the room.

"Oh, it's uh, really nice, but I couldn't accept. I'm sure this wasn't cheap," I said.

"It wasn't, but I insist," he said.

Remembering what he'd said about it being offensive to refuse a gift, I thanked him again and started out.

"Oh Adrian," Marco said. "I don't want Giada worrying about local crime, especially anything happening near the shipyard. She's uh, well let's just say, we've had a hard past relating to some crime there. It's personal to her and to me. So, if you could refrain from telling her what we discussed, I'm sure that would be best."

He had to be referring to his own father's murder. "Of course," I quickly said.

The next morning, I avoided the entire family before work, but when I returned to the house, I didn't even make it out of the driveway without running into Luca.

I greeted him with my head down, but he pivoted to face me.

"Well, if it isn't the man of the hour," he crooned.

"What do you mean?"

"You didn't hear? Your little prosecutorial police sting was a success. Drugs were seized, bad guys were put away."

"Oh, wow. That's good, I guess," I said, a little surprised Marco had discussed it all with Luca.

"Yeah, best of all, the competition is now dead."

"Like gone?" I asked, confused.

"No, dead." He chuckled and grabbed his neck, miming a death. "Geez, don't you read the papers?"

I shook my head. Somehow, I had missed any news reports that day, and Jeremy hadn't been in the office, so I certainly couldn't have discussed it with him.

"There was a shoot-out with police. The owners of the company are dead, and the rest of their employees are in jail. With the amount of drugs seized, they'll be going away for a long time."

"Wow." No other words captured the situation. When I'd brought the tip to Jeremy, it hadn't occurred to me that someone might die, bad guy or not. I replayed Luca's words in my head. "What do you mean about the competition though?"

Luca raised an eyebrow. "You know my family deals in exports, right? JD Douglass is our biggest competitor." He paused and laughed again. "Or rather, *was*. Just goes to show you, it's never a good idea to get on my papà's bad side. Or Marco's, for that matter. I guess we all owe you a big thank you."

I was completely speechless. Luca reached into the backseat of his car and pulled out a fancy-looking box. He opened it to show me neat rows of cigars. "Cubans," he informed me. "Cigars are the one thing they do better than Italians."

He handed it to me, and I shook my head. "I don't smoke."

He continued, thrusting the box at me until I accepted it, but I couldn't even mumble a thanks with how confused I now was.

"Hey, I'm headed to meet Mr. Conti and some of our associates now if you'd like to join?"

I forced the lump back down my throat. "Thanks, but I told Gia I'd meet her for dinner."

"Have fun," he said, sliding into his car.

～

Giada

*A*fter multiple days of Adrian avoiding me and behaving strangely, I'd been looking forward to spending the weekend with him. We lucked out Friday night, as the majority of my family went out for dinner to celebrate some big business deal. It was the first time we'd had the house to ourselves all summer, but even after snuggling beside him on the couch all evening, I sensed a distance between us.

"I have a surprise for you tomorrow," I began. I waited for him to take the bait, but he didn't, so I elaborated. "I thought we could explore the farmer's market."

"I promised my boss I'd be in early tomorrow. They have a big case starting Monday, and they need my help preparing the exhibits."

I nibbled the inside of my lip, trying to hide my hurt over his immediate dismissal of the idea. "You could help with that later. This week is the festival of the roses, and it only happens once a year. It's so beautiful."

"I'll sneak out as soon as I can, but you should go to the festival without me. Take Matteo or meet up with an old friend," he suggested.

"It's supposed to be romantic. I don't want romance without you."

"I'm sorry," he said, brushing an awkward kiss across my forehead. "I should head to bed though."

When I awoke in the morning, he was gone. I texted to ask for an ETA, and he reiterated that I should go to the festival without him, saying he might be working all day.

I let myself pout for only five minutes. I refused to be the pathetic girl waiting in the wings. I pulled on a short denim skirt and a cute flowing tank top that would coordinate perfectly with the gorgeous flowers. I styled my hair, double-checked my makeup, then started outside. Since Enzo wasn't around, I was finally going to get to drive myself somewhere.

Just as I reached the garage, I ran into Luca.

"You guys had another late night," I commented, letting him pull me towards him for a polite kiss on each cheek.

"We were celebrating. The Marino family's biggest competitor in the exports business is no more. Business will be very good from now on." He smiled contentedly. "Where are you headed?"

"Farmer's market. I thought I'd look at the flowers."

His grin widened, showing off his dimples. "You always did like those festivals. The flowers will look dull next to you, though. Where's Adrian?"

"Working," I said, wrinkling my nose.

"You're too gorgeous to look at flowers alone. Come on," he said, motioning towards his Mercedes.

"It's alright. I'll probably run into some people I know."

He laughed. "Like who? I know your high school friends, and they don't live here. Come on. We haven't had a chance to catch up anyway."

I relented and climbed into the car. We passed the drive chatting about my college experience and whether Luca felt he'd missed out on anything by not going.

"Well, yeah," he said, pulling into a parking spot. "No part of my childhood was average or what you'd call the typical experience, so it would've been cool to see what 'normal' feels like, but I've got no real complaints. Don't you think it is similar enough to our high school experience?"

I considered that. "Yes, actually."

As we rolled to a stop at the next light, I felt Luca's gaze on me.

"What?" I asked, suddenly self-conscious.

He clicked his tongue and turned back to the road. "I didn't think your family would take to an outsider, but they seem to like Adrian, especially now."

I wasn't sure what he meant by that last part, but I wasn't going to engage. "He's a likable guy," I said instead. Then I flipped the tables. "Do your parents like your girlfriend?"

He raised a brow. "Girlfriend?"

He looked so confused that I would've translated if I'd known how. "Chiara?"

I watched Luca as he wrinkled his nose. He took his time answering. "She's not in the picture," he finally said, pulling into a parking spot a block from the market. "That was a long time ago."

For some unknown reason, that knowledge made me happy. Even stranger was my decision to push further. "So, who's the new girl in your life?"

He shook his head dismissively, then shut off the engine. As we climbed out, Luca went out of his way to confirm his glove box and trunk were locked, then set the car alarm once we were out.

"It's not exactly a high crime area, you know. I think the car is safe."

He ignored me and placed his hand on the small of my back to guide me across the street and through the crowd. We walked past a few of the local produce vendors and then stopped to buy coffee.

"You had the worst caffeine habit in high school," he recalled, chuckling.

"Still do," I admitted, touched that he remembered. "It's hard to satisfy on campus though. Not a lot of quality coffee."

We kept exploring the various booths, but when I stopped to scope out some handmade scarves, we were separated. Luca returned with a single red rose and an egg roll.

"That's an odd combo," I said.

"When I'm with a beautiful woman, I can't pass by a floral vendor without buying her one."

"And the egg roll?"

"Eh, they're supposed to be the best on the East Coast."

"Where's yours?" I teased, taking it from him and plopping down on the nearest bench.

Luca sat beside me and draped his arm over the back of the bench, his hand lightly touching my shoulder. I bit into the egg roll and groaned. It truly was the best egg roll I'd ever tasted.

"This is amazing," I moaned. "Try it." I held it towards his mouth and waited while he took a bite. We both laughed as some of the filling dropped onto his lap.

"Sorry," I said, patting at him with a napkin for a second before realizing I probably shouldn't have my hand in his crotch.

"Va bene," he said, instantly translating, "It's alright."

As I yanked my hand away, I took in his dark jeans and a T-shirt, much more casual attire than he usually wore. I would've commented on it, but as I glanced up, I spotted someone familiar walking towards us.

"Adrian!" I shrieked, hopping to my feet. His arrival was such a surprise that I felt almost giddy.

"Am I interrupting something?" Adrian asked me, glancing from me to Luca and back again. Clearly he wasn't as happy to see me.

"Nope, just having a snack. How'd you finish so soon?"

"Well, if you answered my calls, you would've known there was a problem with the printer, so we were going to meet up later today to finish instead."

I winced. "Sorry. I must not have heard my phone over the crowd."

Luca stood. "I should go. Enjoy the rest of the egg roll, Giada."

Adrian glared until Luca was down the street. Once we were alone, I turned to him. "That was rude."

"I don't like him, and I certainly don't like coming here to surprise you and seeing that you're already in the middle of some fantasy date with your ex-boyfriend."

"Wow. Okay. You were the one who said I should come without you."

"I didn't mean with *him*."

"What's wrong with Luca?"

Adrian's jaw tightened. "It's the fact that he clearly wants to sleep with you that bothers me."

"He does not."

Adrian plucked the rose out of my hand and held it up. "Exhibit A," he said.

I rolled my eyes, suddenly no longer in the mood to look at flowers.

~

Adrian

Giada stayed annoyed with me the entire drive back to her house. I was starting to regret my childish behavior when she dashed ahead of me into the house. I debated apologizing again, but instead, I opted to head straight back to the office. Once my work was done, I could focus all of my attention on her and deliver the type of apology she'd actually accept. I climbed out of my car to shut the passenger door that she'd left wide open and nearly slammed into Luca.

"I just can't get away from you today," I said. I meant it to sound like a joke, but it came out too bitter.

"I'm sorry about this morning. I wasn't trying to come in between you and Giada. She looked lonely, and I thought I'd keep her company."

"Right," I mumbled under my breath.

"You and I should be friends, or at least get to know one another. Especially now that you're working with Marco."

I frowned. "I'm not working with Marco."

Luca shrugged. "Oh, you know what I mean. He asks favors. You follow through and get rewarded. That sort of arrangement."

"There's no arrangement," I said, shaking my head.

"Nice watch," he replied pointedly. "If only you had a seventeen hundred dollar duffel bag to put it in."

I nearly choked on my spit at that number.

"It wasn't that expensive."

"It was. And the perks of being one of Marco's errand boys will just get better from here."

I shook my head again. "I'm not one of his errand boys. This was a one, er, two-time thing. I don't want anything to do with his business or anything else."

Luca cocked his head to the side. "Yeah, well, it looks like you made your choice, and once you're in, you're in. Maybe you don't know enough about how Marco operates his business yet, but—"

"I'm just here for another couple of weeks so I can finish my internship and spend time with Gia, *my* girlfriend. Then I will be out of Marco's hair."

I started to turn, but Luca continued.

"Except you won't," he said. "Giada's family is a huge part of her life. As long as you're with Giada, they'll be a big part of yours, too. Marco and the whole big Conti family will be counting on you to act like a part of the family. Sometimes that means doing things you're not comfortable with. Unless you're going to walk away from Giada, that isn't going to change."

"You're not scaring me off."

"I'm not the one you should be scared of." He stared at me for a moment, then brushed past me to walk towards the house. "Hey, I know an alternative. Maybe you can convince Giada to move across the country with you and leave her family behind? I'm sure that would go over very well with the whole famiglia." He laughed sardonically before stepping inside.

Giada

*A*drian ended up working the rest of the day Saturday and a good chunk of Sunday. He offered a lame apology Saturday night, but when I woke up to find him already back at work the next morning, I wasn't feeling so forgiving. Part of me still held on to hope that he'd come home by lunch with a bouquet of flowers and some fun plans for the afternoon, but I wasn't going to waste my day waiting around. I went to church with my mom and Matteo, but instead of calming me like mass usually did, it just gave me time to think.

This summer was supposed to be like our time in Florida, with Adrian and I spending nearly every waking moment together. I pictured us exploring my charming hometown, lounging by the luxurious pool, and maybe even taking advantage of my family's huge kitchen so I could learn to cook. I'd known he was going to work, but it never occurred to me he'd spend *all* of his time at the office, not for an internship. And even when he wasn't working, he was different. He was grumpy, distant, and newly annoyed by all of my traits he used to find endearing. I could barely remember the Adrian who took me to the planetarium, sang karaoke, or learned swing dancing with me.

I hoped it was only a phase and not a sign of how the future would be for us. If this was what Adrian would be like in law school, maybe he should've just gone back to Chicago.

After church, we grabbed dinner and then I changed into my fluffy pink bathrobe and ran the water for a bath. I went into my bedroom to gather a few magazines to read while I soaked, when I heard a soft knock on the door.

Assuming it was Adrian, I opened it.

Luca stood there gawking at me. "Wow. Nice robe."

I rolled my eyes and tugged the robe tighter. "What can I do for you?"

"Interesting way to phrase it. I can think of a lot of things *I* could do for *you* if you're so inclined."

He was kidding, but it still annoyed me that he could be so cocky. I needed to shut off the water before I could lecture him though. "Hang on," I mumbled, dashing back to the bathroom.

Luca stepped into my bedroom and closed the door behind him.

"Isn't it ironic? I would've killed for unlimited access to your bedroom five years ago, and now, no one minds if I just wander in and out?" he mused.

"I mind," I said. "I was going to take a bath."

"Clearly. Well, I wanted to apologize for yesterday. I didn't mean to step on Adrian's toes. I just felt bad that he had ditched you, and besides, I like hanging out with you. I understand how he misinterpreted it all. It's my fault for taking you in the first place."

He seemed sincere, but it was so unexpected that I didn't have a response prepared yet.

Luca sighed and continued. "Anyway, I talked to Adrian

yesterday and apologized and told him nothing happened and that I had no interest in reliving high school. No offense."

"None taken."

"I think he still hates me, but I tried."

"He'll be fine," I said.

He gazed at me for a moment and cocked his head to the side. "You sure know how to pick the jealous ones, don't you?"

"Adrian isn't a jealous guy," I said. And it was the truth. Or, well, it had been. Back at school, Adrian didn't mind when I hung out with other guys, he didn't care what I wore around them, and he always seemed to trust me. Lately though, he had been a little…off.

"Sorry, I shouldn't have said anything. Maybe jealous isn't the right word anyway. It's more like, I don't know, paranoid," Luca continued.

"What do you mean?"

Luca shrugged. "He just made some weird comments about your dad. Adrian thinks he stole the watch he gave him or it was some kind of bribe. I don't know. Not my business. You should go anyway before your water gets cold."

I didn't know what to say to that, so I nodded and walked into the bathroom, shutting the door behind me.

~

Adrian

As soon as I finished at the office, I hurried back to the house to see Gia. Preparing for a criminal trial was exhilarating, and I couldn't wait to talk about it with her. Focusing all of my attention on the trial distracted me from everything with her dad and Stefano, and somehow, it restored my faith in the system. She was still annoyed with me for snapping at Luca and for working all weekend, but I was confident I could get her to forgive me. We just needed some time together away from the house to feel normal again.

I took the stairs two at a time, then paused outside her bedroom door. Right as I poised my fist to knock, the door swung open.

There stood Luca.

"Oh, hey Adrian. How are you?" he said casually, as though he weren't inside my girlfriend's bedroom.

I glanced past him but didn't see Gia in her room.

"Giada's in the bath. She was a little upset that you ditched her again."

Before I could say anything, he brushed past me, leaving me standing in the hallway.

I sighed and walked into her bedroom, closing that door, then crossing the room to knock on the bathroom door. "Gia, it's Adrian."

"I'm in the bath," she said.

Despite the ambiguity, I took that as an invitation. I stepped in and closed the door behind me. She smiled up at me, and I was relieved at least to see that bubbles covered her from the chin down.

"I just ran into Luca. He said you were in here."

"Yeah, we were just talking," she said.

I winced. I'd hoped she would tell me he was a liar and that she didn't actually converse with her ex-boyfriend from the bath.

"Gee, you should've invited him in the tub with you. It's big enough," I said.

Gia glared at me. "You know what Adrian? I'm trying to relax. Take the jealousy somewhere else."

I started to say something else, then stopped. She was right. I was too jealous at the moment to say anything nice at all, and talking to her was just going to ruin my good mood about the trial prep.

"I'm sorry," I mumbled. "I'll leave you alone. I should get some sleep anyway. Will you come say goodnight when you're done bathing?"

She nodded, so I retreated to my room and got ready for bed. I climbed under the covers and grabbed a book, determined to wait up for Giada. When she still hadn't come after an hour, I decided to rest my eyes for a minute.

The next thing I knew, there was a tickle on my leg. I smiled even though my brain was still foggy with sleep. It was still dark in my room, but I could still recognize Giada's cool silky slip.

"What time is it?" I asked.

"Midnight. I guess I took too long in the tub. I thought about letting you sleep, but I wanted to make sure you had time for me before work."

"I always have time for you," I said.

"Not lately."

I rolled over, pinning her to the bed beneath me. "I'm sorry. I've missed this. I really miss having you in my bed at night."

"Me too," she said, right before I captured her lips with my own.

After a few minutes of kissing her sweet, warm lips, I worked my way down her body, tugging the slip out of the way as I went. I licked and sucked at her pert breasts until she moaned loudly, clearly forgetting we were in her parents' house. Then I worked my way lower, stroking her damp folds with my finger before switching to my tongue. I could tell she was close by her breathing. Then she thrust her fingers into my hair right as her hips began to buck against me.

I worked my way back up her body, kissing her abdomen, then her neck, then her mouth again, then she nudged me off of her. She crawled over me, placing one bent leg on either side of my legs, and she tugged my pants off. Then she lifted her slip off over her head, offering me a glorious silhouetted view of her breasts. I came first, with an intensity that caught me off guard, but she followed seconds later, moaning so loudly that I reached to cover her mouth with my hand.

"Sorry," she said, collapsing onto my chest. She kissed me for a moment, then relaxed her head against me. "Wake me at 7."

Her breathing slowed to a steady sleeping rhythm before it even hit me that we hadn't really talked at all.

My morning at work went very well, thanks to the fresh memories of Gia in my bed, but at eleven am, I received a call from a restricted number. I answered cautiously, expecting either some emergency or a telemarketer. Instead, it was Marco Conti.

"I hope I'm not interrupting anything important, but I wanted to see if you might be free to meet me for lunch today," he said.

As luck would have it, I was wide open most of the afternoon. The majority of the office was attending the trial that I'd helped prepare for, but no one had invited me along. Marco wasn't my first choice in lunch date, but winning over Gia's family was clearly the best way back into her good graces.

"Will Giada be joining us?" I asked hopefully.

"No, I thought the two of us could get to know each other," he said.

He picked me up an hour later but said he wasn't hungry yet. "Mind if we do a little window shopping first?"

We pulled into a Jaguar dealership before I had a chance to answer.

"Are you in the market for a new car?" I asked.

"I'm never opposed to looking." Marco slid his Range Rover into a spot near the entrance then walked around to the newer models. "Your Accord looks like it's seen better days."

"Oh, well, it still drives fine. I figure it has a few more years at least. Probably won't replace it till after law school."

Mr. Conti frowned. "If you were going to replace it, what would you pick?"

I started to think about the options when he gestured at the vehicles in front of us. I couldn't hold in my laugh. "I doubt my first-year lawyer salary would buy any of these."

"Say money is no object. Then what would you pick?"

I wasn't sure what Marco's game was, but I could still play along. I let my eyes drift from one car to the next, appreciating different things about each of the choices. Finally, I stopped by the mid-size luxury sedan. It was about the size of my current car but had a lot more bells and whistles.

"Probably this one," I said.

Mr. Conti paced around the car, then nodded approvingly. "Good choice. Give me your license. We'll take it for a test drive."

"I don't…" I started to protest, but he shook his head.

"Just for fun."

Within five minutes, we were out on the road. Compared to my car, driving a Jag felt like flying.

"Not a bad ride," Mr. Conti commented, glancing around at everything inside the car, opening all the various compartments, and fiddling with all the controls he could reach.

"No, definitely not. Maybe I'll keep it in mind if I play the lottery," I joked.

He laughed, a little too hard, then gazed out his window. "Hey, I meant to ask you, have you heard anything about the Dalton case?"

I glanced in the rearview mirror before slowing for a right turn. "No, not really. It's a big deal, from what I gather, and they're keeping it all very hush-hush. No one except the attorneys assigned to it and their paralegals seem to be involved."

"Hmm. That's too bad."

"Why?"

"Oh, I just, well, I'm friends with the brother of the victim in the case. He's been trying to get in touch with one of the other guys involved, and I told him I'd see what I can do. I'm sure the other guy is on the witness list, so if I could just figure out a current phone number for him, I could get it to my friend. I think for the two of them to talk would go a long way to help the healing process, if you know what I mean."

"Yeah, I'm sorry. I just don't know. I wish I had access to that kind of information so I could help you out, but…"

"Eh, no problem." He leaned forward and switched the radio station. "So if you were buying one of these, what color?"

"I like the silver. Or metallic gray, something neutral for sure."

Mr. Conti nodded. "Yeah, good choice."

We made small talk about Giada for a few minutes until we neared the dealership. As I handed the sales guy the keys, he asked what we thought. I started to answer when Mr. Conti handed the man his business card and spoke up.

"Work up a quote for us in that color. There's my business card."

The man's eyes widened. "Will there be financing?"

"No, cash purchase. No trade-in. Thanks," he turned and walked back to his Range Rover without another word.

I stood there flabbergasted trying to figure out what had just happened. Surely he wasn't contemplating buying me a car, but…

I scurried behind him, buckling my belt as he took off.

As we hit the freeway, I cleared my throat, tightening my abs as I spoke up. "That really was a great car, but I definitely won't have the budget for it anytime soon."

"It's a drop in the bucket for me."

"I could never let you help me buy a car."

"Have you ever been to the Deli off of Main? It has the best corned beef."

"Umm, that sounds good."

Mr. Conti kept the conversation flowing while we ate. I was trying to wrap my mind around what had just happened at the car dealership, but he pelted me with question after random question, keeping me from focusing on anything. He asked me about my sister, my childhood, and all of my favorite sports teams. Neither of us mentioned anything work-related until we climbed back into his car.

"You know, I bet that paralegal you were talking to as you headed out of the office today has access to those Dalton files," he said.

My mind quickly flittered to Susan. She wasn't an attorney, but she was probably the smartest and most hard-working person in the office. "Yeah, she does. But since they're confidential, she's still not allowed to share any of the information with me. I think some of those people on the witness list are in the witness protection program."

"Oh wow." Marco made a face as though that information surprised him, but there wasn't a doubt in my mind that he already knew everything I'd just told him. "A little phone number wouldn't hurt anyone. My friend wouldn't share it. He's a trustworthy guy."

I suddenly felt very warm.

"And maybe that secretary isn't supposed to share confidential information would make an exception for her favorite intern. I saw the way she was looking at you. I bet she could be persuaded to be very chatty," he said.

I opened and closed my mouth several times without finding any words to come out. I didn't want to jump to conclusions, but it sounded a little like he was asking me to seduce a secretary to get access to contact information for individuals in the witness protection program. I didn't even think that was possible, but regardless, I was positive it wasn't ethical.

"You know, I bet my friend would be so happy with the chance to talk to his old friend that he'd chip in on that Jag."

I fumbled for the window control as the temperature became oppressive. My stomach rolled, and beads of sweat formed along my brow.

Marco continued yammering away as though oblivious to my discomfort.

"The more I think about it, the more I would feel better knowing you weren't driving Giada around in an old Accord."

I focused on my breathing and gazed out the window until we returned to the prosecutor's office. Mr. Conti left the car running with the doors locked and turned to me expectantly.

"So...what do you say? Can I count on you to work your magic? At least give it a try?"

"I'm sorry, Mr. Conti. I don't think I'll be able to help your friend out. Thank you for lunch."

He reached over and gripped my arm. The pressure wasn't much at all, but the intensity of his stare was overwhelming.

"Adrian, it would be great if you could at least try," he said.

"I'm sorry," I said. I climbed out of the car before he could say anything else. I jogged into the office and made it to the restroom just in time to empty the contents of my stomach all over the first stall.

After I'd calmed down, I called Gia and told her I had to work late. I just wasn't sure what to do. I didn't want to stress her out by telling her what her father asked me to do, and I didn't even want to consider the possibility that she'd say I was misinterpreting his request or overreacting.

But I also didn't want to face Marco Conti again anytime soon.

CHAPTER 13

Giada

 drian worked late and left early the following morning. I barely saw him for three days. If not for that trial he was working on, I would've sworn he was avoiding me. Luckily, Matteo was in between girlfriends and happy to spend the afternoons poolside catching up with me. Had I been alone with my mom and aunt all day, I might have really resented Adrian.

He thought the trial would be over Friday, so it was like Christmas morning when he called just before lunch Thursday to say he was headed back to the house. His voice was so strained that a pang of guilt hit me. I'd been so caught up in my own boredom and hurt feelings over Adrian neglecting me that I hadn't even considered how stressful his first trial had been for him. He asked me to wait for him outside, which seemed odd but doable.

I wondered if he'd gotten a new car or something else he wanted to show off. But, he drove up in his same old Honda Accord, looking like he hadn't slept or eaten in days, and dragged me by the elbow towards the woods. He paused to kiss me when we were fifty yards or so from the house.

Then we held hands as we walked the rest of the way. Still, he couldn't tell me what was wrong. Finally, he stopped in a small opening amidst the trees that felt like a mile from my house.

"What's so important that you had to drag me out here to talk?" I asked, grimacing at the mud on the bottom of my new open-toed Marc Jacobs heels.

"I wanted to talk with you in private. Look, Gia, something is going on. I'm going to head back to Chicago early, and I think you should come with me." Adrian's skin was flushed, and he was jittery, like he'd downed too much espresso on an empty stomach.

"I don't understand."

He sighed. "Your dad got me fired from my internship."

"What?"

Adrian nodded. "Earlier this week, when he took me out for lunch, he—"

"You went to lunch with my father?"

His eyebrows furrowed as though he just realized he'd never told me that. "Yes. I'm sorry, he asked me not to tell you." As soon as the words left his mouth, he winced. "Actually, I guess he never said not to tell you about lunch, but…"

"Get on with it," I urged, my annoyance growing quickly.

"Your dad asked me to do a favor for him at work. I said no. I didn't feel right doing it. He wasn't happy. Then today, my boss told me they were ending the internship early and asked me to pack up."

I shifted my feet back and forth, wishing I hadn't worn heels today. "I don't understand. Are you saying you got fired?"

Adrian nodded pointedly.

"But you've been working so hard. You've been going nonstop."

"I know. On Monday morning, before I saw your father,

Jeremy told me how helpful I'd been. He said they never could've prepared so well without me."

I took my time answering. I needed to choose my words wisely. "I'm so sorry about the internship, Adrian. But… what does it have to do with my dad?"

"Jeremy couldn't give me a reason why they were letting me go. He just said they appreciated my efforts this summer, and they'd pay out the rest of my salary but wouldn't need my help anymore."

I rolled my eyes. "So that's automatically my dad's fault? Seriously Adrian, do you hear yourself? My dad got you that job. Why would he get you fired?"

"Because I didn't do what he wanted." Adrian thrust his hand through his hair, then reached for my forearms. "You don't understand. This was big. There's this murder trial the office is working on. They're being all top secret with the witnesses. Your dad wanted me to get some information off the list. He told me to seduce Susan if I had to."

"Who is Susan?" His story was officially more confusing than the Spanish soap operas Gabby made me watch whenever one of us was sick.

"A secretary."

"My dad told you to seduce a secretary?"

"Well, he didn't exactly say…"

"Adrian, stop. I can't even…" I shook my head, then gazed at Adrian, pacing back and forth in front of me. He looked—and sounded—like he was strung out on drugs. He wasn't making any sense, so what was there to say?

"Look, I'm sorry your internship ended early. My father got you your dream job—and a salary. He offered you a place to stay rent-free, bought you a ridiculous watch and gorgeous Italian leather duffel bag and has been nothing but supportive of our relationship, so excuse me if I don't want to stand here and ruin my shoes while you ramble on like a lunatic insulting him."

"He's a criminal, Gia. He's in the mafia. I'm sure of it."

I rolled my eyes so hard that it made me dizzy. I started to turn back towards the house, and Adrian grabbed my wrist.

"I'm leaving for Chicago in the morning."

"Do what you want," I said, shaking free of his grasp.

His expression softened, pulling me in with those piercing blue eyes. "I want you to come with me. I'm worried about you."

I tried to focus on the fact that my handsome boyfriend was asking me to come to Chicago with him and not the fact that he was clearly bat shit crazy. "I can't just go to Chicago now."

"Why not? It's not like you're working."

I gritted my teeth. Adrian knew that was a low blow. "I can't just ditch my family. This is the first time in years that I've been able to spend a decent amount of time with them, and I'm not just going to abandon them because of your crazy conspiracy theories."

"They're not crazy, Gia. You're not listening to me."

"I am listening, Adrian. I just don't know how to respond because you sound insane."

Suddenly, there was a rustling in the trees nearby that caused us both to turn. Out popped Luca, who appeared to be casually taking a walk through the wooded portion of the property.

He glanced from me to Adrian then back again to me. I tried to calm my breathing and quickly wiped under my eye, certain I looked upset.

"Is everything okay?" he asked.

"Yes!" we both replied.

"I thought I heard shouting."

I shook my head. "We're fine."

Luca frowned and stepped closer. "Giada…"

"She said she's fine!" Adrian snarled, his face turning vicious.

Luca closed the distance between the two of them, his expression clear. In an instant, I remembered all the times he'd come to school covered in bruises from various fights he just couldn't avoid. The last thing I needed was for him to attack Adrian.

"Luca, can you give us some privacy?" I asked, focusing all of my energy on leveling my voice.

Luca slowly backed away, but neither Adrian nor I spoke for several minutes. When Adrian finally did speak, I wished he hadn't.

"Is Luca the reason you don't want to leave yet?"

"There's nothing going on with Luca."

"You say that, but then he's always with you, at the market, in your bedroom when you're bathing…"

"I explained all of that, Adrian." I swallowed the lump in my throat and bit the inside of my cheek to hold back the tears. I glanced around at our surroundings, taking in the gently swaying trees and the rays of sunlight dancing between the leaves. This part of the property was gorgeous, and yet I'd never spent much time out here. And now, something told me I'd never again want to stand in this spot.

I took a deep breath and faced Adrian again. "Lately, I feel like I'm constantly explaining myself and I haven't done anything wrong. You used to trust me and now, I don't even recognize you anymore. You've turned into this jealous, paranoid monster."

"Monster," he repeated, wincing.

"I didn't mean…"

He blew out a sigh and paced off to the side for a minute. I waited a respectable amount of time and then went after him.

"Things used to be so easy between us, Gia, and now I don't even know what I can and can't say to you anymore."

I started to reply, but he held up his hand then continued.

"I think maybe you're right. I should go to Chicago alone. I just need some time away from all of this."

"This. You mean…?"

"Away from all the drama, away from your family, from Luca."

"Away from me," I supplied.

He didn't disagree. "Giada, I'm sorry. I don't know how we got here."

Hearing him call me by my full name felt like a knife in the abdomen. I squeezed my eyes shut, praying this wasn't it, that he wasn't actually breaking up with me over some stupid theory that my dad was out to get him.

"If you feel that you need time away from me so badly, maybe I shouldn't come visit you later this month," I said, each word tearing another piece out of my heart.

I held my breath, waiting for Adrian to correct me, to tell me I was wrong and that he would come to his senses by then. I waited for him to realize he was just mad about his job and that none of this was my fault or my father's. I waited for him to remember he loved me, that he couldn't breathe without me in his life.

But then maybe that was just me.

Adrian's cerulean eyes had misted over, but he wasn't reaching for me. By the calmness of his face, I could tell he wasn't even feeling for me. In his mind, we were already over.

"Yeah," he finally said. "You're probably right. Maybe we both need some time apart, and then we'll talk in the fall, back on campus."

I heard myself say "okay," but internally I was trying not to vomit. I could still remember when the thought of three weeks away from Adrian sounded like an eternity, but I was so confident that no obstacle was insurmountable for a love as strong as ours. Now, my soul mate, the love of my life, was calmly suggesting we spend nearly two months apart, as though somehow such a time would do anything but break my heart.

I considered the possibility that I was dreaming, that none of this was really happening. Frankly, that made more sense than the alternative, that our random late-day romantic walk had somehow turned into a breakup. I was too dizzy and nauseous to be sure of anything, but when I finally gathered the courage to look at Adrian again, the steely resolve in his eyes confirmed my worst fears.

"I should go pack," he said softly.

Before I could answer, he started off towards the house, leaving me alone in the woods with my ruined shoes.

~

Adrian

Once back in my room, I began packing in a hurry. I was in no condition to drive back to Chicago, but I sure wasn't staying at the Conti house another night. I didn't want to be around when Giada told her dad and Luca what I said about him having me fired and I knew they wouldn't be happy to know I'd blabbed about the witness list. Even if I wasn't in any actual danger, I no longer felt welcome in their home.

I tried cramming all my belongings into the bags I'd initially packed, but thanks to Giada's shopping habits, it no longer all fit. I was forced to use the new duffel Marco had given me. I gazed down at the shiny watch on my wrist, certain that leaving it on the bed when I departed would be the dignified thing to do, but I couldn't. It reminded me of Giada, and besides, I earned that fucking watch. If I was going to sell my soul to the devil, I sure as shit would keep the payment.

I double-checked all the drawers and peered under the bed, then stopped. If I slowed down just a little, maybe Giada would change her mind. If I gave her another minute, she might just realize how naïve she'd been. She might decide to come with me after all.

I sighed, suddenly aware that my hands were shaking.

Had I done enough to convince Giada to leave? I didn't know of anything else I could do, honestly. She'd made her opinion clear. If she had to choose between her family and me, they'd win every time. Not only would she not come with me now, hell, she wouldn't even come visit me like we'd planned earlier. Apparently, now even a few days away from them was too much for her to handle. How had I so abruptly turned her against me?

Except it wasn't me. I knew it wasn't. It was Luca. From the moment he'd shown up, he'd done everything he could to wedge his way in between us and make her think she couldn't have me without forsaking her family.

I made my way downstairs quietly, not wanting attention from anyone. As always though, the house was filled with people. I passed Leo, but before I could exhale with relief that he hadn't spoken to me, Stefano stepped in my path, frowning at my packed bags.

"Where are you headed?"

"Back to Chicago," I said. "My internship here ended early so I'm going to get situated back home."

"You were just going to sneak out?"

"No." I glanced at the door, thinking how close I'd come to succeeding. "I wanted to hit the road before dark, but I was going to load up my car and then say goodbye."

Martina Conti popped her head around the corner, so I set down my bags and went to her.

"Thank you so much for letting me stay here. I appreciate the hospitality and it has been great getting to know everyone." I gazed awkwardly at my feet. "I should go now, but um, please tell Mr. Conti I said thanks."

She offered me a quick, polite hug, and then I successfully made it out the front door. I tossed the bags into my trunk and climbed into the driver's seat, starting the ignition before pausing for a few deep breaths. I couldn't let myself start to think about everything that had just happened, or I wouldn't be able to focus on the road.

I maneuvered partway down the driveway and then stopped. There stood Giada on the side of the gravel path. Her makeup was smudged, and she made no attempt to hide that she'd been crying. I slowed the car and lowered the window, stupidly thinking maybe she'd changed her mind. Instead she just stared coldly, then lifted her hand in a casual wave, as though I were just headed out for a day at work.

"Drive safe Adrian," she said.

I opened my mouth to respond, but there was nothing left to say. She'd made her decision. I wished I could change her mind, but I couldn't continue to ignore what her family was any longer.

"Goodbye Giada," I finally said, my voice cracking like a pubescent boy's.

I paused another moment, then drove off. As I cleared the gate, I glanced in the rearview mirror. Luca had come to stand beside Giada. At least he waited till I was off the property before moving in on her.

CHAPTER 14

Giada

*S*wallowed in solitude for the next two days, taking my meals in my room and having no contact with the outside world except by phone. It hurt my brain to even think of doing something, going somewhere, or interacting with someone. All I wanted was to wake up from this nightmare and hear Adrian tell me he loved me and that everything would be okay.

Short of that, the only thing that would make me feel better was Gabriella, and she was half-way across the world. I didn't want to interrupt her amazing summer, but it was an emergency. I needed my best friend's voice, at least, if I couldn't have her arms to comfort me. She probably missed a class or two listening to my sob story, but when we finally hung up, I did feel a little better.

I spent the second day post-breakup sleeping, thanks to some Valium I found stashed in the back of my medicine cabinet.

On the third day, I managed to shower and binge watch an entire season of Friends while eating junk food with Matteo.

On the fourth day, I did the unthinkable. I texted Adrian. It was a simple short and sweet "I miss you," but from the moment I clicked "send," I suffered heart palpitations.

Luckily, I didn't have to wait too long for his response.

"I miss you too," was all he said.

I wasn't sure what to take from that. If it weren't the middle of the night in Rome, I would've called Gabriella, but as it was, I was on my own.

"Did we make a mistake?" I wrote.

"I don't know," came his reply.

I was toying with what to say next when he texted again.

"It's not too late for you to come to Chicago."

I considered that. It was so tempting to forget our fight, head to Chicago, and pretend he hadn't ever accused my father of being a criminal or me of cheating with my ex. Once Adrian and I were together, we could work everything out, get on the same page again. Except, well, we'd been together a lot this summer, and the opposite had happened. I'd hate to get half-way across the country, and then have the same devastating fight when I couldn't even retreat to my own bedroom haven.

"I feel like you're asking me to choose between my family and you," I finally wrote. I held my breath, praying he'd reply that he'd never make me choose, but he didn't.

"I'm sorry," was his response.

"I hate that this feels like goodbye," I typed.

"Me too."

"But it isn't, right? This is just a break, and then we'll figure things out at school?"

"Yes. That is the plan."

I supposed that was good, but for some reason, I started crying again and couldn't stop long enough to even type out a rational response. After a while, my phone buzzed with another text from Adrian.

"Sweet dreams, Giada," was what this one said.

I tossed my phone across the room, swallowed another Valium, and slept.

On my fifth day of hibernation, my mother dragged me out of my room. She chose an outfit for me, practically threw me into the shower, then waited till I was dressed to help me with my hair and makeup.

"You can feel sad on the inside as long as you need, Giada, but it's been almost a week, so it's time you look like you're moving on," she said, forcing a thin silver bracelet onto my wrist.

"There's nothing to move on from. We didn't break up. It's just a break," I insisted, more for my benefit than hers.

"Even better," she said. "Now we are going to mass and then for a family dinner at Salvatore's."

I grimaced, hating that she'd manipulate me through food.

Mass was a good distraction, and the family dinner was just my actual family—my parents and my brothers. Still, after lounging in bed for the better part of the last week, being out in public was exhausting. Just remembering to smile took a crushing amount of effort. As soon as we returned home, I hurried upstairs. When I reached my room, though, Luca was there, perched on the edge of my bed waiting for me.

He stood when he saw me, but I shook my head. "I'm not in the mood to talk, Luca. I just want to go to bed," I said. I headed to my dresser and started removing my earrings and bracelets. He came up behind me and unclasped my necklace, slowly lowering the delicate chain around me then lingering, his chest so close to my back that I could feel the heat from his body. I shivered. After days of feeling empty and alone, the sensation of a man standing so close to me was unnerving.

I wanted to nudge him away, but instead, I waited for him to cross the line. He didn't. He waited a minute, then backed up.

"I'm sorry about you and Adrian," he said.

"No, you're not."

He quirked an eyebrow. "Okay, true. But I'm sorry you're sad. I hate seeing you hurting."

"We didn't break up," I told him. "It's just a break."

Luca didn't acknowledge my statement, which was infuriating. It *was* just a break, and there was a huge difference between that and an actual breakup.

"It was your brother's idea to take you out to dinner tonight," he said instead. "He thought it would cheer you up."

"It did," I said.

"He had another idea too, but he couldn't actually make it happen."

"What do you mean?" I tugged the barrette out of my hair and combed the long dark strands until their earlier glossiness returned in its full glory.

"He mentioned how you'd love to spend the rest of the summer in Italy with your friend Gabriella," Luca explained.

I swiveled to face him. "I would!" How had that idea not occurred to me before? It made perfect sense. I had no plans the rest of the summer now, and if I was going to be apart from Adrian, where better to be?

"But neither of your brothers can get away this summer," Luca continued. "And you know your father would never let you travel all the way to Italy alone."

Luca was right, but it wouldn't hurt to ask again. I began mentally planning my persuasive argument. Surely Enzo could fly over with me, but that didn't resolve the issue of where I'd stay. Probably I couldn't just room with Gabby since she was staying in some form of overseas campus housing, and since I didn't speak Italian, it might be hard to…

"Giada?" Luca waved his hand in front of my face, pulling me out of my thoughts. "Can I finish?"

I nodded, exasperated.

"I was getting ready to head back in a few days, so I told your papà that I would look out for you over there if you flew out with me. He said that was fine."

I replayed his words in my brain to make sure I followed what he was saying. "You want me to go to Italy with you?"

Now Luca frowned. "Well, only if you want to. I thought you'd be excited, but…"

"Gabriella is in Rome. Your place is in Palermo." I couldn't recall the precise distance, but it definitely involved a ferry and a train ride, if not a flight, so I wasn't about to commit to making that journey every day.

"My papà asked me to do some business in Rome. There's an apartment we can stay in there."

I bit my lip, trying to contain my excitement. "How many bedrooms?"

Luca laughed. "You'll have your own room. I'd hate to violate any of the rules of this 'break' you're on."

I hesitated, sure there must be a catch. "Will you be spying on me for my dad?"

Now he had the gall to look offended. "Unless you and Gabby do something really stupid, I don't see why your father would have to know, but I'm certainly not going to tell him I'll keep an eye on you and then let you go get yourself killed."

"And I don't have to sleep with you?"

"You wish," he retorted. He started out of my room and then paused. "And I do have to actually work when I'm there, so don't bank on me serving as your personal tour guide or translator."

"Everyone in Rome speaks English anyway," I called after him. Then I flopped back onto my bed and practically shrieked with excitement.

Adrian

wo weeks went by without another word from Giada. I supposed that was good. That meant she was doing fine and well, so was I. I had caught up with my old high school friends, spent some quality time with the family, and was focusing on my work. Well, and researching Marco Conti's business. I didn't think I'd crossed over into the obsessed realm yet. Still, I had spent a decent amount of time on various search engines looking into Marco, his shipyard, and Giada's various other relatives.

I lamented not actually having her make me the family tree she joked about because as I attempted to enter in the names of her many relatives, I realized how confused I was. I could piece together their faces and first names, but adding the right last name was tough. Besides, as unique as Stefano and Luca sounded to me, they turned out to be common Italian names.

I found nothing to disprove my theory that Marco Conti was in the mafia. I had no definitive proof to the contrary either, but I did stumble across a lot of articles about suspicious crimes happening that authorities could never officially tie to the Conti family. On top of it all, I found countless news stories referencing Giuseppe Conti, Giada's grandpa, and referring to his death as a mob hit. It made total sense in light of what Giada had told me.

It also interested me to see that while many articles discussing the Conti business mentioned Marco's two sons, none of them mentioned a daughter. I chalked that up as further support to my theory that Marco sent Giada to boarding school to shield her. He wasn't shunning her from all business-related matters because he blamed her for her grandpa's death, but rather because he desperately wanted to protect her from the dangerous lifestyle.

I hadn't decided yet what to do with all of the information. I hoped that if I brought the proof to Giada in a calm, non-accusatory way, she'd realize I wasn't being paranoid or stereo-typing Italian-Americans. She was a smart girl, and despite the naivety she'd accrued as a result of her sheltered life, she would see the truth.

Still, part of me suspected I'd lose her for good if I told her, and I couldn't handle that.

I missed Giada. I missed her laugh, her carefree way of facing every situation, and the way she sank into me when we kissed like she could never feel close enough to me. I assumed she was sad and missing me too, or maybe just pissed off. Since the day she had texted me, we hadn't spoken. I kept tabs on her through social media, but she'd been uncannily quiet for two weeks.

That next morning though, the drought ended. Giada posted a selfie of her leaning against an airplane window, with a spectacular view of blue skies and white clouds beneath her. She'd captioned it "off to Italy." I smiled at the picture, and not just because she looked gorgeous. If Giada was in Italy, that meant she wasn't at home. Hopefully, she would be with Gabriella, and not her family. Being with her best friend would make Giada so happy. She deserved that, even if I would prefer her to be in Chicago with me.

Over the next few days, she continued her photographic journal of her travels. As expected, there were pictures of her with Gabriella. Locations were never identified in her posts, probably thanks to Marco's rules, but even I recognized the iconic Roman landmarks. I found myself looking forward to the pictures, even starting to think about what she'd say about her trip when she returned and we patched things up.

That all changed on Saturday.

Giada posted a series of gorgeous images of the Mediterranean coast, so I guessed that she'd left the city, probably heading to Palermo for the weekend. But when I toggled to the fourth picture, it was of a man. I clicked on the photo, noting the caption read "finally dragged this guy to the beach," but I didn't have to enlarge the picture to recognize the guy.

It was Luca.

Specifically, it was a shirtless Luca stretched out on a beach-front lounge chair.

His face was expressionless and dark sunglasses covered his eyes, so I couldn't tell if he was aware that she was taking the photo or even awake, but it didn't matter. Jealousy ripped through me like a rabid cat clawing at my flesh. I closed out of the app, fighting a wave of nausea, and then forced myself to stare at it again, needing to absorb all the details. There was only one other chair beside him, and I recognized Giada's bag beneath that chair. The photo was cropped widely enough for me to know there wasn't a third chair on either side, which meant that Gabriella wasn't at the beach. It was just Giada and Luca.

My immediate thought was that by leaving, I'd driven Giada into the arms of the exact man I hated most. But when I left, she hadn't been too keen on him either. And just because they were alone together on a beach on a romantic Italian island didn't mean they were on a date. There could be a rational explanation, sure. And I was man enough to let her have an opportunity to enlighten me as to what it was.

"How's Italy?" I texted. As soon as I clicked send, I panicked, unsure of the time change. Luckily, her answer came quickly.

"It's been good to get away. Having a blast with Gabriella."

"She's in Rome, right?"

"Yeah. It's a billion degrees there, though, so I went to Palermo for the weekend."

"With Luca," I replied.

She took her time answering, and when she finally did, all she wrote was a simple "yes."

I gritted my teeth. There was nothing left to say.

"It's not what you think, Adrian. We aren't together or anything. My dad would never let me come here alone."

"Are you staying with Gabriella?"

"No."

I sighed and started to type, but she quickly added, "we have separate rooms." As if that made a difference.

"You don't have to explain yourself to me," I wrote, tapping the screen so hard my fingers hurt. "You can do what you want with whomever you want. It's not like we're together anymore."

I clicked send before the regret flooded my system.

~

Giada

"What's got your knickers in a bunch?" Luca asked, swiping the apple out of my hand, biting off a large chunk and then returning it.

"Classy," I said. I scowled at my phone then set it down on the counter. "Adrian sent me a text."

"Ooh, a sexy text?"

"No. He saw a picture I posted of you on the beach and completely misinterpreted the situation."

"You put a picture of me online?" His expression was serious now. "Giada you know I don't do that sort of thing."

I cringed. I couldn't deal with both men in my life hating me simultaneously. "I'm sorry. I didn't say your name, and no one would be able to tell it's you unless they're a total stalker."

"Not reassuring."

"I tried to explain, but he got all pissy. Now I think our break is an actual break up. Or he thinks that I think it is, anyway."

Luca was visibly confused, but at least his expression softened. "Giada, I'm sorry. I know you still care about him, but don't you think maybe it is time to accept that you guys just aren't meant to be?"

"You don't know that. You never gave him a chance."

"Why would I? He had no business being with you. Everyone could see that but you."

"Bullshit. Everyone loved him. Even my dad liked him."

Luca laughed so abruptly he nearly spit out the water he'd just sipped. Instead of saying anything, he just gave me a pointed stare.

"What?"

"Why do you think I showed up when I did? You really think I just randomly came over to your house to stay with you? Not a chance. Your papà asked me to come. Practically begged."

I considered his words, then sunk onto the kitchen stool and rubbed my forehead. "Adrian said my dad didn't like him. I called him paranoid."

Luca chuckled. "Well, no one ever said he was stupid." He opened the fridge and pulled out a yogurt. "I see why you went out with him. He was a nice guy, good resume, pretty eyes. But he wasn't right for you. You two were doomed from the start."

I shelved the part about him complimenting Adrian's eyes for another time. For now, I wanted an explanation. "Why?"

"Because you're a Conti. You are la principessa. You are royalty in our world. You should be with someone like…"

"You?" I supplied.

He shrugged. "It'd make your dad happy."

I frowned. "Why?"

"Because he likes me. Most people think I'm a likable guy."

That was patently false. No one would describe Luca as a likable guy. Confident, suave, and manipulative, sure. Influential, maybe. Powerful, probably. But not likable, at least not around most people. When we were alone together, Luca was different. He was relaxed, more approachable, and *almost* always likable; but with everyone else, Luca seemed to maintain a constant barrier between them and any true personality.

"You know our dads used to be competitors, right? When we were kids," he began.

I nodded, although the details were fuzzy.

"A couple of years before my papà sent me to boarding school, something happened and it brought our dads together. After that, they started partnering up on some of their ventures. By the time you were in school and we started dating, rumor had it they were planning some big merger. You and I together was just the icing on the cake. I don't think either of them ever got over the notion of the two of us as a couple."

"Why did you leave me?" I felt silly the moment I blurted out the words, and for a second, I thought maybe he hadn't heard me.

"I had to go to Italy. My papà was serious about training me to take over the business. It's like how your dad is with Angelo."

"We could have made it work." I centered my breathing, determined not to cry over a breakup that I'd gotten over years before. "You were in town that February, and you didn't even come see me. Why?"

"You were the one who told me to stop calling you," he reminded me.

"You know why I said that. Besides, when else have you actually done what I've asked?"

Luca scooted his yogurt away and turned to face me, running his fingers through his still-damp hair. "I don't know."

"Why not just break it off with me?"

"I didn't want to."

"You obviously didn't want to still be with me."

He shook his head. "Giada, come on. I was eighteen years old. I thought I had my whole life ahead of me, and then I realized how wrong I was. My papà had every moment of my career planned out for me before I even graduated and the only thing left for me to decide was my personal life. With you, well, that was all decided too. I just needed a break."

I squeezed my eyes shut, physically pained by his last word. Apparently, everyone needed a break from me at some point.

"Shit, Giada, I didn't mean that. It wasn't…"

I pushed away from the bar, nearly knocking the stool backwards. "No, I get it. It makes perfect sense, actually. I just… I, um, I'm tired," I said, scurrying out of the living room. I tried not to focus on the facts, that the only two men I'd ever loved had come to the same conclusion about me. I was too much, or maybe I just smothered them. Whatever it was, people didn't need breaks from those they truly loved, and that was all that mattered.

Luca's beach villa only had one bedroom, so I didn't anticipate a lot of time alone, but he at least gave me a respectable fifteen minutes or so to cry in solitude before barging in.

I'd lain on the bed with my back to the door. Facing the French door that opened onto a small balcony overlooking the sea, it was hard to be too stressed about anything. The breathtaking view, fresh ocean air and gentle breeze all worked together to soothe my nerves. The door clicked as Luca came in, but he didn't say anything as he came up behind me. The bed shifted as he sat beside me then inched closer, placing his hand on my side.

"I would've come this summer even if your dad hadn't called. Matteo told me you had a boyfriend. I didn't like it. I was a fool at eighteen for letting you go. I've regretted it many times since. But I never really thought there was a chance I wouldn't eventually get you back until I saw you with Adrian."

His hand gently rubbed up and down my side, further calming me.

"I hated it — hated the way he touched you, how he looked at you. And I really hated the way you looked at him. I know the right thing to say is that seeing you happy made it all okay, but that's a lie. It just made me see how much I'd lost."

I tried to think of something to say, but my mind was blank. I hadn't expected Luca to suddenly open up so much.

"And for how dumb I was at eighteen to let you go, Adrian is an even bigger moron for losing you now. He should've known better. No matter how much you're hurting, I'm sure he feels worse." Luca's hand stilled for a moment, his fingers resting along my ribcage. Then he continued rubbing at the same time he resumed talking.

"It never would've worked with you and Adrian. He never could've understood your family, what it means for you to be a part of that family. But I do because mine is the same way."

I rolled onto my back to look up at Luca. He was seated, leaning back against the headboard. I pushed up onto my elbows and scooted over so I could rest my head against his chest. He lifted his arm to hold me close.

After a few minutes of silence, Luca kissed the top of my head.

I thought about everything he'd said about the family, and he was right. I'd never told him exactly what Adrian and I had argued about, but he clearly knew. I cringed at the thought that maybe my whole family realized that they were the root of the arguments between Adrian and me.

Maybe Luca was right. Maybe Adrian and I had been doomed from the start.

Luca forced me back to the beach before dinner time, clearly bored with my sulking. But once I was there, basking in the direct sunlight with the salty air flowing freely into my nostrils, I did feel better. I told myself that nothing between Adrian and I had truly changed. We were on a break until school started again, and neither of us knew if or how we'd fix things when the time came.

What I needed to do in the meantime was figure that part out, to decide if I truly wanted to work things out with Adrian and if so, how. Maybe Luca was right and Adrian and I were never meant to be together. Just because it felt right being with Adrian didn't mean it was. Simply having a successful relationship at college meant nothing. The real world loomed in the very near distance, and if Adrian and I couldn't make it there, well, what was the point?

I shielded my eyes from the sun peeking in above my calypso

blue sunglasses and gazed over at Luca. He was pacing back and forth ten or so yards away, clutching his phone tightly by his ear. I could tell he was stressed by the way he shuffled the sand around as he moved and because he alternated gesturing wildly with his free hand to raking his fingers through his hair.

I continued roaming the beach with my eyes, my gaze next landing on a pair of girls who looked about my age. As soon as they caught my glance, they both looked away abruptly. It took me a moment to realize why—they'd been checking out Luca and assumed they were caught. They were both attractive girls, although I couldn't stare long enough to get too thorough of an opinion since they were both topless and I'd feel like a pervert ogling them much longer. I laughed to myself, hoping poor Luca didn't realize my mere presence was killing his chances with other girls.

I turned back to Luca, trying to view him the way those other girls must. It wasn't hard to see the appeal. He was indisputably good-looking, the quintessential Italian man. Lean muscle comprised his tall frame, long black eyelashes framed his rich chocolate eyes, and his dark brownish-black hair was soft and just long enough to run my fingers through. He carried himself with confidence, and everything about him oozed wealth and power.

I thought about what Luca said, how he'd admitted that losing me was a mistake. Had he actually meant that, or was he just trying to cheer me up? I wasn't oblivious to the way he flirted with me, or the way he unapologetically checked me out whenever he wanted. But that didn't necessarily signal anything except for a deep-seated sense of entitlement on his part.

Years ago, when the flirting first began, I was more susceptible to Luca's charms. Even at sixteen, he radiated control and dominance. The attention he bestowed on me in high school instantly ratcheted up my popularity and made me more sought after by all of the guys, but thanks to Luca's smooth lines and ceaseless flattering, I had eyes only for him.

During the time we'd been a couple, my self-esteem had been at an all-time high. If the coveted Luca Marino loved me, I had to be beautiful, smart, and funny. He wouldn't have wasted his attentions on someone unworthy. Besides, he could've had any girl at our school. Yet, he chose me.

Now, years later, my heart fluttered at the possibility that Luca still wanted me. It was flattering, and it was precisely the ego-boost I needed after watching Adrian leave me for Chicago. But could it be more than that?

I snapped out of my thoughts as I realized that Luca, still on the phone, was now staring at me, his eyebrows furrowed. When our eyes met, he cocked his head to the side and mouthed, "you ok?"

I nodded and gave him a cheesy two thumbs up. He laughed and returned to his call, but as soon as I settled back onto my chair, this time on my stomach so my back could tan, Luca returned.

"It's hard to focus with you ogling me like a piece of meat," he said as he stretched out on his chair.

I lifted my head and turned to face him. "I was not ogling you. Those girls sure were though," I said, pointing.

Luca barely glanced in their direction.

"What are all the phone calls about anyway? You looked stressed."

"Business," he said.

"That's not vague at all."

His nose wrinkled into an adorable mock grimace. "There were some issues with an inspection at the port."

"Here?"

"No, near Rome. I'll straighten it out tomorrow."

I groaned. "I need a few more days on the beach."

"We don't fly back till evening, so you'll have most of tomorrow."

I considered that. I was eager to get back to Gabriella, but she had classes. Besides, a little time alone would be good for me. I reached for my phone to look up flight times. "I'm thinking of staying a little longer. I bet I can find a flight Wednesday."

"No," Luca replied.

I turned to him. "No? You wouldn't let me stay at your place an extra couple of nights?"

"Not alone."

"I'm not going to trash the place."

"I'm not worried about my villa. I told your dad I'd keep an eye on you, and that doesn't involve leaving you in Sicily while I'm all the way up in Roma."

"I'm a big girl. I can handle myself."

"It's not up for discussion."

I gritted my teeth and squinted to see my phone better through the glare of the sun. There weren't any direct flights Wednesday until late, so I selected a Tuesday afternoon one. A minute later, the transaction was complete, and I set my phone down contentedly.

"I booked a flight for Tuesday," I said matter-of-factly. "If you don't want me in the villa, I'll find a hotel."

Luca turned to me and glared. Then he muttered something in Italian and slid off his chair. I watched as he made another phone call. This time he was back in under five minutes.

He pulled out a magazine and began flipping through it. Based on the ferocity with which he turned the pages, I was fairly certain he was still pissed.

"So about the villa…" I began timidly.

He slammed the magazine against his legs. "It's fine, Giada. Forward me the flight details, and I'll arrange transportation to and from the airport."

"I could take a cab."

The look in his eyes as he faced me was terrifying enough to convince me just to let him arrange a car.

"Fine," I said meekly. "Thank you."

"Have you always been this stubborn?"

Honestly, I had never been what one could consider low maintenance, but it was possible I'd gotten a little less malleable with age. When I snapped out of my thoughts, I realized Luca was still staring at me. His gaze hadn't lost any of its intensity, but he no longer seemed annoyed.

"What?" I asked.

Luca shook his head but kept staring.

I flipped onto my side so I could stare back. Two could play at that game. Luca's eyes widened and then slowly worked their way down my body with a thoroughness that should be reserved for a dermatologic exam.

"Excuse me," I said. "You couldn't be a little more subtle?"

Luca grinned. "Why? You know you're hot."

"It's rude."

"You don't mind."

"I might!"

He outright laughed in response.

I stood and wrapped a thin white sarong around my waist. "I'm going for a walk."

"I'll join you," he said, hopping up eagerly.

I didn't refuse the company. We walked side by side for a few minutes before Luca casually tossed his arm around my waist. I stiffened at the contact but didn't protest. It was nice having a man touch me.

As we strolled along the sand, I couldn't help but think back to my time in Florida with Adrian. That trip had been idyllic, and it was only a couple months ago. How had we gone from the perfect couple to broken up so quickly? Was I that impossible to love?

I didn't even realize I'd begun crying until Luca abruptly

stopped walking and swiveled to face me, placing a second hand on my waist. "Oh Giada, it's killing me to see you sad." He used his thumbs to wipe the tears from under my eyes and then he left his hands on my cheeks.

He was staring into my eyes as though searching for something. Then suddenly, his lips were on mine.

With his hands holding me in place, I couldn't have easily moved if I wanted to. But even if I could've, I'm not sure I would have. Kissing Luca left nothing to be desired. It was perfect in every way, even when unexpected and completely inappropriate. His lips were soft and moist, his tongue exerted just the right amount of pressure, and he tasted like a refreshing mint.

When he ended the kiss, I was breathless and disoriented. I needed to say something, but he beat me to it.

"That's better," he said.

"What is?"

"Everything. But especially that you stopped crying."

"You kissed me so I'd stop crying?"

Luca smiled. "I kissed you because I've wanted to kiss you for weeks now, but an added perk is that it distracted you from your sorrows."

I had no idea what to say to that. Luca sounded sincere, but then again, he was a sweet talker. I never doubted his ability to say what people needed to hear to bend to his will.

Luca reached for my hand and continued walking along the beach as though we were two familiar lovers just out for a casual stroll.

"I was crying about Adrian," I said, hoping to remind Luca that he wasn't the one I was pining for.

"I know. And I have to say I agree with Gabriella. The best way for you to get over one man is to get under another."

I stopped in my tracks, mortified. "Oh my God. You heard that?"

He nodded.

"We were not talking about you."

"You most certainly were."

I swiveled around to head back to our chairs. Not that I had any hope of personal space there, either, but it beat this odd walk.

"You kissed me back," he said, jogging to catch up.

I considered denying that, but I was pretty sure I'd actually moaned at one point. "So? You're a good kisser. That's beside the point. You don't think it's a little strange that you're trying to seduce me when I'm still hung up on someone else?"

Now Luca laughed. "If I were trying to seduce you, you'd know."

I stopped again and flung up my hands. "Seriously? You're just flirting and kissing me for fun? You're not even interested in me either?" The day just kept getting better and better. There I was, thinking Luca might still be interested, but no, in reality, no man wanted to be with me.

Luca started to say something, but I shook my head. I couldn't handle another second of the conversation. I turned and jogged back to the chairs. I was already wadding my towel into my tote when he caught up.

"Giada, wait."

I ignored him and started towards the villa.

He reached for my wrist as he caught me. "Giada Francesca, I said wait!"

I looked up to face him. "Well, maybe I don't do everything you say!"

From the look in his eyes, I nearly thought he might hit me, but instead, he just laughed.

I sighed. "Great, glad I'm so amusing to you."

"Giada, come on, baby. You are amusing to me. You are everything to me. How do you not see that?"

Something about his tone made me pause. That gave him enough time to reach for my hand.

"I didn't mean I'm not interested in you, only that I was trying to be respectful and give you time to get over Adrian."

"By kissing me?"

"I couldn't help it, Giada. You are so beautiful. I could look at your eyes for days and when they're filled with sadness…" He shook his head. "You have no idea how much self-restraint it has taken not to just throw you down in my bed and have my way with you. You've always been gorgeous, but now you're all grown up, and it's just breathtaking."

He paused, but I was too dizzy to speak.

Luca reached his finger to trace my lips. "Your lips are my most favorite thing about you. Quite possibly my favorite place in the world."

"My lips aren't even a place," I said, wondering if he'd been in Italy so long that he was starting to forget his English translations.

"They are. I would spend all day in them if you'd let me." He winked, filling my head with all sorts of dirty connotations.

I sighed and broke the stare. "I just can't tell with you."

"What?"

"Do you just want to get me in bed? You want me to admit I like you so you can cross me off your list of conquests?"

Luca cocked his head to the side. "Yes, to both of those things. But then I want to spend every day loving you until you're old and no longer more attractive than me."

I couldn't help but laugh.

"Giada, look at me. I know you're still mad about how things ended years ago, and you're right to be. I screwed that up, and I'm sorry. But I'm not a kid anymore, and I still want you more than I've ever wanted anything else in my life. You can't deny we make sense together. You won't have to change to be with me. We fit."

I swore under my breath before complying and looking up at him. "You're too much, Luca."

"Without you, amore mio, I'll never be enough."

He kissed me again before I could protest his corny over-the-top lines. This time, I regained my wits quickly enough to be the one to break off the kiss. When I did, he gathered up his stuff.

"I need to make a few more calls, but I should be done by seven to take you out to dinner."

"Okay," I said, dumbstruck.

CHAPTER 15

Giada

*D*inner that night was delicious, but I had that nervous unsettled feeling like I was on a first date. Luca, not surprisingly, seemed completely calm and self-assured. He didn't spew any of his seduction spiel though, so in the end, I wasn't sure if it was a date or just a meal like the many we'd already shared since arriving in Italy. As we neared the villa, though, that changed.

"Let's go dancing," he suggested.

"You do not dance."

"I'll make an exception," he said. We parked at the villa but walked towards the beach. As we drew closer, I heard music playing softly.

A dozen or so yards back from the water, there was a slew of candles and a man holding a bottle of wine beside a string trio.

I guessed that was what he meant about how I'd know if he was seducing me.

"I'm surprised you didn't spring for the string quartet," I teased.

"That would've been excessive." He handed a glass of champagne to me before taking one for himself. "To subtle seductions," he said, clinking his glass against mine. "Salute."

Swaying back and forth in Luca's arms, I couldn't help but think of all the other times I'd danced with him. For a man who didn't like dancing, he'd swept me off my feet at every prom and homecoming dance back in the day. He had always been so romantic, the perfect boyfriend in every way. I would've trusted him with my life back then. Looking back, I still didn't think I was wrong to put so much faith in him. He had earned my love. Even though he ended things between us, I knew the chances of our relationship having survived high school and college were slim.

"How'd I do?" he whispered against my ear, sending chills up my spine. "Is this romantic enough?"

I had to admit that dancing under the stars beside the crashing waves was romantic. It didn't hurt that I was still giddy from spending the two prior hours reminiscing about all the craziest high school memories while devouring my favorite foods.

"I'm still not sleeping with you," I told him.

He laughed. "Oh, you're taking the couch tonight?"

I groaned inwardly. The one problem with his villa was its lack of a second bedroom. Luca refused to sleep on the couch since it was his bed, so we'd technically been sleeping together since we arrived in Palermo, albeit in a totally platonic way. "You know what I mean."

"We'll see about that," he replied, pulling me close and kissing me.

In the end, there was a lot more kissing in bed, the slightest bit of groping, and nothing else. Luca was much more of a gentleman than I would've imagined.

When I awoke in the morning, he was already up, standing on

the balcony wearing linen pants and no shirt, pacing around while talking on his phone.

He was hot, and seeing him like that made my body react in less than innocent ways. After a few minutes of me gawking at him, though, he winked and came inside. He was speaking Italian on the call, and I understood none of it until he said goodbye. Then he tossed his phone on the nightstand and plopped onto the bed beside me.

"Ciao bella," he said, appreciatively eyeing my slip before kissing me on the cheek. "How'd you sleep?"

I shrugged. "You're perky today."

"I woke up with a beautiful woman in my bed."

He stood abruptly then reached for my hand. I followed him to the kitchen where an amazing spread of pastries sprawled over the counter.

"You're trying to make me fat."

Luca laughed and handed me a coffee. "Eat, then change into your suit. The white one. I'm taking you out on a boat."

I liked the sound of that, but the dress code was oddly specific. "The captain only allows white?"

He winked again. "No, but that one's my favorite."

I complied and wore the white bikini, and I had no regrets. We spent hours out on the boat, talking, relaxing, and flirting. It felt like we were in high school again, both of us carefree and focused on simply enjoying the day.

Being with Luca was easy. I'd known him forever, so I felt no pressure to pretend to be anything or anyone that I wasn't. I didn't have to try to impress him. He knew the real me, and he was okay with that person, overbearing family and all.

When we returned back to the villa, it was already time for him to shower and head out for his flight. As I kissed him goodbye, I realized I actually would miss him the next few days.

Even with Luca back in Rome, he didn't let up on his whole seduction scheme. Two dozen roses arrived for me that night, and a gorgeous anklet followed in the morning. It was delicate and silver with tiny little charms of various Italian places, the touristy sort of jewelry Luca found tacky but probably guessed—accurately so—that I'd love.

When I was at the beach that morning relaxing on my lounge chair, I snapped a picture of my leg with the bracelet and texted it to him with a short "thank you. It looks good."

He replied quickly. "Best looking leg I've seen all day."

"That's a relief." I replied. We texted back and forth for a few minutes before he said he was headed into a meeting.

I pulled out a book, then glanced around. With the weekend over, the beach was surprisingly empty. I'd been alternating bikini tops all weekend to minimize my tan lines, but without Luca here to ogle my bare chest, there wasn't any reason to keep the top on. I flipped onto my stomach, untied the back of my suit, then began to read. My neck was cramping after only one chapter, but I wanted to keep reading, so I turned over, raising the chair up a bit.

I had finished exactly one more chapter when my phone rang. I smiled when I saw it was Luca.

"Bored already?" I teased as I answered.

"Put your suit on right now," he barked in response.

I glanced all around, trying to figure out where he was. I squinted to see the villa, but I couldn't imagine he was there on the balcony either.

"Where are you?"

He sighed. "Rome. Trying to focus on a meeting."

"Then how the hell do you know…" I stopped talking as it all fell into place. "You have someone spying on me!" My voice came out so loud that the couple down the beach turned to stare at me.

"Yes. And I didn't expect to be forced out of my meeting by a text saying you were naked on the beach."

"I'm not naked, and besides, no one wears a top on this beach."

"Giada, I am not going to ask again. Put it on now."

"No. You are not my boyfriend. You do not get to boss me around."

He sighed loudly into the receiver. "I promised your father I would keep an eye on you. When you refused to return to Rome with me, I had to delegate that task to someone else. I am sorry I didn't tell you, but I figured you would relax more if you didn't know."

"Who is it? What's his name?"

"Ricardo. I believe you've met him before."

I couldn't picture him at the moment, but then again, all of Luca's associates looked alike to me. "He's not watching me inside the villa is he?"

"No, Giada. He's just making sure you stay safe, so I don't have to tell your father you went missing on my watch."

I sighed. "Well, sorry. Tell him to shield his innocent eyes or something because my top is staying off."

"This is not a negotiation, Giada. Put your top on now."

"Or what?" I challenged.

"Giada, your father has plenty of associates in Sicily. If you don't like my methods, I can call him and let him know you wouldn't stay with me, and I'm sure he'll be happy to send one of his guys to keep an eye on you. If you take off your top on their watch though, you might end up shoved in the back of a trunk en route to a nunnery."

I suspected he was bluffing, but he was right about my dad's reaction.

I groaned and hung up, then retied my swimsuit. I took a selfie as proof, flipping off the camera, then sent it to him along with the short message, "happy?"

"Thank you," he replied. "But I would've been happier with a selfie before you complied. I told Ricardo to introduce himself. Be nice. He's just doing a job, and I promised him you only bite in the bedroom."

By the time Ricardo drove me to the airport the next day, I

had made no real progress sorting out my feelings. Luca's grand gestures continued the rest of the time we were apart, and while I wanted to preserve my dignity by rejecting his gifts, he had excellent taste in jewelry and accessories.

Besides, I wasn't even sure how mad I was about the whole babysitter thing. It was the sort of thing I'd expect from my father, so I supposed it made sense for Luca to pull the same crap. From a romantic partner though, I'd have expected a heads up. Maybe I wouldn't have flashed Ricardo had I known he was watching me.

Gabriella met me at the airport, and we went out for a quick dinner to swap stories about our time apart. Of course, I gave her the full rundown on everything with Luca in hopes of hearing her opinion, but I was actually surprised by what she said.

"He's perfect for you. You should start dating him or make it official or whatever right now, Giada."

"He crossed a line by sending a stranger to spy on me."

She shrugged. "He's overprotective because he cares. I think that's romantic. You can't deny you guys make sense together. Besides, nothing is ever going to work out with Adrian if you don't even give it a try with Luca. The only way to truly decide what you want is to explore the options."

She had a point. If Adrian and I did reconcile, I would wonder what might've happened with Luca. If I gave Luca a fair shot now, while Adrian and I were on a break, I could at least make an informed decision about which man I wanted to be with—if either one still wanted me back.

When I returned to Luca's apartment in Rome, he wasn't yet home. I unpacked in the guest room while I waited, but by eleven when I was still all alone, I gave up and decided to go to bed. Right as I was about to drift off, I heard Luca return. Seeing his silhouette in the doorway as he looked in on me, I waited for him to approach. When it was clear he wasn't going to wake me, I spoke up.

"Hi," I said, my voice barely more than a whisper.

"You're awake," he said. He came closer and sat on the edge of the bed. "Good flight?"

"I guess."

"Are you still mad at me?"

"I don't know. Will you keep buying me pretty things if I say yes?"

He laughed. "I could do some things now to convince you to forgive me."

"I'm tired. Maybe tomorrow."

"Goodnight. Sogni d'oro." He planted a soft kiss on my forehead then translated, "Sweet dreams."

I practically swooned against my pillow. "Hey, Luca? If you ask me out on a real date tomorrow, I think I'll say yes."

"Thanks for the tip," he said.

Luca was gone before I woke in the morning but did text me an invitation to dinner. As far as dates went, it was good. Very good. Conversation flowed smoothly at dinner. Afterward we took a romantic walk along a river. Luca was his typical charming self, and I felt like the most cherished person in the world by his side.

My next official date with Luca was on Friday. The weather was gorgeous, and we stopped at a market to pick up a picnic basket Luca had preordered. Then we made our way to Aventine Hill.

"Supposedly, this is the best spot in the city to watch the sunset," Luca informed me.

"Hmm, seems like another one of your romantic ploys," I teased.

We made casual conversation while we ate and drank, but as we packed the remains back into the basket and snuggled together, the discussion became more serious.

"Do you know why they call Rome the Eternal City?" Luca said suddenly.

I shook my head, opting against mentioning that I hadn't even known that it was called that. I'd heard people say it was the city of love, but this was news to me.

"The people believe that no matter what happens, Rome will endure," he said. He paused and gazed out at the sprawling landscape before us. "That makes me think of us. When we weren't together, I always believed we'd somehow find our way back to each other. I feel like whatever happens, we can make it. And if I finally have you back, I don't want to screw it up again."

His voice was raw and filled with sincerity, and the intensity of his gaze made my heart thud awkwardly in my chest. I couldn't possibly speak, so I leaned forward and kissed him. We broke apart just in time to watch the sun drop down behind a church in the distance. As we sat there, holding hands and watching the sun's final rays paint the sky an abundance of pastel colors, my brain kept jutting to one singular thought.

If Luca noticed that I was uncharacteristically quiet during the drive home, he didn't say anything. The drive felt painfully long, and the way he gently stroked the back of my hand with his fingers drove me batty. By the time we reached the apartment, my body ached to touch him. Luca unlocked the front door and flipped on the lights. I watched quietly, as he went to retrieve a bottle of water from the fridge. He took a sip, then offered it to me. I accepted a swig then handed it back.

Oddly emboldened, I decided to make my move. As he turned to kick off his shoes and stow his gun and wallet above the dresser, I slipped my blouse up over my head and slid my skirt to the floor. For some reason, standing in nothing but my lingerie made me feel alarmingly naked, even though Luca had seen me plenty in skimpy bikinis.

Luca froze when he saw me, the bottle of water slipping out of his hand. He reached for it without taking his eyes off me and then walked closer. He set the bottle on the kitchen counter and reached for my hand, holding on to me as I stepped all the way out of my skirt. I started to slip off my shoes, but he shook his head.

"Leave the shoes. The shoes are hot." He sucked in a ragged breath then gazed admiringly at me a moment longer. "It's not fair for one person to be this beautiful."

The intensity of his stare made heat rush to my cheeks, but I wasn't feeling any regret.

Luca's breath came fast and hard as he continued to let his eyes wander all the way down my legs, then back up again. His hands then followed the path his eyes had taken, stroking from my hip down to my calves. I shivered at his touch.

"You're even more gorgeous in real life than in my dreams," he said.

I wanted to reply but didn't trust myself to formulate real words now, at least not without my voice faltering. There was no reason for me to be nervous. I wanted this—a lot. And it wasn't like it was my first time with Luca. Sure, it had been years, but we already knew each other intimately.

"Are you certain?" he asked.

I nodded.

Luca kissed me with a force that made my insides weak. After a minute, he lifted me onto the counter but continued kissing me. Everything was a blur as the rest of my clothing and most of his all came off.

His lips left my mouth, trailing down my neck, then dipping lower, to my breasts, my abdomen, then my thighs. Luca moaned while kissing, licking, and sucking every part of my skin along his path. The look in his eyes was so erotic that I tried to keep watching him, but the sensations were so intense that I felt my eyes flutter shut as my head dipped backwards. My hands reached for his hair, my fingers grazing his scalp while he worked his magic. One of my shoes fell off, then the other as I squirmed against his mouth.

I was already close, too close. I didn't want to come like that. I wanted to feel him inside me, wanted to look into his eyes as we both lost control. But by this point, I was too far gone to even spit out a full sentence.

"Luca, I need..." was all I mustered. My voice sounded breathless and distant.

He gazed up at me for a moment, then pulled away. My body barely had time to register the sudden disappearance of his warm, damp tongue before he'd stood up, yanked off his boxer briefs, and tugged my hips off the edge of the counter towards him.

He drove into me, filling me with one slick movement, his eyes still piercing mine with a wanton stare that left no questions about how much he wanted me. The sudden intensity of the movement was too much for me, and all the desire that had been building within me peaked, sending me into a series of wild spasms around him.

Luca paused, grinning at me like he knew exactly how talented he was with his tongue and his hips. I would've said something to dispel some of his arrogance, but I was too breathless and dizzy.

"Hang on," he mumbled, pulling out and carrying me just across the room to the couch. I reached for him with my arms as my legs wrapped around his hips, tugging him back into place. He moaned my name as he sunk back into me, stilling for a moment once he was in position.

I kissed his neck, jaw, then lips as finally, he began to move. Our hips shifted back and forth in unison, and I was surprised to find the tension within my core quickly mounting again. Luca's hands found my breasts, kneading, tugging, and pinching in exactly the right way to drive me crazy. Our kisses became sloppy as both of us lost focus, our bodies moving with pure animalistic instinct.

My skin tingled at the sensations bombarding me all over. Luca was everywhere—his tongue lapping through my mouth, his hands roaming my breasts, his torso stretched out along my own, and his legs entwined with mine. It was exquisitely intense.

He picked up the pace, and the combination of the deeper movement and the awareness that he was close ratcheted up my own building desire. He ducked his head down, raking his teeth across my nipple while pulling my hips harder onto him, and that was all it took.

I cried out his name, dug my fingernails into his buttocks, and clutched him to me as hard as I could as explosive waves of pleasure shot through me. He was only a moment behind, moaning loudly and shouting something in Italian. Warmth filled my body as he came, and I felt nothing but pure, simple happiness as he collapsed against my chest.

"Gesù Cristo," he murmured, kissing the side of my breast where his face rested.

I didn't need a translator to guess what that meant.

After a minute, Luca slowly eased away from me. "Tell me you're on birth control," he said, wincing.

My breath caught in my throat as I realized what he meant. We had completely forgotten the condom. "Yes," I said. "I get the shot."

I expected this to please him, but instead, he groaned. He left me, returning a minute later with a warm, damp washcloth. He gently dabbed at my thighs then tugged a blanket over us both.

"The shot works better than the pill," I said.

He eyed me warily. "I believe you."

"I thought you'd be relieved."

"I am."

I stared, eyebrow raised, until he explained.

"The fact that you're on birth control makes me think you've done that before, with someone other than me. I don't like that."

I almost laughed at the ridiculousness of this. "Really?"

He shrugged.

"You had to realize that Adrian and I..."

He wrinkled his face up like he was going to be sick.

"Oh, okay, so you haven't been with anyone since high school?" I asked.

"I didn't say that."

"Just one other person?" I paused.

He shook his head.

"Two?"

"I don't like this game."

I stared pointedly.

"More than two. But I can't remember a thing about any of them now, and I'm positive it's never been like that with anyone but you," he said. "It's like your body was made for mine."

I couldn't help but smile at that, but I wasn't about to tell him that I felt the exact same way.

CHAPTER 16

Giada

The next morning I awoke in Luca's bed.

I sighed happily. Over the years, I'd remembered Luca as a talented lover, but then I'd started to question my memory. Maybe, since he had been my first, I didn't know any better. Now, I could confirm that my memory had served me correctly, and a night in Luca's bed was definitely not a disappointment. It also wasn't restful. We found our way to each other two more times over the course of the night, and even though I was sated every time we finished, my body craved more of him within the hour.

By Monday, I felt like Luca and I had been a couple for ages. We'd spent an inordinate amount of time in bed over the weekend, but by the time he left for work again, it seemed like any other day. I hadn't remembered going from being a friend to a girlfriend so quickly before, but with Luca, it just felt right.

I met up with Gabriella for lunch, and we spent the afternoon shopping. Although Milan was the fashion capitol of Italy, Rome had its fair share of designer shops. I couldn't wait to show Luca my haul, but he looked miserable from the moment he walked in the door.

"My papà wants me to accompany him to dinner tomorrow," he blurted out.

I made a sympathetic face, although really, that didn't seem like a big deal.

"He asked me to invite you along."

"Oh," I said, quickly realizing the issue. Luca's father was an intimidating guy, and despite working together, he and Luca didn't exactly get along. "In what capacity would I be attending this dinner?"

Luca worked the cork out of a bottle of red and filled his glass to the brim. "He doesn't know we're dating if that's what you're asking. I'm sure your father asked him to check up on you and see how you're doing."

"Maybe I should just go out alone with him then," I teased.

"Like hell."

"So, do you not want me to go with you?"

He frowned. "I don't want to subject you to my papà, but he's not a person you say no to. It's not so much a dinner invitation as a summons."

I couldn't help but laugh at the analogy. "That's fine. I'm happy to go. And I'll be careful not to say anything that makes him think we're anything more than friends."

Luca sipped his wine then gazed up at me. "I'm not keeping it from him for my sake, Giada. Lord knows he would be thrilled to hear I'm back in your good graces."

"So why haven't you told him?"

"I wanted to talk with you first. Obviously, he'll tell your father."

"Who would be equally thrilled."

Luca nodded. "But then Adrian might find out."

I sucked in my lip. I had assumed Luca realized I wasn't still with Adrian. Unless he thought what he and I had was temporary.

"I'm not with Adrian now," I finally said. "I thought you and I were…together. And exclusive. But if you're not all in…"

He pulled me close and captured my lips with his own. His tongue delved into my mouth as his fingers crushed against my butt. He tugged my bottom lip then tangled his tongue around mine. His kiss was all consuming and left me feeling like I was on fire.

When he finally released me, I was panting and desperate for more, but I no longer questioned whether he was interested.

"So do we keep our involvement from them just to deprive them of the happiness of knowing we're together?" he asked.

"They'll figure it out soon anyway."

"True."

I considered the options. If we told Mr. Marino, it would make dinner much less stressful. A happy Salvatore Marino was much less scary than the normal Mr. Marino. But, if our parents knew we were dating, they'd be devastated if it didn't work out. Again.

"Can you get your dad to speak English around me?"

Luca laughed.

"Okay, well, honestly I guess I prefer we not tell him yet," I said, "but only because I'm not ready to discuss it with my parents."

Luca agreed to that plan.

My hesitation wasn't just because of my parents. If anyone aside from Gabriella knew that Luca and I were dating, it would be official. It made more sense for me to be with Luca, at least now, but my feelings for Adrian hadn't completely disappeared either.

I'd meant what I'd said. Luca wasn't simply a placeholder for me until I returned to Adrian, but I also wasn't ready to accept that Luca was definitively the man for me. I was much too young and far too indecisive for that kind of permanent decision.

The next evening when he returned home to pick me up for dinner, Luca whistled when he saw me.

"You like?" I asked, twirling around in one of the dresses I'd bought the day before. The fabric was thicker than what I usually wore, but the dress was incredibly flattering yet classy.

"I love," he said, pulling me in for a kiss. He groaned as we pulled apart. "It might be tricky keeping my hands off you tonight."

"I'm sure your dad won't notice if we sneak off for a quickie," I said, with a scandalous eyebrow wiggle.

We were meeting Salvatore Marino at an upscale restaurant in Parioli, one of the nicer neighborhoods in Rome. We arrived before him and were about to head to the bar for a drink when he arrived. Two men in dark suits flanked him, but as he neared us, they stayed back.

"Does your dad have bodyguards?" I whispered to Luca.

He shook his head dismissively. "Business associates."

Mr. Marino approached me first. "Buonasera Giada. Sei molto carina. Molto bella."

I could translate *Good evening* and figured the rest were polite compliments. Thankfully, he switched to English then.

"Your father is a lucky man." He leaned forward and kissed each of my cheeks before stiffly greeting his son. "Shall we?"

He motioned to the host, who immediately escorted us to a table in the back corner.

Mr. Marino ordered a bottle of wine for the table then turned to me, lobbing me softballs about my major at the university and what I'd seen in Rome so far. He made some generic sightseeing recommendations, then focused his attention on Luca.

With Luca, his questions were pointed and accusatory. I could tell Luca's resolve to remain calm was further deteriorating after every question. I didn't blame him. By the time we ordered our food, my nerves were frayed, and I wasn't even the one being interrogated.

Most of the topics they discussed were meaningless to me, random details about a business in which I had zero interest. They occasionally delved into Italian, but Luca would then catch my eye and quickly switch to English. For the most part, his father would follow suit.

Mr. Marino seemed particularly annoyed about Luca's failure to follow up on some shipment that had been delayed. "There's no reason why that shouldn't have been resolved that day, Luca. Actions need to have swift consequences," he said before switching back to Italian.

I could tell from the tone and by Luca's paling complexion that his dad wasn't being any nicer in his native tongue.

"You just need to be more attentive," Mr. Marino said. "You can't lose focus for one minute."

When Mr. Marino paused to sip his wine, I jumped in.

"I think it's my fault," I said casually, as though I didn't realize he wasn't already aware of what I was about to share. "Since we've been back together, I've maybe been a little too demanding of Luca's time."

Mr. Marino frowned. "Back together?"

Luca turned to me.

I squeezed his hand under the table. "Yeah, you know, dating, er, whatever."

Mr. Marino stared at me blankly for a moment before turning to his son and asking something in Italian.

"You didn't ask," Luca replied in English for my benefit. "I wasn't aware you were that interested in my personal life."

Mr. Marino appeared to consider that a moment longer.

Then, as the waiter appeared with our entrees, Mr. Marino ordered prosecco. "Apparently, we are celebrating!" he said, his enthusiasm seemingly authentic.

I smiled, relieved at the sudden change in his mood.

"Does your father know this?" he asked me.

I shrugged. "I don't know. After he sort of chased my last boyfriend away, I became less enthusiastic about sharing my personal life with him. I mean, I'm glad he did it, obviously, but I don't need to hear the 'I told you so' quite yet."

Mr. Marino chuckled. "I understand. Your father will be a happy man, though. He likes my boy."

"Yes, he does," I agreed.

As we finished up our meals, Mr. Marino excused himself to take a phone call, so we had a minute alone.

"You didn't have to do that," Luca said.

"He was treating you like a criminal defendant."

"I can handle him."

"I know you can, but you shouldn't have to." I leaned forward and kissed him. I intended it as a quick peck, but I may have lingered a moment too long.

When we broke apart, Mr. Marino had returned and was standing behind us.

Luca cleared his throat awkwardly.

"My apologies for the intrusion," his father said, grinning. "I'll take care of the check. I don't want to keep you two any longer."

"It was good seeing you again, sir. Thank you for dinner," I said, standing as he pulled out my chair.

"Give your father my regards."

"Will do."

Mr. Marino then leaned forward and gave his son a half hug, half pat on the back. "Ben fatto," he said.

As we walked to the car, I reached for Luca's hand.

"What does that mean, 'ben fatto'?"

Luca chuckled. "It means 'well done.' Apparently, even when my business skills are disappointing to my papà, he's still impressed that I can bag a sexy lady like you."

I swatted him playfully. There was a lull in the conversation, and I could tell Luca was deep in thought. I wanted to ask more about some of the things his father had said in Italian, but I didn't press it. Luca already seemed bummed enough.

"My mother had surgery this week," he said suddenly.

That wasn't at all what I'd expected. "Oh my gosh! I had no idea. Is she okay?" I turned to him, but his eyes were focused on the road, his face emotionless.

He blew out a sigh and patted my leg. "Not that kind of surgery. It was um, tummy tuck or butt lift or something elective like that."

"Oh."

"She sounded fine when I spoke with her. She recovers quickly. This isn't her first time having something like that done."

I suspected my own mother had undergone some similar work when I was away at school, but we never discussed it aside from me telling her she looked good and her pretending it was natural.

Luca fell quiet again as he pulled into the parking space.

"My dad has another girlfriend."

"He told you that?"

"He made some comments, but I don't know her name or anything. Mostly I just know because that's the case every time my mother has some work done. It's like their unwritten arrangement."

"That's terrible."

Luca didn't speak as we walked into the apartment. Once inside, he stared at me.

"I don't want to be like my parents."

The pain in his eyes was so raw that I wanted to take this tall, tough man and hug him like an injured toddler, but I knew that wasn't the way to best comfort him.

"We won't be," I said.

He continued to stare at me for a moment, making me wonder if I'd said the right thing. But then he pounced, taking me in such a forceful kiss that I lost my footing and would've fallen if not for his hands behind my back. His kiss was demanding, possessive, and oh so erotic.

He loosened his grip on me so he could wrangle off his suit jacket, and carried me back to the bedroom. He swiveled me around and unzipped my dress, leaving me facing him in just my bustier-style bra and silky slip. I watched his expression as he looked at me. I loved that the sight of me nearly naked still affected him so obviously.

He shook his head and smiled, then struggled with the buttons on the bra. When he reached the slip and slid it off, he paused.

"Do you ever wear panties?"

"I try not to."

He laughed. "So glad I didn't know that at dinner."

He nudged me back onto the bed and climbed on top of me, still fully clothed. He kissed my neck and my collar bone before returning to my lips for a minute. Then he paused, with his face mere inches from my own, and looked at me.

"I love you, Giada."

"I love you, too," I said. I hadn't planned to say it, but I meant it.

Luca smiled and kissed me on the mouth again before dipping lower and roughly raking his tongue across my breasts. A jolt of pleasure shot down my body, and I shrieked, spurring him on to do it more. When I was sure I couldn't take any more of the intensely exquisite sensation, he moved to my belly button, dipping his tongue in before glancing up and grinning at me.

He moved lower, nudging my legs apart and settling between them as he licked along my tender slit. Every nerve in my body responded instantly, and I thrust my hands down into his hair both because I needed something to hold on to and because I desperately wanted him to continue what he was doing. Within a minute, the burning inside me intensified more than I thought possible, and I exploded into a zillion bursts of wonderful sensation, my hips bucking against him.

Luca waited for me to still then worked his way back up my body, settling on top of me. His suit pants pressed against my already-sensitive clit, and I lifted my legs around him, pinning him against me. He smiled.

"You didn't mean what you said, did you?"

I laughed. Even if I hadn't loved him before, I sure would after that orgasm. "Yes, Luca. I love you. But you should maybe take off your pants now. I'm worried they're going to get all wet and smell like…"

Now he laughed out loud. "This is Italy. Everything smells like pussy."

I rolled my eyes at his crassness, then helped him unfasten his belt and pants. He left his shirt on as he drove into me.

I cried out at the suddenness but quickly felt the pressure building again. Luca picked up the pace, relentlessly pounding into me, and I heard myself loudly crying out before I even registered the strong waves of pleasure rolling through me. Luca thrust several more times, then groaned loudly and collapsed on top of me.

The next day, Luca texted me a couple of hours after he left for work, asking me to meet him in front of the apartment. I had just stepped outside when a sleek black sports car pulled to the curb. Right as I thought to myself that Luca would love that car, the tinted window rolled down, and Luca peered out.

"Ready for a ride, Signorina?"

I climbed in. The inside of the car was even more posh than the exterior, with smooth Italian leather everywhere, the tantalizing new car smell, and tons of futuristic-looking knobs and lights.

As Luca zipped off onto the main road, I squealed. "This is a fun car."

He laughed loudly. "For a hundred and fifty thou, it had better be more than just fun."

My breath caught in my throat. "One hundred and fifty thousand dollars? For a car?"

Luca grinned. "It's a Maserati, baby. Worth every penny."

"But…whose is it?"

"Mine. Apparently, I made Papà proud."

I was speechless. Luckily, Luca was the one driving because I would've probably steered into a tree.

"Honestly, I think this was a reward for finally getting back in your good graces."

"Oh, so can I drive it sometime?"

He laughed. "You don't drive."

"I could."

"You don't even have an Italian license."

I couldn't argue with that. Besides, I didn't really want to drive. It seemed like too much pressure. I felt nervous the first time I wore a new pair of Jimmy Choos because I was so sure I'd get dirt on them, so this would be infinitely worse.

"Just wait until we're on the Autostrade. This baby has 450 horsepower and gets up to 187 miles per hour. The engine purrs like a kitten."

I nodded like that meant something to me. It was good seeing Luca so excited about something, but I had some questions.

"What exactly does your dad do again that he can afford a car like this just because you finally got a girl to go out with you?"

He laughed at my phrasing. "Business, Giada. You know that."

"But what kind of business?"

"He owns some property, and we do lots of exports."

"And that makes this kind of money?"

Luca turned to me. "Giada, don't stress yourself out over this boring stuff. We can afford the car, okay? Just let me enjoy it and save the tedious business talk for us men."

And just like that, my good mood waned. "Are you suggesting I'm too stupid to understand what it is you guys do all day?"

"Of course not. I can explain it to you sometime if you want, but there's no point. Pretty women like you don't need to get hung up on all this boring crap."

I gritted my teeth and looked out the window. If I didn't know better, I'd think I was talking with my father. Or Angelo. Or really any of the men in my life.

I sighed.

A moment later, the car swerved across traffic and came to a sudden halt on the side of the road. I turned to Luca in a panic.

"What's wrong? Are you okay?" I gazed around the car trying to see if a policeman had pulled behind us or something.

Luca dipped his head against the steering wheel before turning to me, his expression serious. "I'm sorry," he murmured, reaching to tuck my hair behind my ear. "From the second Papà showed me the car, all I could think about was how much fun it would be to drive with you, and now I've gone and upset you. I just didn't want to talk about work because it's boring and stressful, and I wanted this to be fun. But what you want to know about my business? I'll answer your questions."

His eyes had glossed over, and he looked like a boy who'd just lost his puppy. I pressed my palms against his cheeks, relishing the feel of his afternoon stubble against my skin. I tried to remember why I even wanted to know anything about his boring job or why I was even pouting when I had this beautiful man willing to do anything to make me happy.

"Oh Luca," I sighed. "I love you."

He quirked an eyebrow as his dimples slowly came out of hiding.

"I love the car, and I want to see how fast it goes, but I do have one question."

His expression tensed almost imperceptibly as he awaited my question.

"Do you think there's room for us to make love in this car?" I asked.

We both laughed at the same moment. Luca wiggled his eyebrows before raising my hand to his lips, kissing it tenderly.

"I absolutely do," he said, steering back onto the road.

Adrian

Summer in Chicago was long. Thanks to my unexpected loneliness, though, it was also a highly profitable summer. With nothing else to do, I worked nearly double the hours I'd planned to filing documents at my dad's law firm. Keeping busy made it easier for me to avoid texting Giada after our fight over Luca. Still, I waited for her to call me, to beg me to believe she and Luca were just friends.

Of course, that call never came. I followed her on social media, always "liking" her posts but never commenting. There were no more pictures of her with Luca, or any of Luca at all, or any other men for that matter. So I held on to a sliver of hope that she was telling the truth, that they were just friends, and that we could straighten things out eventually.

Two weeks before I was due to return to campus for law school orientation, I finally got a glimmer of hope that I could convince Giada. I was watching the news while jogging on the treadmill when the newscaster began talking about the Dalton case.

I'd never been involved in the case, but I knew the basic facts. It was the big trial my boss was working on at the prosecutor's office—and the same case that Mr. Conti had asked me to look into. That was the case where, when I'd refused to sneak a copy of the witness list and addresses to Marco, I was mysteriously let go from my internship. Those details made it hard to forget the defendant's name.

I nearly flipped off the treadmill as the anchor spoke. Apparently, one of the witnesses—a key witness who had been in the witness protection program—had been murdered. I'd never confirmed that Susan or my boss Jeremy had a list with the locations of all of the witnesses, but presumably, they did. That was the list Marco had asked me to get for him. I'd refused, but maybe someone else hadn't.

I swallowed the lump in my throat and stepped off the treadmill.

I weighed my options. On the one hand, I could stay out of it. I didn't know for sure Marco played any role in the murder of that poor witness. But, I was certain that Giada wouldn't be safe as long as she lived in a house of criminals. And surely even Giada wouldn't call this evidence coincidental. Obviously, Marco was up to no good. Maybe with that information, Giada and I could patch things up and start anew outside the criminal shadow of her family.

As soon as I got home, I called her. I hoped she would already be back from Italy, but I also knew if I waited, I'd lose my nerve.

I assumed the worst thing that could happen was that she wouldn't believe me.

My assumption was wrong.

The phone rang twice, and then a male voice answered.

"Pronto," he said, completely disorienting me.

It took me a moment to speak. "Hi, I was looking for Giada…"

"Ah yes, she's here," the man said, immediately switching to English. His voice was maddeningly familiar, but it could just be her brother. "Who's calling?"

"Um, it's Adrian," I said, certain caller ID could've told him that.

"Oh hi, how are you? Hang on, I'll get Giada." He didn't wait for me to answer.

"Cara, phone." The man said, clearly making no effort to mask his voice. I cringed, certain "cara" was an Italian term of endearment.

I heard Giada in the background. "You answered my phone?"

"Yes," the man said unapologetically. "It's Adrian."

There was a lengthy silence before Giada came to the phone.

"Adrian? Hi, how are you?" Giada said. Her audible discomfort confirmed my suspicions.

"I'm good. Just back from the gym. You?"

"Doing well."

"Was that Luca?" I asked, skipping to the punch.

Her voice was strained. "Yeah….uh, I was in another room, and um…"

"So, I guess you're still in Italy."

There was a long pause. "Um, no. We got back a few days ago."

"Ah. How's your family?"

"We're in New York," she blurted out. "I mean, my family is good. I'm just not with them. I'm, uh, staying with Luca for a few days before I head home, and then I'll probably be home for a week before I go back to campus."

Nausea swept over me. I was a fool for even entertaining any other possibility, but still, the confirmation of what I'd already suspected hit me like a ton of bricks. "So you and Luca are together now? You're dating?" I asked, not willing to risk my warped mind coming up with any alternatives.

It took Giada an eternity to answer. "Yes. We just…" she sighed loudly. "Nothing happened before the last time that you and I spoke. We went to Italy as friends. It was… well, after you broke up with me, we started spending more time together and then…"

"It's fine. I don't need all the details," I interrupted. Then, her words registered. "Wait, when I broke up with you? That's not how I remember it."

"You made it very clear you didn't want to be with me."

"Yes, because you made it clear you wanted to be with Luca."

"I didn't—" she began, but I interrupted again, remembering the reason for my call in the first place.

"You know what? It doesn't matter. You two deserve each other," I said, surprised at how bitter I sounded.

She didn't answer, so I tried to soften the blow.

"I'm sorry, I didn't mean it to come out like that. I hope you guys are happy together. That's not why I called."

Giada was quiet as I recounted what the news story said. When I had told her everything, the silence continued for another minute.

"I don't understand what you think any of this has to do with me," she finally said.

"Giada, it's not a coincidence that the precise witnesses your father was asking about are now starting to turn up dead."

"You think my dad is murdering people?"

"No, it's probably not him personally, but Giada, you can't ignore the facts. He's involved in something that isn't good. I just want you to stay safe."

She sighed loudly. I'd lost her. I waited for her to accuse me of harboring more conspiracy theories.

"Well, thank you for the heads up, Adrian," she said. "I appreciate the concern. Luckily, I think Luca here will take care of me and make sure I'm safe. So, if that's all…"

I gritted my teeth. "Yeah, that's all. I'll, uh, see you around campus."

CHAPTER 17

Giada

Living in Staten Island with Luca, I felt like a real grown-up for the first time in my life. On the surface, it was similar to our time in Rome. He went to work most days, taking occasional meetings at odd hours, but devoting his free time to me. I spent my days exploring and shopping and visiting with the handful of old friends who lived there.

Unlike in Rome, I could see what our future would look like together. I'd always dreamed of moving to New York after graduation, and I could completely picture life with Luca in the Big Apple. Well, I mean, I assumed we'd have a much smaller house than his parents' home where we were currently living. But, as long as his parents remained in Italy, I had no qualms about settling into their mansion.

On my last day in New York before returning home to pack up for school, Luca took the day off work. I yearned to spend as much time with him as possible, so I didn't protest when he took a call while snuggled up beside me. The entire conversation was in Italian, but listening to Luca speak the romance language was incredibly sexy. I was just about to start distracting him from his call with my hand when I heard him say, "Dalton."

The name stuck out like a sore thumb in the conversation since it lacked any of the flowing characteristics of Italian. Plus, at that point in the conversation, Luca grew visibly agitated. He nudged my hand off his lap and stood, stepping into the other room and closing the door behind him.

I turned to my phone for entertainment until he returned a few minutes later.

"Sorry," he mumbled. "I should be good for an hour at least."

He sat beside me and started to kiss me.

"Well, that won't take a full hour," I joked, pulling back. "Who were you talking to?"

"Work associates."

"No one I know?"

He frowned but shook his head. He pressed his hands against my biceps, gently massaging towards my shoulders and then the side of my neck. It felt so good that I almost forgot my question.

"Just curious. I heard you say something about Dalton. Were you guys talking about that case? Did you hear about that back in Connecticut? The news is saying a major witness was killed while in the witness protection program. My dad mentioned something about it once."

The twitch of Luca's eye was almost imperceptible. "I heard about it on the news. I assume your father did as well."

I shrugged. "So, what were you discussing about it just now?"

His gaze narrowed, and his hands dropped from my body. "Nothing. You must have heard wrong. Last I checked, your Italian wasn't so great."

I stared at him for a moment. I tried to absorb as much as I could from his body language, but Luca was a hard man to read. "What were you talking about?"

"Why the sudden interest in my work, Giada? You getting

bored with all the fashion and design stuff, thinking about a change in profession?"

"I'm trying to get to know you, Luca. You're always so secretive of your work. It reminds me a little too much of my dad."

His eyebrows furrowed. "I remind you of your dad?"

"Not like that."

Luca sighed. "My work isn't always pleasant. Parts are stressful. I don't want to stress you out, and I don't want to think about work when I'm with you. I prefer to keep it all separate. Is that so bad?"

I shook my head. "I just want you to know you can always talk to me, even if you think I'm too stupid to understand."

"I don't think you're stupid."

"Can I ask something else?"

Luca's eyes said no, but his lips said yes.

"How's this going to work, with you in Italy and me in Connecticut?"

"Tesoro," he breathed, planting a kiss on my forehead. His expression immediately softened, just like it always did when he called me his 'treasure.'

"I won't be in Italy long. Two weeks, maybe three. And then you can see me whenever you want. Besides, you have all these school breaks. We could do some more traveling together. Maybe fall break in Sicily?"

"Mmm," I said. That did sound tempting. "How do I know you won't forget about me when you're off in Italy?"

"I could never forget about you, principessa. I am yours, and you are mine."

Before I could respond, he'd shifted over me, and my baser instincts distracted me from any further conversation.

Luca treated me to the most romantic night ever on my last night in New York, complete with a horse-drawn carriage ride and candlelit dinner. The next day, he drove me back home where my entire family was gathered.

Everyone made such a big deal about us "finally" being a couple again that I was uncomfortable by it all. My aunts were the worst, with their constant references to marriage. Sure, things were great with Luca, but even if the rest of the family had been waiting for "years" for us to fall in love, we'd only been together for about a month. And while Luca made his fair share of comments about an eternity with me when we were in private, I recognized that as what it was, part of his over-the-top Italian seduction scheme.

Once he left for Italy, he continued spoiling me. Flowers, jewelry, and even a designer handbag arrived for me, all reminding me of his affection. He sent a fruit basket to my apartment the day I moved in, and a diamond bracelet the first day of classes. The note with the bracelet promised he'd call to check in after my first day, but he never did. It *was* the middle of the night in Italy, so I supposed it was forgivable.

When we spoke the next day, he'd apologized, saying some work thing had come up with a late shipment, and he was out most of the night. I believed him, but I already started to feel the distance between us.

My dad asked Lorenzo to accompany me for the first few weeks of school, just until I was settled. It was completely unnecessary, but my mom said he was nervous about me living alone and that it made him feel better to know Enzo was on campus. With Gabby in a different apartment, Luca in an entirely different country, and Adrian avoiding me like the plague, I relented. It would be nice to have a friendly face in town.

The new school routine provided a welcomed distraction, but after the first full week, the novelty wore off. When I had too much downtime, my emotions ran wild. I missed Luca, but I also still sort of missed Adrian, which in turn made me feel guilty. And then I was also annoyed at Luca for making me feel so lonely. I was supposed to be enjoying my senior year of college, not pining over a boyfriend across the ocean. It all started to feel a bit too much like my high school senior year, especially since I called Luca twice the second week of school, and got only text messages in response.

After a few drinks and some girl talk with Gabriella that weekend, I was done trying to guess if he was just going to blow me off like in high school. I called him, but it went to voice mail, so I hung up. I waited a few minutes. Then at Gabriella's insistence, I called back to leave a message.

That time, however, Luca answered.

"Giada? Are you okay?" His voice was scratchy and filled with sleep.

I cringed, immediately realizing my mistake. "Yes, sorry, I just—"

"Fuck Giada. It's six o'clock in the morning here."

"I'm sorry. I thought you'd be getting up for work now."

"It's Saturday. And I was out late last night."

Jealousy surged through me. "Doing what?"

"Working."

"On a Friday night?"

He sighed. "What do you want, Giada?"

I paused, having so many possible answers for his loaded question. "I wanted to talk with my boyfriend. You didn't call me back this week, and I missed you."

"I was busy. The real world is more time consuming than college, you know." He laughed sardonically. "Actually, you don't know. You will never know what it's like to actually have to work."

I wiped a tear out of my eye and sniffled. I wasn't going to take the bait and start arguing about that. We both knew he had me there. I'd never held a job, and at the moment, I was utterly unqualified for anything beyond trophy wife. But still, for him to throw it in my face like that…

"You told me you didn't want to become like your parents,

Luca. But now I'm here, missing you, and you're way over in Italy doing God-knows-what."

"Working, Giada. I'm working."

"Well, fine. You're over there working, but I don't even know anything about your day because you never call me, and I'm lonely."

He was quiet for a moment. "Fine, you want to talk about things we've told each other? You told me you loved me. Doesn't that mean you trust me?"

He paused, but not long enough for me to answer. "And you say you're lonely, that I'm not doing enough to make you feel loved, but when is the last time you sent me flowers in the mail? Or jewelry? Or a fucking handbag? Or are you not receiving my gifts either?"

The tears began flowing faster, making it hard to answer. He didn't actually want me to send those types of gifts, but I got his point regardless. I was no better than he was, only I had the nerve to call and complain.

"Luca, I'm sorry. This just feels like high school all over again."

"Well, it's not. We're not kids anymore, so don't act like one. I'm sorry this is so hard on you, but I'll be back September twentieth, and we can figure it all out in person. Until then, trust me when I say I'm busy. I'm stressed out about work, and my papà is being impossible, and I just don't have the energy to also worry about you questioning my every move."

"Okay," I said. I was about to say that I loved him, but there was a click, and the line went dead. I started crying so hard that Gabriella thought we'd broken up. But before I could explain what happened, my phone buzzed with a text.

"I'm sorry, baby. I haven't been sleeping much, and I'm so tired. I didn't mean to take it out on you, I'm just not awake yet," Luca said.

I sniffled, feeling slightly better, and then another text came through, again from Luca.

"I miss you. Probably more than you miss me. This isn't like last time. I'm coming back soon to be with you, and I'm thinking about you every minute until then. Ti amo."

I wiped off my eyes, replied that I loved him too, then tried to perk up.

Gabriella stayed the night, and we were both up so late that when my phone rang at eleven a.m., we were still asleep.

I answered without checking who it was.

"Giada? Jesus, you sound terrible."

"Angelo?"

"Ouch. No," the caller replied.

"Sorry," I said, instantly realizing my mistake. I rubbed my eyes and looked at the clock, and I cringed when I saw how late it was. "How's it going Matteo?"

"Not bad. Clearly didn't have as much fun as you did last night. Are you just now getting up?"

"Yes, but it's not what you think. Gabriella is here, and we just—"

"Yeah, I don't need visions of whatever you two do overnight stuck in my brain," he interrupted. "I'm gonna be in town today, so I thought we could meet for dinner. Six o'clock okay?"

I agreed without asking why he was suddenly showing up in town.

That night, Matteo picked me up, and we went to an upscale pizza place near campus. We made small talk for a few minutes, but as soon as we'd ordered, he got to the point.

"So, listen," he began. "Luca called me early this morning."

I rolled my eyes and smacked my fingers on the table. "I wondered why you suddenly wanted to see me."

My brother made a face. "He said you guys had a fight and that you seemed upset and were being all crazy and jealous."

"*I'm* being crazy?"

"He asked if I could check on you and make sure you were doing okay."

"And maybe put in a good word for him while you're here?" I guessed.

Matteo held up his hands. "He's Luca Marino. He hardly needs me to put in a word for him."

"What does that mean?"

"I don't know. He's kind of a big deal. Dad has wanted you two to get together for years."

"Well, that's his problem. You have to admit it's a bit ridiculous. I mean, why is everyone so focused on me and Luca? If Mom and Dad are going to micromanage our social lives, why don't they work on getting Angelo married off first? Seems to me I should be third in line for the pressure."

"If Luca had a sister, I'm sure Dad would be pressuring Angelo to wrangle her, but since the Marinos have no daughters, you are Dad's only hope of getting some formal connection to that family."

I leaned back as the waiter came to refill my water. "You do hear how insane that sounds, right? Dad wouldn't force me on Luca just to seal some business deal."

Matteo didn't look so sure. "You know Dad wants you to be happy. That's most important. I mean, come on. He was accepting of Adrian."

I chewed my lip at the mention of his name. I still hadn't seen Adrian around campus. Now that this long-distance thing with Luca was starting to feel more like the break I took from Adrian, I was beginning to think no man would ever want to be in the same town as me long term.

"Anyway, it's not about Dad. My point is just that since we all know Luca and his family. Maybe you don't have to treat him like you would some other random boyfriend."

"What is that supposed to mean?"

"I don't know, Giada, just that he's an adult. You can't drunk dial him in the middle of the night accusing him of an affair."

"That is not what happened!" I shook my head. "I can't even believe he called you."

"I'm screwing this all up. Look, he didn't tell me to say any of this. He just wanted me to check in and see if you were okay. He thought you sounded lonely." My brother paused. "He really seems to like you, Giada. And he can give you a good life. Mom and Dad aren't going to be around forever, and you need someone who can provide for you, keep you safe."

"Well, since you're clearly going to remain a bachelor, I can just come live with you when I'm old and alone," I said. "Besides, what is this, 1920? I don't need a man to provide for me. I can take care of myself."

Matteo's skepticism was offensive.

Our pizza was delivered, so we focused on that for a minute before resuming our discussion.

"You seemed like you were really into Luca a few weeks ago," Matteo said.

"I was. I mean, I am. Everything was going really well until he left. I just think it's premature for everyone around us to start getting all excited about us ending up together. We haven't even been dating eight weeks."

My brother frowned and set down his pizza. "He's the prince, Giada. You're the princess. It's meant to be."

My head was spinning with all of the ridiculousness. People in my family had made comments like that back in high school when we were together, and it never made sense to me. As best I could tell, they thought it was funny to call Luca that when we first started dating, but I'd never figured out why I got stuck with my nickname in the first place. Our dads were both bigwigs in their business, but surely they could forge whatever partnership they wanted without pimping out their children.

"Can we talk about something else?" I asked Matteo.

He nodded, and we happily started chatting about stuff back home.

I texted Luca to apologize the next morning, and I ordered him a small gold lion figurine. Hard as it was to shop for a man with a limitless budget and refined tastes, I knew he'd think it was cute and would think of me whenever he looked at it.

When he'd received it, he'd called me immediately, gushing over how perfect it was, and then we both laughed at the ridiculousness of a miniature lion statue. Over the next few days, he made more of an effort to call or text regularly, and I gradually started to feel like things were back to normal. It was almost time for him to return from Italy, anyway, and I knew that our reunion was going to be worth the wait.

~

Adrian

*E*very awful thing I'd heard about the first year of law school was true. I'd assumed everyone was exaggerating about how awful it was, that surely, it wouldn't be much different than undergrad. I was in the same apartment, on the same campus, but somehow everything was different.

The first-year law classes were no joke. The quantity of reading for each class was astounding, and my blood pressure skyrocketed from the constant threat of being called on in class to remember a minute detail from any of the dozens of cases I read each night. It didn't help that there were no grades in most of my classes until the final exam. I would have to work my ass off for months with no gauge of how I was doing until that one exam was over.

Thanks to the enormous pressure of it all, my classmates and I bonded quickly. I fell in with a small bunch of friends and had another few students I studied with. Both groups helped me feel slightly less alone.

Unfortunately, the law building was directly adjacent to the building where I'd taken criminal justice classes. That meant I spent an inordinate amount of time a hundred yards from Giada's apartment building.

Despite the time we'd been apart, it was still torture to think about her. It didn't help that I was filled with regret. The more I replayed the events of that fateful day in my mind, the more I realized I'd basically driven her into Luca's arms. He'd wanted to isolate me from her, wanted to make me jealous of him and wary of her family, and I'd fallen right into his trap. Confronting Giada like I had was guaranteed to push her away. I hated myself for letting my pride get in the way of calling her in the days after that argument. It didn't matter that I was right about her family. I would've rather had her than the satisfaction of being right.

Everywhere, there were constant reminders of her. I couldn't go anywhere on campus without seeing someplace we'd kissed or remembering something funny she'd said or done. Every time I left class, I noticed Enzo's car parked outside her building, leaving me wondering why, all of a sudden, she needed a driver on campus. On nice days, my study group often met outside on the side lawn of the law school where there were concrete tables built into the landscape. I never accomplished much at those sessions, always searching for her face coming or going from the building next door.

On Thursday, I finally saw her. She was walking with Gabriella, who was talking in a voice so animated that I could hear the tenor of it, if not her words, from several yards away. I recognized Giada immediately, even though something had changed. She still had the same glossy, dark hair falling halfway down her back, and she still had the same warm, contagious laugh.

My chest physically ached at the sight. I could barely breathe as I watched her happily go about her day. It was pathetic.

After study group, I trekked to the coffee shop for my caffeine fix before more studying. When I bumped into Hillary, the blonde from my contracts class who was always smiling at me and laughing whenever I said anything even remotely humorous, I knew what I had to do.

I approached her before I lost my nerve. "Hey, listen, I was thinking I need a break from all this studying. Any chance you'd want to grab a bite to eat with me this weekend?"

Her smile instantly widened. "I'd love that. Friday night?"

We exchanged numbers, and I promised to pick her up at seven. I felt better already.

CHAPTER 18

Giada

The following week, I was on the phone with Sarah, a girl from my latest design class, as Enzo pulled up in front of my building. I covered up the mouthpiece on the phone to thank him for the ride and to tell him I was staying in the rest of the night so that he'd know he could head home. Then, repositioning the phone against my ear, I started into my building.

I stopped for my mail, smiling as I noticed the large manila envelope with Italian postage. I rushed the rest of the way to my apartment, already trying to guess what Luca might have sent me.

But instead of a gift or sweet note from my boyfriend, all I found inside the envelope were photos.

"I have to call you back, Sarah," I said, disconnecting without waiting for her response.

My phone dropped to the floor with the rest of the mail as I looked closer at the pictures. At first glance, it appeared to be Luca—my Luca—with some leggy blonde bimbo. In two of the photos, they were kissing. Another showed his hand on the small of her back, and the most sickening of all was the one where he was whispering into her ear while she laughed.

I raced to the bathroom, and emptied the contents of my stomach. I returned to the envelope, staring at the photos again before dialing Gabriella. I needed a voice of reason, or at least a friend. She'd gone back home for the weekend, but thankfully she still answered my call. I struggled to explain the situation in between sniffling and hyperventilating.

"Giada, calm down," she said in her even-toned voice. It reminded me of the way someone would try to soothe a rabid animal. I would've been offended by that, but it did relax me.

"You need to look for clues. Try to figure out who the girl is, where the pictures were taken, and who sent them to you. Then, when you're calm, you need to ask Luca about it."

"He'll just deny it."

"They're photos, Giada. He can't deny anything when you have proof, but it's probably not what you're thinking anyway. For all you know, they could be photoshopped. Just stay calm, and don't do anything crazy. I'll be back tomorrow, and we will figure this out together."

I agreed to her plan, but once we hung up, I snapped photos of the pictures and texted them to Luca.

Even though it was nearly midnight in Italy, he replied immediately. "What is this?"

"These pictures were in my mailbox today," I typed back.

I barely had time to blow my nose before my phone rang. I made no effort to mask that I'd been crying as I answered.

"Giada, I don't understand. Who sent you that?"

"I don't know. There's no return address."

He swore under his breath. "I'm so sorry, tesoro. I have some enemies, former business associates, competitors, etcetera, that might want to mess with me, but I don't know why anyone would want to hurt you with these lies."

"What lies?"

"Tesoro, you know I'm not kissing some other woman when I'm here in Italy."

"Pictures don't lie, Luca. This is most definitely you, and you are most definitely kissing some other woman."

There was another pause. "It's not what you think. Those aren't recent pictures. That happened last spring when you were with Adrian."

I considered his explanation, oddly determined to find fault with it. But I couldn't. The photos were undated, and there were no clues in the background that would tell me when they'd been taken.

"Tesoro, I'm so sorry someone did this. I hate to think of you hurting. I'll find out who sent these, and—"

"What's her name?" I interrupted.

There was a long pause. "Why does that matter? I haven't seen her for maybe six months. She doesn't even live in Italy."

"I want to know."

He sighed.

"Please Luca. It'll make me feel better."

"Mila Burgin. She's a Swiss model I met a while back — dumb as rocks and had an annoying laugh like a hyena. I never would've touched her if I'd ever known I'd have a chance with you. She was nothing compared to you, amore."

We talked for another half hour. By the time we hung up, I'd stopped crying, and my heart had stopped racing. I felt calm and, oddly enough, even closer to Luca than I had earlier in the day. I had jumped to conclusions and assumed he was not only cheating but also dumb enough to publicly flaunt it. In a way, it was endearing that he hadn't been offended or upset with me for that insulting assumption.

The crying had exhausted me to the point of no return, so I went to bed shortly after we hung up. I awoke early to the sound of my stomach growling. I reluctantly crawled out of bed and poured myself a bowl of cereal, then glanced over at the awful pictures. Luca had told me to burn them, but that seemed dramatic. I started to toss them into the trash, and then I paused.

Taking my cereal over to the sofa, I pulled out my phone and googled the woman. Yes, it was petty. But I wanted to know everything I could about the women Luca dated before me.

Everything he had told me about her checked out. She was a Swiss model, and she did sound dumb, based on the various fleeting mentions of her in random fashion magazine articles. Looking at photos of her on the runway, it was obvious that her legs were actually too long. Creepy-long, like a spider.

I clicked on a link about last week's fashion week in Milan and was pleased to see she was not modeling there. She had, however, attended a few of the shows as a guest. I clicked on a photo of her arriving at the show of a French designer, and then I froze.

My cereal stuck to the back of my throat, and I fought back the urge to vomit again. I slowly rose from the couch and carried my phone to the counter. Comparing the photo of her with Luca and the photo of her at the runway show, I couldn't ignore one nauseating detail—her dress was the same.

No fashion model would wear an old dress to a designer show.

That left one possibility.

Luca had lied.

I reached for my phone to call Gabriella before I hyperventilated, but before I tapped on her name, I paused. Gabriella would tell me to take a step back, not to do anything rash. Her motto was think first and act later.

Well, screw that philosophy.

Luca deserved my full, untethered wrath. I didn't want to talk to him, didn't want to hear even one word of another lie, or give him even the slightest opportunity to weasel his way out of the trap again. So, I sent a text, one that I thought reasonably short, if not so sweet.

I wrote, "How was fashion week, you manipulative prick? I hope your fucking car rolls into the Tiber River."

I clicked send and then blocked his number.

Adrian

I knew I shouldn't answer the phone when I saw "Gia" pop up on the caller ID, but I couldn't resist. Her voice sounded distant and uncertain as she launched into a minute of pleasantries. It made me wonder what was going on and why she was calling.

"Is everything alright, Giada?"

"Oh. Yes," she said in a voice that undermined her words. She paused. "I was just wondering if you'd want to go to dinner with me tonight. I know a lot has happened since earlier this summer when we said we'd get together and talk once school started, but I was hoping we could still be friends."

I took my time answering. "I'm not sure Luca would approve of us meeting up for dinner." He did not strike me as the type of guy to let his girlfriend fraternize with an ex.

"Well, he's in Italy now."

I laughed and the consistency of her naivety. "Something tells me he'd still find out. Isn't Lorenzo in town?" I cringed the moment the words left my mouth. Hopefully she didn't think I was stalking her, since I just admitted to knowing her driver was on campus.

"Yes, but Luca and I broke up, so..." Her voice trailed off, leading us into yet another awkward silence.

"Oh," was all I could think of to say.

"It turns out he was only dating me to appease his dad. So, um, joke's on me."

Well, that explained why she sounded so awkward. I didn't

believe for a second that Luca hadn't had real feelings for Giada. I saw the way he looked at her back in Connecticut, but I also didn't doubt Luca would use Giada—or anyone, for that matter, to get what he wanted.

A smarter man would stay away. I was finally getting over Giada, and there was a very real possibility that I'd get trapped in her web if I saw her again. But I did want to see her again. I missed our friendship almost as much as our relationship, and I wanted to confirm for myself that she was okay.

I didn't want to hurt her by telling her I had a date that night, so I spewed the first lie that came to me.

"I can't do dinner tonight. I have this big project for my civil procedure class, so I'll be studying all weekend. Maybe coffee next week?"

"Sure. Good luck on your project," she said. Her voice was filled with disappointment.

"How about Monday afternoon?" I suggested so she'd realize I wasn't blowing her off.

"Yeah, that works. Want to meet me at my apartment? Just text when you're done with class, and I'll come out."

I agreed, and we hung up.

～

Giada

When Gabriella finally got back that evening, she dragged me away from the couch, where I'd been planning to wallow with a tub of ice cream and bad TV. She found the sexiest dress in my closet then made reservations for us and two of our other girlfriends my favorite Italian restaurant.

"I can't go to Marzetti's," I reminded her. "Adrian and I went there on a date, and it'll just make me sad to be there."

Gabby rolled her eyes. "Tonight is about forgetting Luca the douchebag. You have no reason to be sad about Adrian. You have a coffee date with him Monday," she said as we headed out of the building. "What you needed was a break from Adrian, a time for you to see if there really was anything between you and Luca, and you did that. Now you know what you want. Now when you and Adrian get back together, you won't have to wonder whether you were meant to be with Luca."

"You think so?"

"Absolutely."

We headed downstairs to where Enzo was waiting in the car. As much as I'd protested when my dad sent him to campus with me, I had to admit it was nice having a reliable DD whenever my friends and I wanted to go for drinks.

Our friends had beat us to the restaurant, so we hurried back to the table and quickly chugged our first round of drinks to catch up. I'd gotten about halfway through my second drink and a few bites into my meal when I stood to head to the restroom. The girls were already plotting where we'd go next on our night of distractions and debauchery, and frankly, I didn't care where we went as long as it didn't make me think of Luca.

I caught two guys checking me out as I walked past and was feeling much better about myself when I saw *him*. Adrian. He was at a table by the window, and he wasn't studying. He was with a woman — specifically, a pretty blonde woman who was laughing at something he said and flirtatiously touching his arm.

I froze, unable to move or even to stop staring. Clearly, Adrian had moved on, and my plans to get back together with him were stupid. Even more disturbing was the fact that he hadn't told me. Why had he said he was studying? Clearly he was on a date. The sick reality that both the men I'd loved were lying to me washed over me like a tidal wave.

A waiter bumped into me and jostled me from my panic. He apologized and asked if I was okay, but I merely shook my head and sprinted to the bathroom. I took my time in the bathroom, only leaving when I realized I'd start sobbing uncontrollably if I was alone for another minute. I walked back to my table just as Adrian and his date stood. He smiled and wrapped his arm around her as they approached the door.

He obviously liked the girl. If they'd been photographed at that moment, the pictures would look about the same as the ones of Luca and his Swiss slut.

I watched him leave as I processed my reality. Neither Adrian nor Luca wanted me. Somehow, I'd gone from having two men in love with me to no one even willing to eat a damn meal with me.

I returned to the table and chugged the rest of my drink.

"What's wrong?" Gabby whispered.

I shook my head in lieu of answering. My situation was literally so pathetic that I couldn't even tell my best friend.

"I'm not feeling well. I'm going to go," I said, standing abruptly.

Gabby stood too. "Let me have them wrap up our food, and I'll go with you. You shouldn't be alone."

"No, it's fine. You stay. I insist. Enzo will get me home safely," I said. Before she could protest further, I dashed out the door. I stepped around the corner, ready to text Enzo to come get me, when I spotted the car.

"It's just me," I said as I climbed into the passenger seat. "Just go, quickly."

He obeyed, pulling the car out into the road and starting off down the darkened street.

"Where are we headed?"

"I don't know. Just drive."

"Why don't I take you home?"

"No," I said. My phone had already begun ringing, so I retrieved it from my purse and switched it off. I couldn't handle any more sympathy from Gabby at the moment.

"Are you alright?" Enzo asked. He sounded concerned, which frankly just made me feel even more pathetic.

"I need a drink," I told him, ignoring the soft crease of worry in his forehead as he gazed at me.

There was a pause before he answered. "How much have you already drank?"

"Not enough," I said. I wasn't sure if there was enough alcohol in the world to deal with my shitty love life.

"Giada, it's late, and—"

"Lorenzo," I interrupted, signaling that we were now speaking as employer-employee and not friends, "Either you can take me to the Pearl Street Bar, or I'll call a cab and go alone."

He sighed so loudly that I didn't think he'd do it, but a moment later he pulled the car to the back entrance of the bar.

"I'm not drinking alone," I said, as though the notion were preposterous.

He paused, then pulled into a parking spot. I climbed out of the car without waiting for him to open my door for me. Enzo raised an eyebrow at my outfit.

"You're going to freeze," he said.

"Not if you hurry up," I replied, annoyed that he didn't at least compliment the outfit for which I was sacrificing my comfort.

He walked around the car and draped his suit jacket around my shoulders before bending down and hiking up his pants leg a few inches. I was about to question what he was doing when he stood, clutching a handgun.

"Enzo!"

He bent over in the passenger side of the car and punched in a code to open the glove box, then deposited the gun next to what appeared to be a second gun.

"It's illegal to carry concealed in a bar," he explained, not addressing why he had a gun—or two—in the first place.

"Do you always have that with you?"

He nodded, then placed his hand on the small of my back and guided me towards the bar. It was a small dive bar frequented by a random collection of locals with whom I had nothing in common. Enzo and I stuck out like sore thumbs, but at least I didn't have to worry about running into anyone from school or anyone who knew Luca.

"I've never felt this out of place before," Enzo said with a grimace, taking in our surroundings.

I nodded towards two stools at the end of the bar. He followed but eyed me skeptically as I draped his jacket over the back of the barstool and climbed up onto the seat.

"Luca would have a heart attack if he saw you wearing that dress when he wasn't around," he said, his eyes lingering on the newly exposed part of my upper thigh. "So would your father, for that matter."

"Well, luckily, you're enjoying the view too much to rat me out," I replied.

Enzo laughed.

"Oh, come on. I've had a shitty night, and I keep fishing for compliments. I certainly didn't wear this dress because it's less fabric to wash. I could use the ego boost."

He sighed but glanced over again, giving the dress a more thoughtful inspection. It was a strapless rose gold sheath, fitted but stretchy. The hemline fell halfway between my hips and knees when I stood. It barely covered my ass as I sat.

"You know you look amazing," he said finally. "That dress looks like it was made for you. Every man in here is staring at you now."

"Okay, that's too over the top. Keep it plausible."

He lowered his eyes and rest his hand over mine. "Giada, you are stunning in everything you wear, and that dress is no exception. Luca is a fool if he lets you slip away."

There was no masking his sincerity this time, but before I could reply, the bartender appeared. Enzo turned to me. I ordered a vodka martini, dirty, and with extra olives.

"Just a club soda for me," Enzo then told the bartender.

"He'll have a whisky neat," I said. "Something top shelf."

"I'm not drinking when I'm about to drive you home," he said after the bartender left.

I rolled my eyes dramatically, hating that I now felt like a petulant child. "I know for a fact that you drink with my father when you were on duty. One drink will not impair your driving. Besides, it's my treat," I said, holding up my platinum Visa.

Once the drinks arrived, we made small talk for a minute before Enzo jumped right in.

"So, are you going to tell me why you're so determined to make bad decisions tonight?" he asked as I neared the bottom of my first martini.

I lifted the toothpick garnish from my drink and used my teeth to slide an olive into my mouth. "Adrian was at Marzetti's tonight, with another girl."

"You went out with Luca, so why isn't Adrian allowed to move on too?"

"Of course you'd take the guy's side," I said, holding my empty martini glass up and motioning for a second one. I noticed that Enzo had barely sipped his drink.

"Not always."

"He took his date to *my* favorite restaurant, after he told me he'd be studying."

"Marzetti's has good food, and it's not like he knew you'd be there. Anyway, you can't leave a guy for another man and then complain when he tries to move on. Besides, I liked Adrian."

"You don't like Luca?"

"I never said that."

I snorted. "You don't have to."

"Luca's the man you're supposed to be with."

"Luca's screwing some Swedish girl."

"Swedish?"

I accepted the new drink from the bartender, sipping quickly while shaking my head at Enzo. A bit of the drink swished out over the side, so I licked the side of the glass with my tongue. "No, Swiss."

"He told you that?"

"He told me she was Swiss. And I looked her up."

"What?"

"Yeah, apparently she's some fashion model over there. Obviously not attractive enough to make it in the U.S. Weirdly long legs," I added.

"No, I mean, did Luca tell you he's sleeping with someone else?"

"Oh," I said, laughing that I hadn't understood his questions sooner. "Someone delivered an envelope of pictures to me. Luca with some lanky blonde bimbo."

"And they were having sex?" he lowered his voice at the end.

"No, not in the pictures. They were kissing in one, but that's not the point. When I asked him about it, he admitted it all, but he said the pictures were six months old."

"You weren't even together then," he reminded me.

"Yes, but the pictures weren't actually that old. They were taken after a fashion show last week. In pictures from the fashion show, she's wearing the same outfit that she wore in those photos. No fashion model would attend a show in old designs."

Enzo downed a large swig of his drink. "Sorry. That sucks."

I swirled my olives around the edge of my glass. "Luca practically begged me to come back to him. And for what? So he could leave the country a month later to hook up with random sluts?"

"I'm sure it's not that simple. He screwed up. I'm sure he'll make it up to you though."

I chugged the rest of my drink, and Enzo did the same with his. Out of the corner of my eye, I saw him motion to the bartender for the bill.

"Hey, I wanted another."

"Not a chance."

He held out his credit card for the bartender, but I quickly gave the guy mine instead. "You didn't even want to come, so no way you're paying. Besides, you actually work for your money. It's more fun spending money that isn't earned."

He made a face at this but let me pay.

"I'm not even jealous about Luca and the other woman. Mostly I'm just pissed off. He's supposed to be mine, and there he is publicly pawing some floozy. But second, why? Why drive a wedge between Adrian and me to start with if he doesn't really want me? Does he just think I'm that stupid that I won't notice he doesn't truly love me?"

"No one thinks you're stupid."

Everyone thought I was stupid. And they were right. Tears started to well up in my eyes. When the bartender returned, Enzo signed the receipt before hopping out of his seat to help me. Someone whistled as we walked out of the bar, and Enzo quickly tossed his jacket back over me in response.

"Hey, at least someone appreciates my assets," I mumbled.

"Everyone appreciates your assets," he said. "And your ass, apparently."

He glared at several men checking me out as we exited.

Flattered, I mustered a smile. But as soon as we were back outside, the tears started to fall. Enzo looked panicked, but I couldn't stop the deluge now.

"I thought I loved Luca, but maybe it was just some rebound from Adrian or remembering how things used to be back in high school. We were good together then. I know we were. Luca never would've cheated on me then," I cried, pausing as I recalled how he did, technically, leave me. "And I thought I loved Adrian, and it was just all so perfect, but then it just all went to shit. God, I don't even know what love is. I suck at relationships, and I fucked everything up with Adrian. But now that it's obvious I've gone from having both of them wanting me to neither wanting me…"

I paused to wipe my eyes on the tissue Enzo handed me. "What is so wrong with me? Why does no one want me?"

He unlocked the door, tugged the jacket off my shoulders, and tucked me into the passenger seat before tossing his jacket into the back. He walked around to climb in beside me but didn't start the ignition.

"Adrian doesn't think he has a chance with you, and Luca is an idiot. Neither of those mistakes reflects badly on you."

I laughed. "It's not me, it's them?"

"Exactly."

"Yeah, well, that theory might hold water if not for the fact that it's not just them. No one wants me."

"Tons of guys want you. Did you see the looks on those guys' faces when you walked into that bar? They were all shooting daggers at me all night wondering how I got so damn lucky."

I sighed. "Fine, I will concede I look good in a tiny dress, but that's not the same thing. Those guys don't know me. They aren't interested in me, just my body. But is that supposed to make me feel better? Knowing lots of guys want to sleep with me, but none of them actually want to date me?"

"It's not you, Giada."

"Really? If I'm not the problem, why is it that no man still wants me once he gets to know me?"

Enzo's breathing came fast and loud, but he didn't answer immediately. Instead, his eyes lingered on mine for a minute. "I know you," he finally said. "And I still want you."

My heart fluttered at the possibilities. *God*, the sheer number of times I'd fantasized about hearing him say such things over the past few years... And I had just enough alcohol in my system to ignore the niggling doubt in the back of my mind.

"You don't mean that. You're just trying to make me feel better."

He dragged his hand through his hair.

"You look at me like a little sister."

His eyebrows shot up. "If you could be inside my head right now, you'd know I don't think of you that way."

"You've never said anything."

"What am I supposed to say? I work for your father. You're dating the—" he paused abruptly, as though he'd been about to say something damning. "You're dating Luca."

"Not anymore," I said. "I already told him it's over." I stared at Enzo, overwhelmed by his words, mystified by how I could be so enamored by this man for so long and never once realize he had any such thoughts about me.

His eyes—his big beautiful dark brown eyes—locked on mine, and my insides turned to mush. I was done thinking, done feeling pathetic and sorry for myself. I was ready to feel good. I shifted my body towards him and began to lean in. He figured out where I was headed and met me halfway, our lips crashing together forcefully.

His lips were soft and warm and bore the slightest taste of whisky. I leaned closer, needing more of him, and he must have felt the same because he wrapped his arm around my back. I raised myself up onto my knees, and Enzo lifted me towards him, helping me straddle him.

He deepened the kiss as his hands shifted from my hips to my thighs, then slid back up again. My legs were bare, the movement having jarred the dress practically to my waist. There was something deeply erotic about the position, being pressed between Enzo's firm torso and the steering wheel. I was trapped, with nowhere to go but closer to him.

My skin was on fire, my breasts felt heavy, and every ounce of me ached to be touched, devoured, and claimed by him. His erection pressed firmly against my sex, taunting me as it strained against the thin material of his pants. I tilted my head back, letting his lips find my neck while his hands roamed my back before settling against my ass.

I tried shifting slightly, desperate for friction against my clit to relieve the pressure quickly mounting inside me. Enzo moaned my name against my lips before working his hands between us, caressing my eager breasts as best he could from the position. Soon I was the one moaning, and I was done waiting.

I reached for his fly, stroking him through the material. I was panting with need as I began unzipping his pants, inching the zipper down slowly so as not to hurt him.

Suddenly, his hand clamped over mine, and his lips pulled away. Cold air hit my face without his warm skin against me.

"Fuck, Giada, we can't do this. We can't." Enzo dropped his gaze so I couldn't read his eyes, but I knew he didn't mean it. He was still rock hard beneath my hand, and his breathing was still labored.

I glanced at the windows, which were fogged over. "No one is here. No one can see us. I want this. Don't you?"

He breathed a laugh. "More than anything, but we can't."

"Luca and I are done." I said. "And no one will ever have to know."

Enzo shut his eyes. When he opened them, his answer was obvious even before he spoke. "We can't, Giada. I'm sorry. It's not right. I want this…I want you…but we can't."

I sighed, scooted back into my own seat, and fastened my belt.

Enzo started the car and drove me home in silence. I was grateful that my hair was long enough to block his view of my face as the tears started coming down again.

When the car slowed to a stop, I was ready to bolt, but Enzo reached for my hand.

"Giada, hold on. Are you okay?"

No part of me was okay, but I knew what he meant. "I'll be fine, Enzo. I'm a big girl."

It was obvious he wanted to say something else, so I waited.

"Are you, um, going to mention any of this to anyone?"

I couldn't believe he even thought he had to ask that. "Of course not!"

"Thanks. Your father would kill me."

Despite my misery, I had to laugh at that.

I glanced out my window once inside my apartment and saw that Enzo's car was still there. I switched off the lamp, not wanting to give him a show, then collapsed on my bed to sob.

A text jolted me out of my funk a half-hour later. It was from Enzo.

It said, "I'm sorry. I meant what I said, but I shouldn't have done that tonight. I know you're mad at Luca—just please don't give up on him yet. Maybe he's not perfect, but he can keep you safe and give you the life you deserve."

I couldn't envision a more infuriating text. But instead of crushing my phone in my hands or telling Enzo he was a moron, I simply replied, "Goodnight."

CHAPTER 19

Adrian

$\mathcal{A}$s I neared Giada's apartment building for our coffee date, I spotted Lorenzo's car. I groaned. Coffee with Giada was one thing, but further interaction with anyone in her family was a whole other matter. I started towards the side entrance to avoid him just as another car pulled up behind Lorenzo. I paused behind a tree and watched three men from the second car approach Lorenzo.

The tallest man knocked on the driver's window, and from where I stood, he looked an awful lot like Luca.

I swore under my breath. Whether they were broken up or not, I wasn't stupid enough to take Giada to coffee with Luca right there. I texted Giada, asking if she was sure Luca was still in Italy. Her reply was immediate.

"Positive. You here?"

"Almost. Don't come down yet," I replied. I needed to buy time to figure out what was going on before I decided if I was even going to go through with the coffee date. I watched as Enzo stepped out of the car. He held up his hands defensively, turning to the guy who looked like Luca. It was obvious even from a distance that Luca's look-alike was not happy to see Enzo. He nodded his head to the side, then took off on foot, with Enzo following, and the other two men bringing up the rear.

I inched closer as the men walked towards the hidden enclave next to the building that housed the trash dumpsters. I could tell the men were arguing about something, but the only word I could make out was "Giada." I kept watching even though every fiber in my being ached to run away. Something bad was going on. I just knew it.

Only a few minutes passed before the first man reappeared. I got a good look at him as he checked his phone, and I would've bet anything that it was Luca. A moment later, he ducked back into the enclave, and the other two guys reappeared. They were both straightening their suits and moving quickly back towards their car. Luca joined them, and I stared as they drove off. Enzo's car remained empty, its driver still nowhere to be seen.

"Shit, shit, shit," I mumbled between gritted teeth. I jogged back to the alley, hoping against all certainty that Enzo would simply be standing there taking a phone call or something else equally mundane.

Instead, he was sprawled on the concrete. His eyes were closed, and he wasn't moving, but his cell phone was next to him. I dropped to my knees beside him to check for a pulse, and his eyes flitted open with terror.

"Thank God, I thought you were dead. Hang on, I'll call for an ambulance."

"No!" Enzo croaked. "No police, no ambulance. Even if I pass out, I need you to promise that."

"You need help," I said, glancing around me. I started to wonder what I'd do if Luca and his friends came back, but we were less than ten yards from a busy part of campus. People maybe couldn't see us here, but they could hear if we screamed.

No sooner had I entertained that thought than it hit me. Enzo hadn't screamed. From where I'd stood, I would've heard, and he'd said nothing. As far as I could tell, he hadn't fought back either. What the fuck was going on?

"No police. I need you to swear it."

I ignored his words and reached for his phone to call 911. "Jesus, they texted Gia from your phone. She's going to come down here. What if it's a trap?"

"Tell her to stay in her apartment."

I did, not even bothering to work up an explanation.

I looked closer at Enzo. It was a miracle he was even conscious, let alone talking right now. His entire face was a bloodied mess. "You have to get to a hospital. You need stitches. They might have broken your nose."

Enzo appeared to consider this for a moment. "Drive me." He tried to sit up and winced, clutching his ribs. I prayed they were just bruised and not broken from the kicking.

"I don't have my car here. I walked."

"Take mine."

I leaned over and helped him up, draping his arm over my shoulder and placing my own arm around his back to support him while we walked. Somehow, no one seemed to notice this bloodied man hobbling along the sidewalk. Or if they did, they didn't care. I helped him into the backseat, then started the ignition. Enzo was so quiet that I kept looking in the rearview to ensure he was still conscious. His eyes kept slipping shut then blinking open again a few moments later.

"I was coming to meet Giada for coffee," I said. "I saw Luca and those other guys come up to you."

"Luca is in Italy. You did not see him. You did not see anything," he replied through gritted teeth.

There wasn't a doubt in my mind that the man I'd seen was Luca. Not even an identical twin could mimic that pompous smirk and holier-than-thou posture. "I did too. Why did you go with them? Even I could tell they weren't there for a friendly chat."

"Adrian, listen to me. No matter what happens, you did not see Luca. You did not see anyone."

I bit my lip. He wasn't thinking clearly through the pain. "How will you explain your injuries?"

"I was in a bicycle accident. I went down a hill too fast and crashed into some steps."

He sounded so calm that for a moment, I wondered if *I* was the one not thinking clearly. But then he tapped my shoulder with something.

"Take this," he said. "I can't have it in the hospital."

I turned towards the object and swore, swerving out of my lane at the unexpected sight. It was a gun. When I didn't reach for it, he tossed it into the passenger seat. I yelped, half expecting it to go off upon impact.

Enzo spewed out a six-digit code to unlock the glove box. At the next red light, I did so, desperate to have the weapon out of sight.

Inside the glove box were two switchblade knives, another gun, and two stacks of money. I swore again, tossed the gun in, and slammed the glove box shut.

What the fuck had I gotten myself into?

"If you had a gun, why did you let them do that to you?"

Enzo groaned. I was in awe of his pain tolerance, even being able to speak at all with such extensive injuries.

"I did something I shouldn't have," he said finally.

"To Gia?" I asked, positive I'd heard her name when they were arguing.

"Not *to* Giada," he clarified.

"Is something going on between you and Gia?"

"No. Giada is with Luca. Giada needs to stay with Luca."

I detected a hint of sadness in his voice as he repeated the stupid claim. I couldn't think of a single reason Gia should stay with a monster who would do that to anyone, no matter what he'd allegedly done to justify it. "What if they come after you again?"

"They won't. It is resolved."

"How do you know? Jesus, what if they come after Gia?"

"They won't. La principessa is untouchable. No one will hurt her, especially not il principe."

"She hates when people call her that," I said, in lieu of commenting on how insane it all was. "And she deserves to know what kind of man he is. She could be in danger."

"I don't want her getting hurt any more than you do, so stick with the story, and she will be fine. You did not see Luca. You found me after I fell off my bike."

"What about Marco? I know he can protect you."

"No one can know, especially Marco. Don't keep asking questions, don't poke around. It's fine. Everything is resolved now, so let it be!"

We reached the hospital, and Enzo was taken away for stitches and an x-ray. Two ribs were broken, and an obscene number of stitches were required to patch up his face and chest, but they said he'd recover fully.

I texted Gia to let her know I'd found Enzo after a bike accident and that I hadn't meant to stand her up. Within the hour, a friend dropped her off at the hospital.

I couldn't make eye contact with Gia as Enzo spewed the ridiculous tale of his bike accident, but she seemed to buy it. She crouched by his side, brushing his damp hair off his face.

"I didn't even know you rode a bike," she said.

A goofy grin crossed his face. "Well, obviously I don't, not well anyway."

She shook her head instead of laughing, then bent over and placed a soft kiss on his forehead. "Next time you run into concrete steps, lead with your arm or something. I don't like seeing your pretty face all mangled."

He nodded, then shooed us out, assuring us he'd be fine.

Once we were alone in the hall, I wanted to warn Giada, but Enzo's words kept replaying in my head. Enzo had never given me reason to question his loyalty to Giada, so if he said she was safe, well…

"So much for coffee," Giada said, jolting me out of my panicking thoughts.

"Yeah. Raincheck?"

She nodded and smiled. "Gabriella is coming to pick me up. You want a ride?"

"No, I'm fine." I hesitated. "It's not my business, but Enzo seemed to think you and Luca weren't broken up for good."

Giada's eyebrows rose. "Wishful thinking on his part, maybe."

We walked side by side towards the elevators.

"When he gets back from Italy, I'm sure I'll have to talk with him again, but there's nothing he could say that would change my mind."

"Oh," I said, struggling to pretend I was somewhat disinterested. "Wait, he's not back from Italy yet?"

"No," she said, the odd expression on her face reminding me that I'd asked her that earlier.

"Do you think he'll be okay with that, breaking up, I mean?"

She laughed, but her eyes filled with sadness. "Well, he already started seeing someone else, but I do think he wants to keep me in the wings to please his father."

I cringed at my next question, but I had to say it aloud. "You're not scared of him, are you? I mean, no matter what you tell him, you don't think he'll react…"

Giada turned to look at me, and the intensity with which her eyes locked on mine made me feel like she could see my thoughts.

"Why would you ask that?"

I forced a casual shrug. "I just wanted to make sure. I know you think I'm paranoid, but there are a lot of suspicious things about Luca that just don't add up. If you notice a red flag or you sense that maybe he's not being upfront with you, listen to your instincts. You're smart, Giada, so if you're sure you don't have to worry about him, I trust your judgment."

She kept walking. "Luca is a manipulative jerk, but that's it. My dad would kill anyone who hurt me, and Luca knows that."

She waved goodbye as she reached the door. I found myself wincing again, this time at the way she talked about her father killing someone, much like any other daughter of an overprotective father might joke. Except with Giada, I wasn't so sure her father wouldn't take it literally.

~

Giada

I went to visit Enzo the next morning. He seemed well medicated, and though his injuries looked worse, he assured me he was doing quite well and would be discharged later that day.

I perched on the edge of the bed. "Can I get you anything?"

"A new bike," he said, offering a crooked half smile, thanks to his stitches limiting his movement.

"That better be a joke."

"It is. Never again," he promised. "Hey, um, you didn't tell your dad, did you?"

"No, but he'll be fine with you taking some time off. As much as I like your company, I don't need a driver on campus."

"You know that's not why he keeps me around."

"Yeah, but I don't need you for that either. It's not exactly a high crime town."

He nodded. "Well, if you don't mind, please don't tell him about my accident or that I was in the hospital. It's too embarrassing. I'd been planning to go visit my mom and sister for some time now, so I'd rather just take the week off to do that and not let him know he's hired a total klutz to drive his daughter."

"Of course."

He grimaced, and my stomach clenched. I hated seeing him in pain. I glanced around his room for a moment, and then he spoke again.

"When will Luca return?"

"Um, tomorrow, I guess."

"You didn't answer my text the other night."

"You didn't ask a question."

He sighed. "I'm not trying to boss you around. I just…"

"You just think you know what's best for me. Just like every other male in my life."

His eyebrows furrowed. "Have you spoken with him since…"

"Since you rejected me? No. But just because you don't want me doesn't mean I'll run right back to him."

He stared past me towards the hall. I didn't see anything beyond the small window, and with the door closed, the room was relatively silent.

"I told you it wasn't like that. In a different world, I would jump at the opportunity to be with you, but that's not reality. I'm older than you, and I work for your father. Your boyfriend is one of your father's biggest business associates. And besides, you were drunk and hurting. I couldn't take advantage of that."

"I know. I get it," I said, even though I could've argued the point. "I'm not going to slit my wrists or sit around pining for you just because you wouldn't hook up with me. I just thought it would've been fun was all. Awkward as hell at the next family get together, but hey, I can keep a secret."

He reached for my hand. "Don't break up with Luca just yet. Give him a chance to explain in person. You two belong together."

I swallowed uncomfortably. Somehow, Enzo's accident had ensured things didn't get weird between the two of us after our little makeout session. But now, the awkward tension was making me sweat. I wanted to forget I'd ever thrown myself at him, let alone been rejected by him. The last thing I needed was a lecture from him pushing me back to another guy who also didn't want me.

"There's nothing Luca could say to ever make things right between us. At this point, I don't even want to speak with him ever again." I shook my head.

Enzo winced but didn't reply. After a few more minutes, I excused myself so he could sleep before being discharged.

CHAPTER 20

Giada

*A*s I approached my apartment after class the next day, two men in suits stood beside a sleek black car in front of the building. They turned to watch as I neared. Something about the attention was unsettling, so I paused to see if I recognized either man. They were too old to be students, and I didn't recall seeing them at the building before. As my eyes paused on their faces, they each met my gaze. I shivered, certain something was off.

I reached for my phone to call Enzo, then stopped. He was out of town. I was on my own.

Keeping my phone in my hand, I pushed through the double doors, continuing on as though I weren't scared shitless. I tapped the elevator button, praying a handful of students would join me, but they didn't. I stepped in all alone. I quickly pressed my floor button then jabbed the "close doors" button and held my breath while I waited for the doors to close. I half expected some bloody hand to thrust into the elevator.

Of course, that didn't happen. I chided myself for being so

silly, but I still had no idea what I would've done if the men had forced their way onto the elevator with me. I reached for the rosary beads in my purse and said a quick prayer that no one would jump out when the doors opened. Thankfully, the hallway was empty, and nothing appeared out of the ordinary.

I exhaled the breath I'd been holding, but kept peering over my shoulder while unlocking my door. The adrenaline pulsing through my veins made my hands unsteady, and it took me longer than normal to maneuver the key through the lock. Once I did, I stepped inside cautiously.

Everything appeared just as I had left it. I locked the door behind me then made my way to the window across the room. Peering down, I could still see the two men there. I chastised myself for being so cocky and assuming their presence had anything to do with me.

Just as I was about to turn and head into the kitchen, a hand reached around my face, covering my eyes.

I froze, despite every fiber in my body telling me to scream, kick, and bite.

"Hey baby," a deep voice said. "Miss me?"

I swatted the hand away and swiveled around. "Luca? Jesus Christ you nearly gave me a heart attack!"

He laughed. "Who else did you think it would be?"

I had no answer for that question because, of course, it was dumb for me to have gotten so worked up in the first place. I'd just been so on edge the entire day. I shook my head as I put it all together.

"Are those your goons out front?"

"I don't have goons. They're friends, colleagues. We have a meeting near here but I wanted to see my girl first. I told them to wait for me. I didn't realize you'd be so late."

"I have classes," I reminded him, "but please, don't keep them waiting on my account." I brushed past him headed towards the kitchen. I'd completely lost my appetite, but he didn't need to know that. Maybe if I busied myself with dinner preparations, he'd leave sooner.

"Giada, don't be like that," he said, grabbing my hand and tugging me to him. "I missed you."

"Is that why you fucked a blonde?"

He flinched at my language. "I told you that was last spring. You were pretty cozy with someone else then, too."

"Nice try. The photos were from fashion week. Didn't you get my text?"

The asshole actually laughed. "Yes, and I've assigned round-the-clock security to my precious car ever since." He paused and cocked his head to the side, an odd expression crossing his face. "Besides, I'd say we're even now, wouldn't you?"

He raised his thumb to my lips, wiping my lipstick off as he sometimes did before kissing me. I turned my head roughly.

"Not even close." I snarled, unsure what he thought I could have possibly done to even come close to his level of betrayal.

"Tesoro, it's true. My last night with her was ages ago. I couldn't even think about another woman when I knew you were here waiting for me. No one compares to you."

I stared into his eyes to find he looked completely sincere. Did he just assume I was that stupid, or had he actually fooled himself into thinking his behavior was somehow acceptable?

He pressed his lips against mine, and I did nothing to resist. I wanted him out of my apartment as soon as possible, and arguing would only make him stay longer.

"I brought you something," he said as he ended the kiss. He reached into his pocket and pulled out a jewelry box. Inside was a pair of emerald earrings. Of course, they were gorgeous.

"They're beautiful," I said. "Thank you."

"Anything for my princess." He glanced down at his watch. "I would love to stay and give you some other gifts, but I really do have a meeting soon."

I tried not to gag at his implication of these other gifts, focusing instead on his impending departure.

Suddenly, he reached for my phone. He quickly unlocked it, spurring me to make a mental note to change my password, then he went to my calls. He snooped through my list of calls, unblocked his number, then handed it back.

"Now you won't miss any more of my calls and texts." He paused and smirked at my eye roll. "Hey, I noticed Lorenzo wasn't outside. How'd you get home?"

"I walked. Class is only a few blocks."

"Where is Lorenzo?"

"Visiting his family. He'll be back in a few days," I said, keeping my tone casual. If Luca knew about the bike accident, he'd tell my dad.

Luca nodded. "I'll send someone else over to drive you until he returns," he said.

I opened my mouth to protest, but he placed a finger over my lips. "It's no trouble, and you're so jumpy. I don't want you feeling uneasy all the time."

Adrian's words, advising me to look out for things that seemed odd, pressed to the front of my mind. "How do you know people who are free to just hang out outside your girlfriend's apartment?"

He flashed me a cocky grin and leaned in for a kiss. I tilted my head down, so his lips landed on my forehead. "Most people find me a likable guy. Apparently not you." Luca snatched his suit jacket off the back of a nearby chair and a roll of bills fell out. I lunged towards the ground and grabbed the cash.

"Papà forget to pay your Amex bill this month?" Luca chuckled. "It's fine, Giada. Keep it. Business is good."

I glanced down at the money, attempting a guesstimate at the total and trying to memorize any other pertinent details. "People pay you in cash?" I asked, holding it out for him to take.

He nudged my hand away. "Seriously, keep it. I would've just spent it on you anyway," he said, ignoring my question. "I'll be back in a couple hours, and I can stay the night, but then I'm headed into the city tomorrow."

"New York City?"

"That would be the one. Wait up for me?"

"I'm still mad. I'd rather you stay somewhere else. Maybe you could head to the Big Apple tonight?"

He squeezed my forearms. "Baby, I'm so sorry those photos stressed you out. If I knew who sent them or why, we'd have a long chat, but I promise you nothing happened with that woman on this trip. I don't even know what country she's in now. I have eyes only for you, and even though I didn't do a damn thing to apologize for, I will keep groveling as long as it takes for you to forgive me."

"Can you grovel from the couch?"

He dropped his head down. "Giada, come on. I need you tonight. If I'd actually cheated on you, maybe I wouldn't be so desperate, but as it stands, I've gone way too long without it. Besides, you have too, unless you've had someone else in your bed since I left."

"Seriously, Luca?" I jerked my arms free. "The only reason you think I wouldn't sleep with you is because I'm cheating?"

"I don't know. You seem to think everyone is a cheater these days."

I rolled my eyes. "I have never slept with someone else when you and I were together, and the fact that you'd even accuse me otherwise…"

Luca looked like he was going to say something, but he stopped himself. He kissed my hand and turned towards the door. I thought about Enzo and what I'd been willing to do, and suddenly, I felt bad.

"Fine. I'll wait up, but if I'm not in the mood, nothing is happening."

He smiled. "It's always your prerogative to say no, baby, but you and I both know you'll regret it if you do." Luca kissed me one last time, then left.

I watched him through the peephole till he reached the elevator, then went to the window to see him rejoin his cronies. After a minute, he got into a car with one, leaving the other behind. A babysitter.

I sighed.

I sat on the couch with the roll of money, then started to think about the whole babysitter thing. That was a huge part of the role Enzo played for my dad, but did Luca have someone watching me too? He had at least once. When I'd insisted on staying in Palermo, he'd asked Ricardo to watch me without my knowledge. Since Luca had done it before, it definitely seemed possible that he would've done it again.

If someone had been watching me the last week, Luca might know that I went to a bar with Enzo, might even know what happened between us in the car after.

I shook my head at the ridiculousness of it all. Somehow, I'd just let Adrian's paranoia about his competition permeate my subconscious. Criminal or not, there was no way Luca would just let it go if he knew another man touched me. Even in high school, he'd been possessive. He'd probably kill the guy, or at least beat the shit out of him.

I considered Enzo's ridiculous story about a bike accident, then shuddered. What if it hadn't been a bike accident? What if…?

"No," I said aloud, my voice echoing in the empty room. First off, there was no way Luca was *that* big of a jerk. Cheating on me and lying about it to my face was one thing. Paying someone to spy on me was another. But beating up a guy for kissing me was a whole different level of evil.

Still, I couldn't shake the feeling that something was off. I toyed with calling Adrian and telling him my concerns, but I quickly dismissed that idea. With the way he'd been acting that summer, he would praise my theories as credible even if they were completely off the mark.

What I needed to do was to prove to myself that Luca wasn't violent, that I hadn't been completely wrong about him all along. I unrolled the money he'd left and counted it, finding exactly eleven-hundred dollars in fifties. It seemed like a lot of cash to carry, and I noted that the bills bore sequential serial numbers. The money could've come straight from the bank, but then why was it rolled instead of crisply stacked in envelopes?

For the next hour, I delved into researching Luca's father's business and Luca's role in it. For such a profitable company, I found surprisingly little information online. Maybe the lack of information hinted at something sinister, but more likely it was because the company was based overseas. That dead-end left me with one possible remaining source of intel—Luca's phone. And to access that, I'd have to give Luca exactly what he wanted.

If I wanted Luca to let his guard down, he'd need to believe that I'd forgiven him. As long as I was still fighting him, he'd never trust me. Since Luca seemed to think my forgiveness could be purchased, I located a necklace online for exactly eleven hundred dollars. I printed a picture of the piece and placed the roll of money on top of it, certain he'd pick up on the hint.

Then I opened some wine, filled two glasses, then dumped half the contents out of one so he'd think I started drinking without him. If I could convince Luca I was a little drunk while actually remaining fully cognizant, it would be even easier to get my way.

Finally, I checked my calendar, selecting an event six weeks away and made a mental note to ask him about it. If that didn't convince him we were good, nothing would.

When Luca arrived an hour later, I was ready for action.

He knocked rather than simply using his key like he apparently had earlier. I opened the door but walked away, not wanting to appear too interested.

He shut and locked it behind him, then chuckled. I turned to see his eyes on the wine.

"Get thirsty waiting for me?"

I turned away so he couldn't see my satisfaction that my plan was working.

Luca refilled my glass and handed it to me, sipping his own. He shrugged out of his jacket, making no effort to hide the gun holster over his shoulder. He set it on the counter before draping his jacket over the chair.

"Why do you always carry that?"

"Umm, because the Second Amendment says I can?"

"Seriously, Luca. I noticed that you left one of your friends here to babysit me too. Is my apartment in a bad neighborhood or something? What are you afraid of?"

"I'm not afraid of anything, and you shouldn't be either. But I'm in a high-profile business, and I carry a lot of cash, and I want to be sure I can keep you safe." He stepped closer and wrapped his arms around my waist.

I inhaled slowly, momentarily distracted by how damn good he smelled.

Luca tilted his neck back and smiled. "You like that cologne, don't you? See, I don't forget your favorites."

I gritted my teeth, annoyed at myself and him. Luckily, he spotted the money over my shoulder and pulled away.

"Giada, you shouldn't leave a wad of cash out like..." he began. Then he reached for the paper under it and laughed.

I shrugged timidly when he turned to me. "I mean, if you're serious about groveling."

Luca stuck the paper over by his jacket, not touching the money. "I am serious about wanting to make you happy, and if this does that, I'll be doing some shopping."

He paused and tossed back a healthy swig of his wine, refilling his glass before joining me on the couch.

"Hey, speaking of shopping, there's a fundraiser at the end of next month that my mom wants us to attend. If I get a pale blue dress, will you get a tie to match?"

He wrinkled his nose. "Baby blue isn't exactly my color."

I made a pouty face. "Please? I'll buy it."

Luca sighed. "Does this mean you're forgiving me if you're signing us up for coordinating outfits?"

I smiled at how well my plan was working. "No, but it means I'm open to letting you persuade me."

Luca wiggled his eyebrow then tackled me, kissing me roughly before pulling back to loosen his tie. I watched as he undressed from the waist up, remembering how much I'd wanted him in the past. It was such a scam, for such a terrible human to be packaged in such a deliciously perfect body. I made a mental note to only date ugly men going forward.

As Luca switched his focus to undressing me, starting from the bottom and working his way up my body, coating me in kisses everywhere that he uncovered, I started to think about Enzo. He certainly wasn't ugly, but he also seemed like a genuinely good guy, not that I was such a good judge of charac-ter. Based on the way he'd kissed, we would've had fun together. And what I'd felt pressing against my thighs when I straddled him, well, it had definite potential.

I closed my eyes as Luca's lips reached my breasts, imagining Enzo's mouth on my skin. What would it be like if it were Enzo's hands roaming my body, his tongue invading my mouth while his fingers pressed lower... I continued thinking about Enzo, about what could've happened if we'd kept going that night. So, when my body betrayed me and caved to Luca's expert touch, I told myself it was because I was thinking of Enzo.

When I opened my eyes, it was Luca's proud grin inches from my face.

"You're still not forgiven," I quickly said.

"Good, because I'm not done yet," he replied, scooping me off the couch and carrying me to the bedroom. I waited until he had fully undressed and joined me on the bed before launching into the next part of my plan.

"I want music," I said. "But my phone is in the kitchen."

He'd never leave the bed to go fetch my phone, so as predicted, he reached for his phone. I'd hoped he'd tap in the code so I could see it, but instead he used his thumbprint. But that was okay, I could still work with that.

I tried to focus on Enzo again, but this time my thoughts drifted to Adrian. Ironically, the song Luca was playing was the same song as the first time I'd danced with Adrian. That memory was soothing, not erotic though, so I still had to exert a lot of energy to convince Luca I was enjoying myself way more than I should.

As predicted, once we were done, Luca was exhausted. Between the international flight, work, and now the wine, I'd known he would be. He settled down into the bed then pulled me close. I curled against him, then reached for his phone on the nightstand.

"Can you switch the song?" I asked.

"I'm tired. Let's just turn it off."

"I can't sleep yet. Can we talk?"

He winced. "Baby, it's late. We can talk in the morning."

"Can you get my phone so I can listen to music then?" I asked, grabbing my headphones off the nightstand.

Luca groaned but unlocked his phone and handed it back to me. "Just use mine, but don't kill the battery. I need that seven a.m. alarm."

I kissed his forehead, then started to browse his music files. I changed the song to something soothing, then set the phone beside me, careful to touch it every forty seconds or so to ensure it wouldn't lock again. Once Luca was asleep, I inched away and sat up so he wouldn't be able to see what I was doing if he woke.

I scrolled through his photos first, finding nothing too interesting. There were a lot of me, and a few of some artsy-looking sights in Italy. Nothing that screamed "drug dealer" or implied he would hurt Enzo. None of Mila the Swiss slut, either.

There were a few random shots of people I didn't recognize—all men, but they were all taken as the subject was walking. None were posed or head-on shots, even. I wondered if he had been photographing something in the background or if he'd inadvertently taken the shot. But if that was the case, why not delete them? I couldn't think of any reason, crime-related or otherwise, that he'd save photos of strange men going about their daily routines.

I looked into his notes and files next, bummed to realize that aside from an old shopping list, his notes were all password protected. His calendar was similarly useless, with lots of dates and locations recorded for various meetings or events but no helpful descriptions. An inordinate number of meetings occurred at night, but that was the same with my dad, and I knew the explanation for that. Shipping docks ran 24/7.

His emails were similarly disappointing. By some miracle, he had nothing resembling spam, and all of his remaining emails were sorted neatly into different legit-sounding categories. I clicked on each category and scrolled through a few, boring quickly. The last group looked promising, but the file demanded a password. *Damn.*

Discouraged, I went to his texts. I skipped over the majority of ones in Italian. If my only hope was to decipher text messages in a language I didn't speak, I was screwed. Many of the names in his contacts were familiar, but a lot were labeled simply with initials. He had a lot of texts with "AR," but they were almost entirely in code. They kept talking about LP, almost as though recounting a schedule for something or someone.

I was about to set the phone down and go to sleep when something struck me. Five days ago, there were more texts than usual. The first of the day said, "LP not at class." Luca had replied, "find out why," then AR had replied an hour later, saying "@cafe."

I had skipped class that day. I had met Gabriella for brunch.

LP was me—la principessa. And AR, well that must be Luca's friend, Alessio Rizzo.

I swallowed the lump in my throat and went back to the start of the text stream, realizing with dread that AR—Alessio, had clearly been watching me and texting my every major movement to Luca. When I reached Friday evening, when I'd gone to dinner, there was a note that I left early and seemed upset. After that, it said I went into the bar with my driver.

The next text from Luca said, "send pics to burner then delete." The next text was in all caps from Luca and read, "CHIA-MAMI." Even with just my measly two semesters of Italian, I knew that translated to "call me."

Shit.

A wave of nausea washed over me, and it took all my self-restraint not to slap the man sleeping peacefully beside me. I reread the texts, trying to determine if there was any chance I wasn't LP or any other explanation for these messages. Finding none, I had one last thing to check.

I went to his travel folder and clicked on the latest airline ticket, but it was for the flight this morning from Rome to La Guardia. If he'd taken that flight, Luca wasn't even in the country when Enzo 'fell' off his bike. Except…that flight didn't arrive until five pm. When I'd returned after my last class, it was only six, and Luca was already at my apartment. He couldn't possibly have gotten here that fast.

Unless he'd actually taken an earlier flight.

I wanted to look for proof of another flight, but I'd now been snooping for well over an hour. If Luca woke and saw me on his phone, I'd have no plausible explanation. I closed out of every-thing I'd opened then dropped his phone on the nightstand by his head.

I settled back into the bed facing him, too scared to turn my back to Luca after what I'd learned about him. As my eyes adjusted to the darkness of the room, I stared at his face. Luca looked so peaceful in his sleep, not to mention handsome. His bold, dark features relaxed as he dozed, leaving only a cluster of impossibly thick eyelashes and full lips for me to stare at.

None of it made sense. I'd known Luca as a kid, I'd stared at his face before he was old enough to shave it. I'd fallen in love with him—and his beautiful face—before he'd gotten the scar just above his left cheekbone. I'd long since memorized every detail of his stupid, perfect face.

I'd thought I knew everything about Luca. One week ago, I would've said I knew him better than I knew anyone else.

Now, I wasn't sure I knew him at all. I had thought he was intense, but passionate. Possessive, but adoring. Cocky, but self-loathing. I never believed he was perfect, but I sure thought he was perfect for me.

Now I realized I had no idea what horrors he might be capable of.

I started to recite the prayers of the rosary, certain I'd never fall asleep, not with the man who'd lied right beside me. Except somehow, I did.

When I awoke, the sun was up, and he was gone.

My stomach was still filled with dread.

What was the point of knowing Luca wasn't the man I'd thought he was if there was nothing I could do about it?

CHAPTER 21

Adrian

On Saturday afternoon, I went to mass. I'd literally never attended church by myself before, only having gone when forced either by my mother or Gia. But I needed to see her, needed to warn her, and I was certain she'd be there.

I arrived early and waited outside, watching each parishioner arrive as I pretended to be focused on my phone. When I saw a black Audi pull up, I was sure it was her. She stepped out, gazed around, then smiled. She looked gorgeous and sophisticated, with her hair straight down her back and her navy blue dress barely visible between the folds of her long, unbuttoned coat. A necklace that probably cost more than a month's rent rest against her delicate collar bone.

From that vantage point, I saw why they called her the princess. She fit the role perfectly. She looked exactly as I'd expect her to, and the visceral response in my body to seeing her was also just as I'd expected.

What I hadn't expected, though, was him. Luca stepped out of the back of the car and walked around to her. He tilted his head to say something to her, and she smiled sweetly in response. He placed his left hand on the small of her back, guiding her towards the building while keeping his right hand free to shake the hands of several men who approached them.

Seeing his hand on her, seeing how physically close she was to that monster…I felt ill. How could Enzo say Gia was safe with Luca? We both knew what he was capable of.

I didn't realize Gia saw me, until she turned and flashed me a sweet smile, combined with a half wave. Her eyebrow rose, and I assumed she was curious why I was here. She knew me well enough to realize this wasn't my ideal Saturday afternoon. I shrugged, making my way into the church where I could hide amongst the crowd in the back. I didn't think Luca had seen me, and I wanted to keep it that way. From behind, I was forced to watch every time he leaned close or touched her. I imagined he was holding her hand, maybe even had his hands resting on her thigh. It was sickening.

After the service, I stopped in the lobby. I still wasn't sure I'd get a chance to catch her alone, but I had to try. When they walked out, Luca kissed her cheek then scurried off with two other men. Gia waited in the lobby, watching him go, before turning to me.

"I didn't expect to see you here. Trying to repent for something?" she teased, her tone light.

"Something like that," I said, glancing to confirm Luca was still outside with his guys. "Listen I really need to talk with you. It's about…" I nodded my head towards Luca.

A flicker of emotion crossed her eyes and then vanished. "He's finally back in town. Isn't that great?"

"He got back early." I said, widening my eyes to signal the significance of my words.

Gia opened then closed her mouth without answering. Her expression was still unreadable.

"There are some things you need to know about him." I lowered my voice. "You can't keep seeing him."

"You left me, Adrian. You can't stop me from moving on."

"Gia, you don't understand," I began.

"You're the one who doesn't understand," she interrupted, raising her eyebrows and glaring pointedly. After a beat, she looked away. "It was good seeing you. Let me know how that civil procedure class goes," she said casually.

She started to turn, and I saw that Luca was returning. He met her halfway, but his eyes darted past her and locked on me.

"Look who I ran into," she said, pointing to me.

"How's it going?" Luca asked, offering me a cold, firm handshake.

"Not bad," I said.

"Didn't know you were much of a church man."

"We all have our secrets, don't we?" I replied.

Luca's eyebrow raised, but then he turned to Gia. "I need to go straighten some things out. Alessio will drive you home, okay?"

"Sure babe," she said. She leaned in for an uncomfortably long kiss. As Luca scampered off, I expected her to stay and finish our talk, but instead she simply waved and walked to the car.

"Good to see you, Adrian," she called.

Giada

*L*uca didn't return that night until after I was asleep, and when I left for class in the morning, he was still asleep. Alessio wasn't out front either, so I caught a ride to class with Gabriella. I stayed at the art building for an extra hour, sketching out some new designs, and then I headed back to the apartment for lunch. I assumed Luca would've already left for the day, but as soon as I entered, he stood from the couch. It didn't take a genius to infer his mood from his expression.

"Where the fuck have you been?"

"Class," I said, plopping my backpack by the door and slipping out of my coat.

"You just walked?"

"Gabriella took me. I guess you kept my driver out too late last night. Maybe I should be asking you where you were."

His expression softened. "How long are we going to keep this up?"

I had no idea what he meant.

"I saw the way you were looking at Adrian yesterday."

"And what way was that?"

"Giada, if you're still pissed, tell me what to do to fix it. Don't run around fucking every man you know."

"Excuse me?"

Luca didn't look the slightest bit apologetic. "Don't pretend for a minute you don't know what I'm talking about. You and I both know Lorenzo didn't force himself on you like he said he did."

I felt like the room was spinning. "What? Why would Enzo say…?"

Luca shook his head. "I know you, Giada. You saw the pictures, and you were pissed off and embarrassed. You wanted to make me feel the same way. You've always been impulsive."

I sunk onto the couch, worried I'd pass out. I couldn't even process the magnitude of what he was admitting, let alone the significance of what it might mean that he was actually confessing. "Nothing happened with me and Enzo."

"Sure. And nothing happened with me and Mila."

My energy returned in a flash. I stood up and slapped him. "Bastard!"

He gripped my wrist firmly, too firmly, but quickly released it. "I told you I was sorry about that. I didn't realize you'd ever see, and…" He shook his head dismissively. "But you are my girlfriend, and you can't go around screwing your driver, your exboyfriend, or anyone else."

I started to protest, to tell him again that I didn't want to be his girlfriend, but I started to think about Enzo. I couldn't believe he told Luca he'd forced himself on me. Had he been that worried Luca would hurt me, or did he just assume one scapegoat would be better than two? And God, if Luca nearly killed Enzo, someone he knew and liked, what would he do to Adrian?

"You're right about Enzo. I thought you loved me, that we were meant to be together. You broke my heart, and yes, I was mad. Enzo was there, that's all. You shouldn't have hurt him for that." I held my breath, praying he'd deny it. I desperately needed him to tell me he hadn't hurt Enzo. That he would never hurt anyone.

But he didn't.

"You didn't leave me a choice, Giada. I have an image to protect, and when all of my associates know you're fooling around with your driver, someone has to pay. Honestly, they all think I went easy on him by letting him live, but I figured I owed the guy some gratitude for not letting them think you were a slut."

"You're an asshole, and I am not a slut. I didn't sleep with Enzo, and absolutely nothing is going on with Adrian. We literally just said hi."

"Right. So, you didn't make a coffee date with him?"

"He's seeing someone else now, a blonde, just like you are, so you don't need to worry."

"I'm not seeing her or anyone else. Jesus, Giada. What do you want me to do to make it up to you? More jewelry, some new shoes?"

I felt like vomiting, but luckily, my brain worked overtime when stressed. "I want Enzo to drive me again when he's back."

"No."

I shrugged. "Well, then I guess we don't have a deal."

Luca rolled his eyes. "How would that look, me leaving you alone with him?"

"It'll look like you trust your girlfriend and like your 'associates' are loyal. You don't actually think Enzo will ever touch me again, do you?"

He blew out a sigh. "Fine. But you cooperate with Alessio until he returns, and I don't want you seeing Adrian at all. Not on campus, not for coffee, and not at church."

"This isn't going to work if you don't trust me."

"Trust is earned, sweetheart."

"Fine. No more Adrian."

"Good. I'd hate to have to chat with him like we did Lorenzo."

My stomach clenched. "If you ever touch him, there is nothing you could ever do to get back on my good side."

Luca raised an eyebrow but didn't disagree.

Dizzy and nauseous, I started towards the kitchen for some water. Everything was so surreal. I was painfully aware of Luca watching my every move. Finally, he followed me into the kitchen.

"I didn't want it to be this way with us," he said. "I meant it when I said I was sorry."

"For which part, Luca?" I asked, taking my water into the bedroom and shutting the door behind me. I had no clue what my next step should be, but as long as that door stayed closed, I could at least panic in peace.

Adrian

The next night, I was just finishing up dinner and mentally preparing myself to study when there was a knock at the door. I glanced in the peephole, surprised to see Giada.

She stepped in quickly when I opened the door, shutting it firmly behind her. She wore a baggy sweatshirt, and as she lowered the hood I could see that she'd been crying.

"Gia! Are you okay?"

"I'm fine," she said, looking anything but.

I didn't know why she was there, but it might be my only chance to warn her. I couldn't waste any time, and I couldn't let her leave until she'd heard me out.

"I'm glad you're here. I need to talk to you. Lorenzo told me not to say anything, but I'm worried that you—"

"I know about Luca. I know what he did and who he is," she interrupted, shaking her head. "I want to get away. And I'm sorry to drag you into this, but I need your help."

The End

~

If you enjoyed reading this book, I'd truly appreciate if you took a moment to click the links below and leave a review. Even the shortest of reviews helps me tremendously!

Retailer Reviews: Mafiosa Princess

Goodreads Reviews: Mafiosa Princess

Click here to join my email list and get a FREE book: Newsletter Signup

And read on for a sneak peak of the second book in the Mafiosa Princess series!

SNEAK PEAK OF BOOK 2

MAFIOSA PRINCESS: SACRIFICE

Giada

"I know about Luca. I know what he did and who he is. I want to get away. And I'm sorry to drag you into this, but I need your help." As soon as the words left my mouth, a wave of nausea washed over me. I dashed to Adrian's bathroom, but there was nothing in my stomach to expel. So instead, I sobbed.

What had I done?

All of my mistakes rushed over me like a fog. I'd had the perfect boyfriend—Adrian—but then we'd broken up because he had all these insane theories about my dad being a criminal. I fell for my high school boyfriend, Luca, again, only to learn that he actually was a criminal. And then I made out with my driver, Enzo, which prompted the evil boyfriend to beat him up and lie about it. Now it was too late for Adrian and me to get back together, but he was also the only person I trusted to help me get away from Luca.

Except now, I'd put Adrian in harm's way.

The whole way over, I told myself it was okay, that I had covered my tracks and that no one would ever know I was at Adrian's. But what if I was wrong? I hadn't realized anyone saw me with Enzo, and he almost died for my carelessness. I couldn't risk that happening to Adrian.

I rushed out of the bathroom and slammed directly into Adrian's firm chest. Before I could move, his strong arms roped around me, holding me so tightly I couldn't catch my breath.

"You're okay now Gia. I won't let anyone hurt you. You are safe."

I relished the fleeting sensation of comfort, tried to let myself pretend he was right, but it was futile. I pushed back and shook my head. Even if I were safe, he wasn't. Not if I stayed much longer.

"Adrian, I'm so sorry. I should've never dragged you into this." I started towards his door, but he scrambled around and blocked my path.

Gazing into his piercing blue eyes framed by the most handsome and sincere face I could imagine, I remembered why I went to him in the first place. Adrian was someone I could trust. Perhaps he was the only trustworthy person in my life. I'd known the entire way over here that if I could just get to him, he'd help me. Adrian was that kind of guy, the kind who would help, even though he was seeing someone else now, and even though he had every reason to hate me.

But now that I was actually here, in the safety of his apartment, I saw how selfish my thinking was. He'd help me even if it endangered himself, and that wasn't fair for me to ask.

"No, Gia. You're not leaving like this. I'm not scared of Luca right now. If he shows up, we'll call the cops. But you are not going anywhere. Not until you tell me what is going on."

"Adrian, really. I shouldn't tell you any of this, but Luca is… a monster. Do not trust him or any of the guys he brings around. Don't go anywhere alone with them, don't let them near you. Do you understand?"

As he nodded, sadness filled his eyes.

"Do not tell anyone anything about him, okay? And stay away

from me. Don't call, don't text, don't come to see me. Don't even wave if we pass on the street. Okay? Can you do that?"

The creases around his eyebrows deepened. "No."

"You have to promise, Adrian. He won't hurt me, but he…he nearly killed Enzo, and if he knows you're talking to me, you'll be next."

Adrian expelled a large breath, as though this information provided some relief. "You know about Enzo," he said.

"Yes, it was Luca. Well, actually it probably was his asshole associates and not him, but it was Luca's way of punishing me for…"

"I saw him," Adrian interrupted. "I was early to pick you up for coffee. I would've told you the truth sooner, but Enzo made me swear I wouldn't."

I squeezed my eyes shut, wishing I could turn back time and not throw myself at Enzo. God, how that man had suffered all because of my shitty self-esteem and low alcohol tolerance. I'd known my boyfriend was a jealous, possessive man. But, I honestly hadn't realized he had someone spying on me *or* that he would hurt Enzo.

"Wait, why would Luca hurt Enzo to punish you?" Adrian asked, returning to my statement he'd interrupted.

I winced, embarrassed to have him know the truth. If Adrian didn't already despise me, he would after hearing what I'd done. I tried to minimize how horrific my behavior had been. "I kissed Enzo. It was after I learned Luca was cheating on me and lied about it. I was upset and I'd been drinking. Enzo stopped it before anything really happened and I didn't realize anyone saw, but apparently one of Luca's stupid friends was spying on me and told him."

Adrian shook his head. "I saw Enzo go with them willingly. He had to know what they were going to do."

"Enzo told Luca he forced himself on me," I said, embarrassed to even hear the ridiculous notion out loud.

The transformation in Adrian's face was dramatic. "He forced himself on you?"

"No, no. *I* kissed *him*. Enzo only said that so Luca wouldn't be mad at both of us." I paused, flustered. "I'm sure Luca knew he was lying, but I guess it did help Luca save face in front of his guys or whatnot"

"Gia, between what I saw and what you know, we have more than enough for the police to charge Luca, even if Enzo doesn't come back to corroborate it all. You should get a restraining order against Luca."

I shook my head, trying to swallow the lump in my throat but finding my mouth too dry. "Adrian, I can't do that. You don't understand. Luca's father is…well, all those things you kept saying about my family, it's all true of Mr. Marino."

I paused a moment as Adrian's expression changed yet again while he processed this new information.

"Luca works for his father, and I don't know if his father is in the actual mafia or whatever, but it's definitely something like that. Luca carries huge wads of cash wherever he goes, he's always armed, and he doesn't go anywhere without a body guard. He has guys following me around too."

I glanced down at my cell phone. It was late. Sneaking away for a few minutes was one thing, but being gone for over an hour would raise questions. Apparently, my indirect route to Adrian's apartment took longer than I'd anticipated.

"I have to go. I snuck out the back entrance of the library and then took a cab and then walked the rest of the way so that no one would know I left, but if I don't get back there in a reasonable time for Alessio to drive me home, Luca will know something is up."

"Who is Alessio?"

"He's one of Luca's associates. I think you met him last summer. He's been driving me."

"Giada, you can't just go back to Luca!"

"I don't have a choice. If I disappear, there's no telling what Luca would do to you or Gabriella or my family…"

"Don't worry about your family, Giada. They can take care of themselves."

I really wanted to strangle him. Yes, Adrian hated my family, but I didn't think he was insensitive enough to bring that up when I was so stressed out already. "I don't want to hear it, Adrian. I would never do anything to put them in harm's way."

"I know, Gia. I just mean I don't think your family is in danger. Your father and your brothers are tough guys." It was clear he wanted to say more, but he stopped and just shook his head. "You need to look out for yourself."

"I can handle Luca. I just have to do what he wants until he gets sick of me and breaks up with me. As long as I don't embarrass Luca again, I don't think anything will happen."

"You don't *think*? Gia, do you hear yourself? This is insane. You need to go to the police!"

"I can't." I squeezed my eyes shut, struggling to remember why I had come to Adrian in the first place. I felt safe around him, but what was the point? Had I really thought telling him what was going on would somehow bring up a solution? "I'm sorry I dragged you into this. I know you've moved on, and I promise I'm not trying to come between you and your new girlfriend. I just felt like I needed to tell you."

Adrian still looked confused, but I started to the door.

"I don't have a new girlfriend," he said suddenly.

"Oh, well, new friend. Whoever she is," I said. It was apparent he still didn't know what I was talking about and I just didn't have the energy to pretend I hadn't seen him on a date. "I saw you at Marzetti's with some blonde girl. The night you said you were studying. Right after I found out Luca was cheating and right before I went and threw myself at Enzo. Anyway, it's totally fine. I don't want to mess that up for you."

"Hillary is her name. We aren't going out again, and it's not because of you, so don't worry."

"Oh. Well, I'll go now," I said, pulling my hood back up.

"Giada, call one of your brothers. Or your dad. Promise me you'll get someone you trust that Luca hasn't forbid you to see and have them come up this weekend. Or better yet, head home for the weekend."

I considered that. I could never tell my family everything that was going on, but having Matteo around for a few hours would make me feel better. "Maybe. But they can't know any of..."

"If you told them, they could help you. I'm sure of it. But even if you don't want to tell them the truth, just promise me you'll spend some time with them."

I nodded, then left.

When I returned home, Luca wasn't even there. Nervous energy flooded me, but I wasn't sure what to do with it all. He already knew I was upset with him, and he'd admitted hurting Enzo, so there was no point for me to act normal around him. But I didn't want him to see how scared I was either, in case that made him feel even more powerful.

I slumped onto the couch and rubbed my forehead. How had I ended up with the type of man who got a kick out of terrorizing me? Adrian had been the perfect boyfriend in every way and I'd left him for a bully.

I was a fool. Even looking back, I couldn't figure out where exactly I'd gone wrong. I wanted to identify all the signs I'd missed and berate myself, but I couldn't. There had been no signs. Luca had been completely perfect.

Until he wasn't.

I waited up for a while, too anxious to sleep anyway. When I finally did go to bed, I propped a stack of books a few inches from the door. It wouldn't keep Luca out of the bedroom, but it would topple over and make enough noise to wake me when he returned. Even with the alarm system, I woke frequently throughout the night.

In the morning, my head pounded and I felt achy and tense. But I was still alone. As I finished my second cup of coffee, Luca texted and told me he would be in Manhattan for business for a few days and that I should "behave" during his absence.

As infuriating and offensive as his terminology was, I felt nothing but relief.

I replayed my conversation with Adrian in my head, and decided that of all of his suggestions, involving my brother did make sense. Luca couldn't possibly find fault with me seeing my own brother.

I called Matteo before I changed my mind. We chatted for a few minutes and then I asked if he could come meet me for lunch the next day.

"I'd love to see you Giada, but I'm really busy. Is everything okay?"

"Yeah," I said, trying to mask the disappointment in my voice. "I'm just feeling a bit homesick this week."

"Oh right, I forgot that Luca is down in the city too."

"Too? Who else is there?"

"Angelo. You know, your brother? Tall, dark haired guy with receding hair line and bad attitude."

I had to laugh at Matteo's description of Angelo. Angelo was taller than Matteo, and while his hair was shorter, I definitely didn't think his hairline was receding. Aside from those minor differences, my brothers were identical, and the general consensus of women seemed to be that they were both good looking guys. I didn't disagree with the bad attitude comment though, since Angelo had been intense, grumpy, and at times intimidating, pretty much as long as I remembered.

"Things must be going really well with you and Luca if you're missing him already," Matteo continued.

I cringed. "No, actually they're not. We had a fight before he left and honestly I don't think he's the person I thought he was."

"A fight? Like you hit him?"

Now I was exasperated. "Why would you assume *I* hit *him*?"

"Because you have a temper and Luca would never in a million years lay a hand on you."

I rolled my eyes, annoyed that my favorite brother would take sides with the jackass micromanaging my every move.

"He didn't, did he?"

I sighed. "No. No one hit anyone. I guess 'fight' was the wrong word. We argued. The point is I don't think we should be together anymore and I wanted some sympathy from my brother."

"Gi, you can't break up with Luca."

Okay, not the response I was looking for. "Why not?"

"Because you'll regret it. You and Luca belong together. You've got all that history together and you're a perfect fit." He paused. "Besides, no one else would put up with your level of crazy like he does."

"Why do you keep implying I'm crazy?"

"I just know you that well."

"Look, Matteo, I know you're sort of friends with him, so I don't want to put you in a tough spot, but I really need some support here. I can't tell you all the details, but trust me when I say Luca is not a good person. He's bossy and jealous and controlling and…well, he's done some really bad things."

"Did he hurt you?"

"No, but…"

"Giada, listen to me," he interrupted. "I'm not saying Luca isn't perfect and I see what you're saying about him being a little too possessive, but he acts that way because he cares about you. He doesn't want to lose you and he doesn't want to see you get hurt. I've known him as long as you have and he's not a bad guy."

"You don't know him the way I do," I snapped.

"I'd hope not." He paused. "Is this about Adrian? I wasn't going to say anything, but I heard that he's been hanging around your building some and waiting for you at church, and honestly I think Luca's been pretty tolerant of that given your history with the guy. How would you feel if he was still flirting with his ex all the time? You just can't keep flitting back and forth from one to the other, Gi. I'm not saying you have to settle down and have kids yet but you do have to act like a grown up. You made your choice, now stick with it."

The firmness with which Matteo spoke brought tears to my eyes. He had always been the one I could talk to, my personal champion when everyone else in the house treated me like a child. Now, he was clearly siding with all of them. I didn't know what to say. I realized I needed to know if Adrian was right. If it came down to it, could I count on my family to protect me from Luca?

"Matteo, what if I told you I was afraid of Luca? What if I wanted to break up with him but was scared of what he might do or how he would react? Would you help me then?"

There was a lengthy silence. "I love you, Giada. I'd never let anyone hurt you."

"Okay, well…"

He cut me off before I could finish. "But if you said all that, I'd tell you that you were overreacting, that it would be a huge mistake to break up with him, and you should just appreciate what you have and everything he can give you."

I sucked in a breath, feeling my hands shaking already with the effort of trying not to cry. I had thought Matteo would be on my side. I'd assumed he'd be concerned for me, that he would comfort me. I hadn't expected a lecture. I gave him one more chance.

"Matteo, are you seriously telling me to stay with a man that I'm afraid of? That's how you want me to live?"

He took his time answering, which gave me hope.

"No, of course not. I'm telling you that you shouldn't be afraid of him. Luca won't hurt you."

I swallowed the lump growing in my throat.

"Look, I have to go. Just don't do anything stupid, okay?"

I was crying too hard to reply.

Click here to purchase Mafiosa Princess: Sacrifice.

FREE DOWNLOAD

She's on the clock to win him back

Sixty Days for Love is a "Fun and flirty" full length contemporary romance novel with NO cliffhangers

Get your free copy of "Sixty Days for Love" when you sign up for the author's VIP mailing list. Get started here:

https://www.LizaMalloy.com/registration

PRAISE FOR LIZA MALLOY

Praise for *Hollywood Endings*:

5 stars for this "refreshing" "lifelike story of [a] normal girl dating a celebrity."

- I Like Books Best book blogger

www.ILikebooksbest.com

Praise for *The Brothers' Band*:

"Liza Malloy weaves together music, great works of literature, family relationships, and romantic relationships into this page turner."

- Verified Amazon Review

"Fun romance book, I couldn't put it down! Steamy love scenes and a great back story."

- Verified Amazon Review

Reviews of *For Love and Italian:*

"A fun, lighthearted and steamy romance, *For Love and Italian* is sweet, romantic, and naughty in the best ways. I was entertained the entire time and was quite sad when it was over. Liza Malloy knows how to write addictive and satisfyingly charming

romance stories that will surely give you plenty of swoons and feels…I can't wait to see what she writes next."
    - Karen Jo Custodio, Book Blogger.
    www.SincerelyKarenJo.com

Praise for *Legacy: The Awakening*:
    It is "so easy to get lost in the story and the characters" and "hard to put [] down"
    - Verified Amazon Review

Praise for *Legacy: The Revelation*:
    "Really enjoying the series. It's…a great way to escape during these crazy times. Highly recommend."
    - Verified Amazon Review

Praise for *Forbidden Ink*:
    "Get comfortable, you won't be able to put the book down!"
    - Amazon Customer Review

Praise for *Sixty Days for Love*:
    "A perfect late-at-night after the kids are in bed escape. The heroine is fun and likeable and the hero is sexy and loveable. What more could you want?"
    - Verified Amazon Review

CONTI FAMILY TREE

Others

- Leonardo Ricci ("uncle")
- Giovanni Romano (brother of Bianca Romano-Conti)
- Stefano G. Bruno (Marco's cousin)
- Federico Giordano ("cousin")
- Giorgio Lomba ("cousin")
- Antonio Ricci (son of Leo and his ex-wife Noemi)

ACKNOWLEDGMENTS

Oh boy…getting this story from a vague idea in my head to a full-blown series has taken a lot of hard work and I couldn't have done it without the support of so many people.

Thank you to Sarah P for all your work copyediting and proofing this (and an extra thanks for not deleting too many of my commas).

Thank you to JD Designs for the stunning cover for this book… and for the first 72 versions that I rejected for various reasons. All I can say is that hopefully you agree it's all worth it when we have 10+ books in the series with equally gorgeous covers.

Thank you to all my beta readers, critique partners, and friends for offering feedback and gentle criticism of this massive project. A huge thank you to Lisa H for always texting me your feedback, especially on cover art and fonts.

Thank you to my parents, sister, kids, husband and cats for understanding when this creative endeavor steals my attention from you at times.

And last but not least, thank you to all my readers! Without you guys buying my books, reviewing them, and telling friends without them, I could never afford to pay any of the people listed above :) I especially appreciate everyone who has helped promote my book on social media, whether by reviewing / sharing on your own blog or even just sharing and responding to my posts. Huge shoutout to Xpresso Tours for the cover reveal for Mafiosa Princess and Goddess Fish Promotions for launch publicity.

ABOUT THE AUTHOR

Liza Malloy writes contemporary romance and women's fiction. She's a sucker for alpha males, bad boys, dimples, and muscles, and she can't resist a man in uniform. Liza loves creating worlds where her heroine discovers her own strength and finds her Happily Ever After. When Liza isn't reading or writing torrid love stories, she's a practicing attorney. Her other passions include gummy bears, jelly beans, and the occasional marathon. She lives in the Midwest with her four daughters and her own Prince Charming.

Visit her website at www.LizaMalloy.com

Join her email list at http://eepurl.com/gnuROD

ALSO BY LIZA MALLOY